MANAGEMENT BY VICE

MANAGEMENT BY VICE

A Humorous Satire on R&D Life in a Fictitious Company

C. B. Don

STERLING TER LIBRA
YORBA LINDA, CALIFORNIA

First printing 1999

ISBN 0-9670084-4-1

LCCN 99-93787

ATTENTION CORPORATIONS, UNIVERSITIES, COLLEGES, AND PRO-FESSIONAL ORGANIZATIONS: Quantity discounts are available on bulk purchases of this book for educational purposes. Special books or book excerpts can also be created to fit specific needs. For information, please contact Sterling Ter Libra, 18032-C Lemon Drive, PMB 625, Yorba Linda, CA 92886.

CONTENTS

Disclaimer

The Company and all characters are fictitious
and any resemblance to actual persons living or dead
is purely coincidental.

With a crash like the sound of thunder,
The Company split asunder.
It lost its even keel,
And its shares began to reel.

What caused such a miserable fate?
Why were all the measures too late?

Here's a confidential disclosure,
But don't lose all your composure,
If you see your reflection,
Don't yell, "No connection!"

This perspective comes from the R&D bench,
That's most often blamed for all manner of stench!
Yet, long before The Company was dead,
The stink first arose right from its Head!

GRAB AND RUN

Want promotion in a trice,
Whatever the cost, at any price?
Try Management by Vice!
For honest hard work, loyalty,
Will never bring prosperity.
Don't be a fool,
It's plain to see, just take the opportunity!
Then grab and run with all your loot,
Before your Bonus is the Boot!

Executive jobs in the high-technology arena were hard to find. A high-level position in a corporation as well known as The Company was an opportunity not to be missed.

Dr. Bill Gambill was a chemist turned self-made manager. He felt no need for an MBA degree to excel as a quick-witted, highwayman on the road to success.

He heard about the lucrative position available at The Company while teeing off at a corporate golf tournament in Bermuda and quickly outmaneuvered his "best" friend, a close contender. It was easier than he had thought to sabotage his friend's game. Of course, Bill Gambill was most apologetic when his swing faltered and the golf ball injured his rival's right wrist. This most unfortunate stray shot on the practice green put his opponent right out of commission. Having thus cleared the playing field, Dr. Gambill commiserated with his colleague and glibly promised to put in a good word for his challenger, assuming Dr. Gambill was not too busy impressing the Executive Vice President of R&D of The Company, Mr. Phil Fox.

By a stroke of sheer luck, the aspiring vice president then scored a magnificent hole in one. Henceforth, Dr. Bill Gambill was viewed as a man with executive vision and after a brief interview in the Club Room, Mr. Phil Fox recommended him highly to The Company President, Mr. Wally Steen. Thus, three years ago, Dr. Gambill joined the managerial elite of The Company to hold the exalted position of Vice President of Future Development Technologies, abbreviated FDT.

Since that time, Bill Gambill had acquired a fine taste for the kind of expensive lifestyle that was a natural part of his high-ranking position. So much so, in fact, that he realized he needed to supplement his income. Then a couple of years ago, a once-in-a-lifetime opportunity presented itself–not exactly on a silver platter, but in the mundane Petrie dishes within Dr. Herman Salzer's microbiology laboratory.

At a project review meeting with Bill Gambill, Dr. Herman Salzer had disclosed that the metal complex, synthesized by Dr. Alan Hawk, had some very novel properties. Minute amounts of the amazing complex added to the bacterial cultures in the Petrie dishes were able to kill a type of dreaded bug that had become resistant to antibiotics in hospitals. Wow! A novel drug to wipe out opportunistic infections! What a money-spinner!

"What an opportunity!" thought Dr. Gambill. He only hoped Dr. Hawk's metal complex would not adversely affect opportunists! Hence, the vice president of FDT had promised to champion this project as if it were his very own. In fact, in his mind, it was; and he knew precisely where to transfer it so it would have every chance to fulfill its promise of enormous profits to line his pockets. Dr. Gambill was satisfied that everything was going according to his executive plan, except for the dogged persistence of the two pestilent researchers, the Drs. Hawk and Salzer.

Bill Gambill sighed as he lounged behind his desk, perusing his meeting schedule. Those pesky R&D guys wanted yet another meeting this morning to discuss patenting the medical use of the precious metal complex. He simply did not understand why those two did not view their invention as one of many run-of-the-mill Company projects. Most of them were destined to fizzle out anyway from lack of upper-level management interest. It wasn't as if they would get any monetary compensation for all their efforts. Couldn't they see? The Company took blatant advantage of them; and Dr. Bill Gambill was very faithful to the corporate philosophy!

Heavens above, how he had tried to fob off Dr. Salzer during the past year, Bill Gambill pondered and bit his lower lip in annoyance. He tapped the bald patch at the back of his head with nervous, fidgety fingers. Smoothing down the remaining circlet of reddish hair, he frowned. That Salzer guy was much too determined and Bill Gambill was fast running out of excuses.

"Ouch!" he murmured, pursing his lips at the persistent pain in his stomach. "Damn! Those R&D bods are giving me an ulcer!" he whined to his secretary, who had peeped 'round his office door.

"You have a meeting with–" she began to say.

"Yes, yes, don't remind me!" Bill grimaced, pushing his chair back to stand up, knocking over a potted plant. "You're always placing plants where they can do me some grievous bodily harm, Jo!" he complained.

His secretary did not bother to respond because she knew her boss never really listened. Instead she stepped out of his way as he snatched a handful of the cookies from the plate beside her computer she had prepared for him. Jo was very much accustomed to her boss' cantankerous manner and the cookies were meant to be a pacifier whenever his nervous ulcer bothered him.

"Dr. Gambill!" she called after her sour-faced boss, as he was about to turn to his left at the door. "The workers haven't finished the connecting corridor to the conference room yet. You'll have to go the long way around. Through the R&D departments and back up in the elevator again. I'll see you there with the coffee and cookies."

Bill Gambill groaned. "The things I have to put up with in this Company. A promotion is the least I deserve out of this place for all my efforts!"

Jo rolled her eyes behind his back as the VP strode toward the elevator that would take him to the R&D labs on the ground floor.

Thank goodness, Bill thought as the elevator doors closed, it would not be long now for his gamble to pay off. In the meantime, he would meet his tiresome R&D combatants halfway and then exert just enough of his vice presidential authority to accomplish all his personal objectives!

Satisfied with this strategic plan, Dr. Gambill began his trek along the R&D corridors, hurriedly stuffing cookies into his mouth.

▲

"*I* can't understand Bill Gambill's attitude, Alan!" Dr. Herman Salzer's Austrian accent became more pronounced as his frustration boiled over. "Damn it! I've completed all thzee experiments and Frieda has done all thzee documentation and...," he waved his hand over the two laboratory patent notebooks and a thick ring-binder brimming with notes, "...all thzis work is still not enough for our...pea-brained management!" He threw his hands out in a gesture of helplessness. His youthful face, topped with silver hair, was a picture of utter despair. "In all my fifty years, I have never faced such a vacillating attitude, hot and cold and hot and cold, but always when I try to move forward, we hit a brick wall!"

Dr. Alan Hawk, principal research scientist, frowned in sympathetic understanding. In the ten years of their acquaintance, Alan had grown used to Herman's bluntly expressed opinions and straightforward manner. Unfortunately, The Company managers preferred the indirect language of corporate politics.

Alan threw a cautious glance at the frosted glass window of the dark green office door and noted the outlines of several people standing in conversation in the corridor outside.

"Ah, let thzem hear, Alan! I don't give a damn anymore!"

Alan nevertheless lowered his voice. The management rumor mill could be vicious and had often been unfair to Herman. He was a dedicated and hard-working scientist, a mind-set few Company managers truly appreciated.

"But Bill Gambill has expressed great enthusiasm for our joint project all along," Alan said. "At our recent project review he agreed once again that this is a potentially fabulous opportunity for The Company!"

"Yet he still hasn't given his approval for the attorney to draft a patent application," Herman shook his head. "Can you imagine? He said we should collect more data and try thzee effect of the complex on several unrelated strains of bugs. In my opinion, we have done more than enough for a patent application."

"I agree. I don't know what bug came into his head at the chemistry project review meeting last week. He told me to synthesize more variations of the complex. His suggestions made no sense at all. All this delay is totally unnecessary."

"Do you think he may be using our invention to promote himself up thzee ladder?"

Alan shrugged uncertainly. "Waiting for the right moment to present it at an executive review meeting in front of Phil Fox, you mean?"

"I'm not sure. Our managers play all kinds of political games," Herman shrugged. "Thzee bottom line is, thzee way Bill works things here in thzee FDT department our hands are tied! FDT. What a name! *Future* development technologies–and we can't even push this through tomorrow! Thzee Legal won't touch it without his go ahead to The Company patenting office."

"I still can't understand why he wouldn't at least make some *bona fide* effort to push it through." Alan quickly scanned the familiar text of their in-house invention disclosure. "In my scientific opinion, it is definitely a brilliant, novel application of our complex and should be patented as soon as possible."

"Thzat's how I feel, but…well," Herman Salzer glanced at his watch. "Since you were unable to attend my last meeting with Bill, I asked you to come to thzis meeting with me to see for yourself and listen to Bill Gambill's excuses. I don't know anymore if I'm too close to thzee bench to see thzee business side or…," his light brown eyes lit up mischievously behind his horn-rimmed glasses, "…well, I feel, as we say back home in Vienna: *Bin Ich ein Esel oder Du?* That is, 'Am I the donkey or are–'"

"–Are you?" Alan confirmed his understanding with a laugh. Opening the door he gave a pointed nod in the direction of the vice president of FDT, Dr. Bill Gambill, who at that moment appeared around the corner, struggling to salvage a cookie, crumbling in his hands, by stuffing it into his mouth.

"In this case, Herman, it's not hard to guess who is the real ass!" he quipped as the object of their private jest came hurriedly toward them, still struggling to swallow the remnants of the cookie. He opened his mouth to speak but choked on a crumb and coughing with exaggerated motions that he was about to suffocate, dashed past them to the drinking fountain along the corridor wall. He slurped noisily, splashing his whole face in the process.

"Oh, Lord! That was close!" he called out as he walked back to the two scientists, wiping his mouth with the back of his hand. "I swear my new secretary, Jo, is out to kill me! She said she baked these darned cookies especially for me and the next thing you know, the crumbs nearly choke me to death!"

Dr. Bill Gambill critically scanned his surroundings and grimaced with obvious distaste. "What a hell hole! If the cookie didn't do the trick, the sight of the labs will! Takes me back to my old lab days...slogging behind the bench...pipette, pipette, ...weigh, weigh...prepare smelly reagents...gaze at formulas and waste your time over boring results...all day long, day after tedious day!"

Alan shook his head then interjected lightly, "But you forget all those tedious lab chores are just a means to an end. If you understand your goal–"

"I know, I know–and my main goal was to get the heck out ASAP!"

Bill visibly winced as they passed by the long row of laboratories, illuminated only by fluorescent overhead lights. It was familiar territory to both scientists, almost a second home. Alan Hawk found it quite amusing to see how Bill Gambill, despite his Ph.D. in chemistry, felt as out of place in the research labs as quartz in a diamond mine. Everything, the assorted instruments, laboratory equipment and the army of white-coated technical staff standing so much at ease or sitting by their workbenches, pipetting, weighing, calculating, taking measurements or simply engaged in lively discussion groups, somehow irked Bill Gambill.

"When did you abandon thzee scientific circles?" asked Herman Salzer.

Alan glanced sideways at Bill, his eyes full of mirth as he remembered the enlightening conversation with Bill's Ph.D. supervisor, the now-retired professor and past Company consultant. At the time Bill Gambill was hired as vice president, he just shook his head and dryly commented he hoped The Company was explosion-proof in more ways than one, then promptly canceled his consultation contract!

"I'm still part of thzee scientific circles!" Bill gave a half-joking, exaggerated imitation of Herman's accent. "Very much so! I'm not VP of Future Development Technologies for nothing!" he objected and added in a self-important tone, "It's just that during the years of slaving away to complete my thesis, I wised up! But I never really forsook…forsaked…left science, not in theory I mean and that's what counts! I've done it all…chemistry, physics, immunology.. and all other 'ologies,' but a man also has to move up in the world!" He pressed the "up" elevator button with managerial flare and glanced impatiently at his Rolex gold watch. "Slaving behind the bench is okay for you guys. It's your hobby, but not for me. I want much more out of life!"

He banged again on the elevator button. "Where's that damn elevator?" he said impatiently. "Gee, it's slow! Are all your instruments so slow? Is there anything else you guys need down here?"

Alan smiled at this offer. "Our dull little lives here would certainly be improved if some labs and offices had daylight. We've been waiting for the promised facilities for the past eight years and Building G still isn't ready to move in."

Gambill threw his hands out and hit the button for effect. "That's not my monkey! I've only been here three years. Why didn't you guys sling that monkey, or should I say chicken, into Phil Fox's staff meeting earlier this year?" He chuckled at his own joke. "He's the money bags around here! Executive Vice President of R&D!" Bill obviously admired the title with an anticipatory gleam in his eyes, his aspirations clear to all who knew him.

"Thzat we could not do! We weren't invited!" Herman Salzer replied with a meaningful glance at Alan.

"Well, you're both veteran scientists; you've got at least fifty years between the two of you. You should learn to barge in! See, that's the trouble with you eccentric scientist types, you're too shy of taking the bull by the…horns…." Bill's voice petered out as a sudden thought jogged his memory. "Damn elevator! We haven't got all day!"

Alan wasn't about to let him change the subject. "Bull's-eye, Bill!" he said with a touch of sarcasm. "It's impossible for us to barge in; if you recall, the staff meeting was off-site. In Spain, I think. Madrid, wasn't it? Excellent golfing and bullfight shows. Phil told everyone after you all returned!"

"Yeah, it was our International Marketing VP who insisted on this location. Hmm…we all learned a lot of fascinating business sense by watching the matadors. You know, all about how to bait the customers and get them all excited about our products until they charge for it and want to buy all you offer!" Bill Gambill had a challenging, defiant look in his eyes. "It's hard competition in the managerial arena! Very hard work!"

"I can imagine; it must have been difficult avoiding all the bullshit!" Alan Hawk commented, but his words were drowned as the elevator doors rattled open. Bill Gambill rushed inside, off-handedly returning the cheerful greetings of several research employees.

As soon as Alan and Herman stepped inside, he pressed the fourth floor button and asked, "So, guys, what's this meeting all about?"

"We wish to discuss the status of our patent application on thzee use of our metal complex," Herman Salzer replied.

Bill impatiently motioned him to stop, lips twitching in his habitual, nervous manner. "You've got one-track minds," he accused and sighed as they stepped out of the elevator into his domain, the sunlit, plushy carpeted corridor that led to the reserved executive conference room. "Now isn't this better than those smelly R&D labs!" he commented over his shoulder, and at the sight of a young, petite woman walking in the same direction, called out, "Hi, Ellen! You know Ellen, don't you?" Bill asked the two scientists. "She recently joined The Company as an assistant patent attorney in Hugo Lawson's department. Ellen, these are two of our brainy R&D folks.

Dr. Alan Hawk and Dr. Herman Salzer. So, what brings you up here?"

Ellen smiled uncertainly at them and flicking a strand of long, glossy blonde hair behind her ear, explained, "Mr. Lawson couldn't come," she said in an apologetic tone. "So, he asked Les Suggs to deputize, but as I report to Mr. Suggs, and he had some important files to look into, he sent me."

She was still new and clearly in awe of the vice president. It was quite obvious in the self-conscious manner with which she shifted her large leather folder from one hand to the other, then smoothed her tight-fitting, purple and gray mini-dress. The white teeth she flashed did not distract Bill Gambill from a quick survey of her sturdy legs encased in black tights as he opened the conference room door and gallantly indicated for her to enter.

Alan suppressed a chuckle as Bill quickly reassured, "I'd much rather have you here than Les Suggs, also known as 'Slugs'!"

Ellen dissolved into laughter. Bill had another opportunity to eye her exposed body parts. "Great outfit, Ellen! A very professional look!" he complimented, indicating the way to a seat by the windows at the far end of the long conference table.

Gambill's slim, brunette secretary rushed to fill several plastic cups with coffee and placed them on a tray beside a plate full of those life-threatening, crumbly cookies. With a cynical eye, Alan observed the young patent lawyer as she wriggled herself onto a chair held out by Bill Gambill and attempted to cross her legs, pulling her tight, constraining mini-skirt up higher in the process. She was attractive and about the age of Alan's own daughter. He could not help wondering with a touch of mature mischief, which profession this young lady could be aspiring to by sliding her skirt almost up to the…he recalled with a quiet chuckle his own daughter's description of her trendy skirt, "Dad, it's real cool! Right up to the watermark!"

Bill Gambill sat down and took a careless gulp of the piping hot coffee. "Ouch! Now she's trying to scald me!" he motioned with his head toward the departing secretary. "Well, let's get on with it!"

"Look, Bill, last month you said–" Herman Salzer began but was cut short by Bill's gesticulations.

"Don't remind me what I said last month…last month was last month and as I always say, 'Timpos fogits,' or something like that."

Alan's eyes danced. "I think, Bill, a Roman would tell you *Tempus fugit.*"

"Fogits, fugits, fuc…," Bill Gambill stopped in mid-sentence and laughed, pleased at the knowing smile that appeared on Ellen's lips. "They live in a world of their own down in R&D, " he remarked to the young legal representative. "Okay, Herman, Alan. What were you guys saying?"

"What Herman was trying to say, and I agree with him one hundred percent–"

"See, Ellen, there you have a scientist talking! Nothing but percentages and equations!"

Ellen was trying hard not to laugh.

Alan's ire was rising. He noticed his friend's compressed lips and continued, ignoring the VP's nonsensical chatter. "Okay, Bill, let me make myself clear. Herman and I both believe that the novel use of the metal complex has definite merits. It warrants patenting."

"And all thzee technical data, including thzee graphs necessary for Legal to write up a draft of the patent application, have been completed," added Herman, thinking this would prevent the vice president from objecting that it was not ready. He was mistaken.

"It is not complete without the results of your experiments on the other strains of bugs and a thorough checker-board study in combination with all of Alan's recent variations of the metal complex," Bill persisted.

"We have sufficient data already, Bill!" Alan protested. "Besides, we can add the results of these ongoing experiments later to the patent as a continuation-in-part."

Bill Gambill leaned back, scratching the bald circle at the back of his head. He was unaccountably uncomfortable, Alan noticed with puzzlement. Even his ears were turning red. "What do you lawyers have to say about this?" he turned to Ellen.

Ellen opened her folder and withdrew the invention disclosure, a precursor to the patent application, filed a year ago. "It wasn't approved by the patent review committee. As far as I can see here, it isn't rated as material worth patenting."

Bill wanted to kick himself. He wished he hadn't brought Ellen into the conversation. He had gone to a great deal of trouble to sabotage the progress of the invention disclosure. He was beginning to wish her inefficient boss had come instead. *This woman is much to eager to please,* he thought, frowning.

"What?!" Herman Salzer exclaimed in outrage. "I know you said it had been reviewed! Thzat is why we went ahead and wrote down all the technical data relevant for a patent application. And you said it was all in thzee mill!"

Bill made an impatient gesture. "Stop telling me what I said. I know what I said and if I'd said it, I'd say I had. Good heavens! You're too Teutonic, Herman! Relax, will you?"

Alan and Herman exchanged a look of shared frustration. Bill Gambill's frenzied talk and management style irked them both to distraction.

"I guess I'm not surprised," Alan interjected to defuse the situation. He decided to exploit the animosity between Bill Gambill and Dr. Victor P. Barron, the vice president of Applied Research Technologies, ART. "The patent review committee couldn't tell a nugget from fool's gold anyway!"

Bill Gambill nodded in wholehearted agreement. "Worthless! With Barron heading it up you're better off just keeping it in this department." *And a CEO would be better off with a seizure of corporate raiders,* he chuckled to himself.

Dr. Salzer interpreted the smile on the VP's face to mean Bill was finally more receptive. "Well, thzen, let's apply for thzee patent!" Herman said eagerly. "We all know it is novel. Alan and I have extensively reviewed thzee scientific literature and patents, and nobody has published anything remotely similar," Herman Salzer turned to Ellen. "All thzee relevant literature is appended to our technical report."

"Thank you, Dr. Salzer, that will be a real help…."

"I don't think Ellen will have time to draft your patent application," Bill Gambill hurriedly interjected. She was much too keen, he decided. With her writing the draft, they might even get the patent out by the end of the year. "Aren't you all very busy in the patent department with the ongoing litigation at present, Ellen?"

"Yes, actually we are, Dr. Gambill, but I could still–"

"In that case, I'll make a recommendation to Slugs for an outside attorney to do the work," Bill Gambill determined. "It will cost us plenty. Those outside attorneys' fees are enough to bleed The Company dry!" The VP leaned back in his chair and grimaced at Alan and Herman. "I don't want you guys pestering Legal about this. Stick to doing what you know best. Behind your benches, okay? When Legal finds a suitable patent attorney, Ellen will let you know in her own good time." A very, very long time, Bill hoped, if he knew anything about the inefficient way in which The Company's legal affairs were handled.

Hawk and Salzer also knew. They were not pleased at all about this decision, although they realized they had little alternative but to acquiesce to their VP's wishes.

After a suitable pause, designed to add emphasis to his indisputable decision-making authority, Dr. Gambill added, "The subject is closed!"

"Not until we have thzee patent safely filed," Herman commented.

"I don't see any reason for your annoying impatience!" Gambill groaned. "Those 'opportunist bugs,' or whatever they are called, can wait to get killed. What's the hurry?"

"Opportunistic bugs, Bill!" Alan threw in crossly. "And, if we don't apply for the patent soon, some human opportunists will beat The Company's opportunity for a money-spinner, right out of our Petrie dishes!"

Bill Gambill suddenly stood up and walked to the wide panoramic view of the Pacific Ocean and overhanging cliffs. He turned his back on them and thoughtfully scratched his nose. They couldn't be hinting at his motives, could they? No, impossible. Researchers were too damn honest and naïve to suspect his interest in this high-stakes business game!

He turned a poker face on them. "You've spent too much time with your nose to the bench, Alan. You're becoming a paranoiac!"

With a wave of his hand he dismissed Alan's warning. "It's highly unlikely anyone out there would even think of using the weird metal complex to kill bugs." Clearing his throat, he added, "Of course, we all know people do often think alike in research and come up with the same ideas at the same time, but there's no need to kick up such a fuss." He turned a benevolent smile on the scientists, whose frustration was mounting rapidly. "Even if a competitor did beat us and patent your idea, you can still publish all your research data. That's what you guys in R&D really care about, isn't it?"

They wanted to tell him how wrong he was, but Bill continued. "Look, will it make you feel better in the meantime, if I buy you another instrument—a toy for your new project—and I'm sure you'll soon invent something else. Ideas pop up a dime a dozen in your heads!"

Alan could not pinpoint what his sixth sense was trying to tell him but something was fishy about Bill Gambill's highly agitated manner and evasive attitude. A similar thought must have crossed Herman Salzer's mind for he exchanged a questioning look with Alan as they stood up to leave. Herman was right, Alan decided. Bill was not just a brick wall. He was reinforced concrete.

"Well, folks, that's settled then!" Bill Gambill chatted with a great show of cordial joviality, while herding them out of the conference room. "How would you like to visit my wife's gift shop sometime? There's a fascinating selection of knickknacks. Stop by, we're open from ten to six every day, six days a week!"

As the scientists had feared, five more months passed by before Ellen finally informed Drs. Hawk and Salzer that Mr. Suggs had found an outside patent attorney to compose a draft for their patent application. Bill Gambill's signature, approving the expense of hiring the attorney was required on the document, which she enclosed with the memo. To the scientists' frustration, Bill Gambill was nowhere to be found at The Company.

After some compliments and coaxing, Bill Gambill's secretary, Jo, paused long enough between the click of her knitting needles to disclose Bill's whereabouts to Alan, in strict confidence, of course.

Her "hardworking boss" had taken advantage of what she referred to as "one of those managerial perks" that is, ten days of unofficial leave to help out his wife at their gift shop. She set her knitting aside to retrieve the address from the computer file, took a gulp of coffee then resumed her own creative hobby, a self-assigned perk as the "VP's personal secretary."

Alan and Herman decided to take the authorization document and personally bring the good news to Bill Gambill at his shop over the lunch hour.

"Babe's Gift and Thrift!" Herman pointed to the fancy Gothic letters over the gift shop entrance, neatly positioned between a high-fashion boutique and a mom-and-pop Italian restaurant.

They stepped aside to let three women, wearing expensive-looking outfits, to exit with their bulky parcels and shopping bags.

"Not a bad location," commented Alan as he glanced around the busy, open-air shopping center with its water fountains, palm trees and exotic floral displays. "It seems an expensive, high-rent location," he commented, indicating the if-you-ask-you-can't-afford-it price tags on the outfits displayed in the boutique windows next door.

The chime of the doorbell that accompanied their entrance into the gift shop sounded to Alan like a subliminal reminder of the cash register. A heavy, fruity fragrance filled the air and wrapped the assorted array of colorful knickknacks with an aura of quality. There were knickknacks to celebrate every imaginable occasion from the cat's first meow to your beloved's birthday.

A salon-enhanced redhead, clearly on the losing side of a weight loss program, flashed her pearly white teeth at the newly arrived customers.

"May I help you, gentlemen?"

Her affected, childish, high-pitched voice, very much at odds with the woman's mature age, surprised and instantly annoyed Alan.

"We came to see Dr. Bill Gambill," Herman Salzer said. "We were told he is here in his wife's shop."

"I am his wife," the woman replied. "But let me guess," she tittered, "you must be Dr. Herman Salzer, working for my husband at The Company?"

Herman would have liked to tell Mrs. Gambill in no uncertain terms that her husband was as much an employee as they were at The Company. In fact, no one worked *for* him. Indeed, Alan and Herman had both worked in R&D for many years before Bill Gambill had put in his puffed-up, neurotic appearance on their project.

For the sake of politeness, he simply replied, "Yes, we *all* work for Thzee Company, but how did you know…?"

Mrs. Gambill burst into a gale of adolescent chuckles. "Bill said you've got that *javohl-mein-Herr* accent! It's so cutely Germanic!"

What a perfect match for Bill, Alan decided. A hen-witted spouse with the same silly, uncivil sense of humor.

"Actually, Mrs. Gambill, my accent is Austrian," Herman said with his customary kind smile.

"Oh, I see! Bill and I stayed in Vienna two years ago at the famous hotel that served that delicious chocolate cake. What's it called?"

"The Sacher Torte served at the Sacher Hotel, right in the heart of old Vienna. A very exclusive and expensive hotel."

"You bet it is!" Mrs. Gambill gave him an arch look. "The Company would never expect Bill and the other VP's to stay in anything less when they travel overseas."

"Why not?" murmured Alan, sotto voce. From the ironic twist to his colleague's lips, Alan could see he was not the only one to recall their recent conversation with Bill regarding travel expenses.

"If you insist on attending the meeting," Bill had informed them with a scowl, "remember The Company can't afford fancy, high-priced accommodations for technical staff. Our travel budget is *very* limited." Thanks to Mrs. Gambill, the mystery of the depleted R&D travel kitty had now been solved!

Mrs. Gambill turned her large hazel eyes on Alan. Her puzzled and questioning gaze was framed by eyelashes heavily weighed down with dark mascara.

"Dr. Alan Hawk, also working for The Company," he introduced himself.

"Oh, yes, I've heard about you too, Alan," she smiled coquettishly and after a brief pause added, "you're one of those scientists, aren't you, with loads of ideas and no money…I mean, never enough research funds…yes, well…Bill tells me you're another Einstein!" She giggled like a silly teenager.

"We need Bill to sign a legal document," Alan said, ignoring her witless remarks.

"Oh, Bill has a very low opinion about all those legal things, but if you two promise me to browse around the shop and maybe pick a gift, I'll fetch Bill. He's in the backyard polishing my new sports Mercedes. Can't keep his hands off it! Bet he's sorry it's not his!"

The two scientists exchanged meaningful looks and barely had time to survey the antique dolls and lacy fragrance bags, when a woman in her mid-thirties swept into the shop. With a wide smile she asked whether there was anything she could do for them?

Alan explained the purpose for their visit.

"Oh, how interesting!" her eyes lit up and she broke into confiding chatter. "You are scientists then? So is my husband! He's Bill's cousin, you know. A clinical chemist, but not nearly as important as Bill is at The Company. Well, at least my husband is his own boss in his own small company, Concord Labs Incorporated."

"Oh, thzat's very interesting," Herman said wryly.

The young woman shrugged. "Well, almost his own boss. There's only one major investor to please at any rate…." She turned back as Bill Gambill and his wife entered through the back door. "Speak of the devil!" she chuckled.

Alan thought he must have misunderstood. After all, The Company employees, especially those in high managerial positions, were not supposed to have a vested interest in a company with products that were possibly in competition with those of The Company. Unless Concord Labs was just a clinical testing laboratory. But didn't she say her husband was doing research?

"Hi! Alan, Herman!" Bill greeted, wiping his hands on a paper towel. "What a surprise! What d'you think of my wife's little free enterprise?"

"Very enterprising," Alan quipped and glanced at his watch. "Bill, would you sign these patent authorization papers?"

Bill hesitated. "What's the hurry? Give me more time…."

Herman, sensitized to Bill's delaying tactics, quickly interjected. "Ellen said we have to decide quickly. Otherwise the outside attorney will take on work for someone else!"

Bill rubbed his nose. "Give me a break, guys, and let me first finish what I'm doing! Leave the document with me and I'll get round to it. See, babe," he turned to his wife, placing an arm around her plump shoulders, "that's how a VP is constantly harassed. Nothing gets done if I'm not there!"

"In which case, Bill, why don't you shake off some aggravation and place your autograph on the dotted lines here and here," Alan held out the contract.

"I don't have a—" Bill pulled a disgruntled face and fumbled around his shirt pockets.

Alan Hawk was prepared. He promptly offered Bill his own pen, thoroughly enjoying the scowling look on the VP's face as he grudgingly placed his signature on the document with an exaggerated flourish. "I don't see why you're so insistent?" he glanced at Alan with an angry frown.

"We're just looking after the interests of The Company," Alan said on a dry laugh. "After all, it is the only organization I know of at present that provides our wages and your bonus, Bill!"

"All for one and one for all!" Herman Salzer interjected with a sharp twinkle in his eyes.

Bill Gambill, his face flushed, banged down the pen on the counter top and shook his head, as if in disbelief. "Look at these people, babe. They're always championing others. There's little to be gained by doing so, folks. Take my off-duty advice, look after your own ass!" he said with a cynical sneer. "Now come along, you two, and support my wife's clever enterprise! I'll give you a bargain price on top of the sale discount! You wouldn't want this sweet babe here to go bankrupt, would you?"

That evening, Alan Hawk's wife placed the heart-shaped potpourri Alan had bought in the garage. Alan could not stand the sickly smell and any reminder of Bill Gambill in his house.

*D*r. Alan Hawk was tired. His legs were not made of youthful steel anymore but were beginning to feel more like two sticks of well-chewed gum.

For the past three hours, he had been walking around the extensive exhibition halls, browsing through one exhibit booth after another. Each booth displayed new and old, tried and tested products, from the latest in solid-state technology to environmental and clinical assays and instrumentation for rapid, high-sensitivity analyses. This was the most extensive worldwide meeting for small and large companies on the West Coast, from the internationally reputable to those aspiring to expand their reputation and profits such as small, upcoming enterprises.

Alan Hawk poured himself a cup of coffee at the buffet table and with a sigh of relief sat down on a chair in the refreshment area. He placed the heavy stack of glossy brochures, advertising products of interest to his current projects, on the Formica tabletop. Sipping his coffee, he stretched his aching legs and idly watched the chattering crowds, engineers, and sales people in the booths eager to answer the endless stream of questions from curious and genuinely interested visitors.

A brightly colored display in the booth diagonally across the carpeted aisle caught his eye. He craned his neck to catch a glimpse of the company name between the milling crowds. Refreshed, he suddenly felt ready once more to take a look at the exhibit in this eye-catching booth. Stuffing the pile of gathered brochures into the conference shoulder bag, he strolled casually to the well-positioned booth at the corner. He raised his brows as he read the bold, orange, fluorescent letters advertising the product name. It was strangely familiar. Dr. Hawk quickly turned his badge over to hide The Company name since some exhibitors were known to be reluctant to discuss their products, if they saw an attendee belonged to a possible competitor company, instead of academia or the medical community.

"Are there any questions I can answer for you?" A pleasant voice, belonging to a smartly attired woman in her early thirties, diverted his attempt to read the displayed products. She smiled and asked with a forthright, business-like manner, "Are you familiar with our Concord Labs' products?"

"No, I couldn't say I know much about them," Alan replied and again focused on the advertised product name on the board behind the representative. "But I'm interested in products for clinical microbiology."

The young woman beamed. "Well, let me tell you all about our company products, then." She drew a deep breath and enumerated a range of disposable products from membranes to sterile pipettes, all of which the company was marketing as a middleman for some oriental manufacturer. They must make a handsome profit, thought Alan, as he glanced over the price list.

"But we also have two of our own major products on the market. FastProbe was launched by Concord three years ago and is a rapid detection method for bacterial contamination in foodstuffs. It's very successful! But our latest product, launched here, is truly a miracle!" she enthused, proudly handing him a two-page, glossy brochure.

Alan's eyes widened in surprised recognition as he read the product trademark name and advertising statement aloud, "Opportune! Don't miss it! Take the opportunity and kill those opportunistic pathogens!"

The young marketing representative chuckled. "A most appropriate name, isn't it, for such a unique compound that can prevent *Pseudomona*-induced infections?"

Alan nodded. He was speechless. Their patent application was barely in the process of being drafted and here was their product on the market. It would certainly be no *gamble* to guess who was the originator of this compound! He controlled his anger while the woman continued. "As I'm sure you know, these bacteria are the most common source of hospital-acquired infections in patients suffering chronic illnesses and cannot be eliminated with the usual broad spectrum antibiotics. Our novel chemical compound is sure to become a major pharmaceutical blockbuster!"

"Fascinating!" Alan said with a forced smile, a sickening feeling in the pit of his stomach. "Can you tell me more about the chemical composition of this compound?" Detecting a slight hesitation he hurriedly added, "Surely you must have patented this unique bug killer?"

The woman betrayed her vocation as her enthusiasm for the science overcame her sales pitch. "Oh, yes, the patent application was just approved and the patent will soon be issued."

Damn! Alan Hawk swore to himself. In his mind's eye, he saw the poorly written draft of their patent application as they had last left it on the desk of the worst patent attorney he had ever dealt with. Ellen had told him later, this attorney was the best Legal could find, given the limited financial resources Bill Gambill had been willing to spend.

"I haven't had a chance to look at the patent in detail," the Concord sales representative continued blithely, "but I'm from the microbiology department. Our chemist synthesized the active compound. We only tested its effectiveness, and I've never seen anything like it!" She paused and inquired, "Are you working in research?"

"For as long as I can remember," Alan smiled at her. "I'd love to hear more about this fascinating compound. I'm interested in clinical research and I'm sure many physicians and clinical chemists I know would be equally enthused about your Opportune product."

Prevarication was not Alan Hawk's second nature, but he had to be certain.

"Well, I guess since it's just been patented, it's okay?"

Alan gave a reassuring nod and the lady took her queue. "We microbiologists don't really know the precise formulation, but I heard through the grapevine that our major investor, Dr. Bill Gambill, brought it in through some highly confidential, outside development deal. Someone said it's based on a unique metal complex. I think…selenium, germanium and something like that. Anyway, my assistant and I evaluated it, and it's very potent. So please tell your doctor friends that Opportune will get all those opportunists!"

"Not quite all!" Alan murmured through clenched teeth and waving a hand in greeting quickly walked away as he spotted Bill Gambill hurrying toward the Concord booth, accompanied by a younger man–probably his cousin, Dr. Conrad. Alan waited to see them join the sales representative, who was already engaged in explaining their products to a group of newly interested attendees, and then left the exhibition with a splitting headache.

The following day, when Alan returned to work he immediately set out to write a note to Herman Salzer to arrange an urgent meeting. He had just started to compose the note when Dr. Salzer flung the door open and burst into the office, waving a bunch of glossy adverts.

"Alan, Alan!" he gasped, his face flushed with anger. "Am I glad to see you! *Mein Gott!* Just look at thzis…just look at thzis!" he pointed to the text on the four glossy adverts, which he had dropped on Alan's desk.

Alan stood up and closed the office door.

"Read it, Alan! Look at thzis advertised product!" Herman said, his voice trembling.

"I know what it is, Herman. It's a product sold by Concord Labs., called Opportune."

Herman was stunned. "I got thzis through thzee mail. It's an advertisement announcing a new bug-killing drug! Where did you see it?" He gasped and almost shouted, "No wonder thzat two-faced Bill Gambill kept throwing obstacles in our way! He sold our work to Concord Labs!"

"Waylaid, leaked and stole it!" corrected Alan and explained how he had discovered all the facts at the exhibition.

"What shall we do, Alan? I'll go and confront him now!"

Alan shook his head. "No, Herman. But I'll arrange a meeting with Wally Steen immediately."

"The Company president? Are you sure? I never talked to him. Our project manager will not like it," Herman hesitated.

"I don't give a damn what that useless man likes. With his degree in workplace psychology, he seems to think that we are treating mental depression in bugs!" Alan quipped angrily. It also bothered him that middle-managers were allowed to create a wall between the technical staff and the CEO-level management so that even senior scientists, such as Herman, were afraid to approach the President of The Company without their approval. "For pity's sake, don't look so awed. I've known Wally since his early days in The Company when he was only a junior accountant. His rise was meteoric after he married the very rich daughter of one of our major shareholders with whom he shared a passion for yachting. He's not a god—not even a 'demi' one! Though he may like to imagine himself as the mythological sea-god, Triton!" Alan laughed to cheer up his colleague.

▲

*A*t their appointed mid-morning hour, the President of The Company, Mr. Walter Steen, better known as "Wally", gave them a cordial welcome as they were ushered into his luxurious, CEO suite on the top, tenth floor of the impressive corporate headquarters. The office decor reflected his nautical interest with valuable seascape oil paintings and yachting trophies. Two computer screens displayed alternating stock market reports and updated announcements on swells, knots and yachting regatta reviews. They were in perfect keeping with the spectacular ocean-front view through the full-length panoramic windows that made up one whole office wall.

Yet, all the luxurious splendor of the executive office filled Alan, not with envy, awe or even confidence, but with a sense of uneasy concern. What would become of a Company that was led by a CEO/ President who was far more occupied with planning sailing routes to distant tropical isles than the future goals of the organization?

"What can I do for you, gentlemen?" Wally asked, tearing his eyes from the weather chart displayed on the computer screen. His lean, suntanned face and the polished brass buttons on his navy blue jacket were more characteristic of a seasoned sea captain aboard a luxury ocean liner than of a company president.

With a casual wave of his hand he invited them to sit down on the two chairs opposite his huge captain's desk. "Alan, I haven't seen you for a long time. What do you think of our new corporate building?" He swept his hand around his spacious, deluxe suite.

Alan looked straight into Wally's blue eyes. "It sure is impressive, but I'd rather have more updated laboratory facilities!"

Wally Steen barked a laugh. "A typical reply from a workaholic scientist! You have to look at a wider horizon, Alan. This building represents our image and that's what keeps The Company cruising. Always remember that in the world of big business, it's representation that counts! That's what our customers like to see!" He gave a dismissive wave. "Okay, Alan, don't look so cross-eyed. Your super-luxury benches will come eventually. But at the moment we have some other more pressing business priorities to spend our profits on!"

"Dr. Salzer and I didn't come up here to talk to you about lab facilities," Alan steered Wally's ship back on course.

"Good! I can't waste my time on the research labs' furnishings," Wally said, focusing his attention on the Swan 57 *Duchess II* 1979 yacht advertised for sale on the computer screen.

Alan waited patiently. He had no intention of wasting his words on the salt breeze blowing through Wally's head at that moment.

"Well, get on with it, Alan!" Wally's mind sailed back to his office. "Maybe you can speak up, Herman?"

Herman Salzer eagerly handed him the glossy adverts of the new "Opportune" drug. "We came because thzese people from thzee Concord Labs claim that thzis is their latest product and have applied for thzee patent! But they have violated The Company's priority rights!"

"Then why come to me?" Wally raised his brows. "We pay damn good salaries to those guys in Legal to help you with this. It's up to Hugo's people to take care of any litigation. Or are you saying they ran foul of their anchor?"

The eagerness in his voice did not pass unnoticed. Alan knew that, although he was not a malicious man, Wally mischievously delighted in clipping his VP's sails.

"There are special reasons why we wanted you to know first about this case before we inform the Legal department, Wally," Alan interjected. "You see, the subject matter of our own patent application, which is still being prepared by The Company's outside patent attorney, describes exactly the same invention—my unique metal complex and its use to stop the growth of antibiotic-resistant opportunistic infections, as Herman has discovered."

"But what's the problem?" Wally asked, puzzled. "We go out and buy the license to manufacture it, if it's really so good. Have you talked it over with our Dr. Bill Gambill? What does he think about it?"

"Thzat's the problem, I mean, thzee point, Mr. Steen," Herman launched into excited explanation. "You see, Bill Gambill stole our invention and applied for the patent through his Concord Labs venture."

His words had seized Wally Steen's complete attention. He raised his hand stopping Herman in mid-sentence. "Ahoy there! Hold on!" he said waving away the advert Herman held out to him. "Do you realize what you are saying, Herman? This is a serious allegation against an upright, experienced member of my management staff! We don't do this kind of thing. It plain doesn't happen!"

Alan had to raise his voice to interrupt the sudden tirade in defense of his untouchable management troops. "Wally, we have proof! I, myself, talked to a scientist from Concord Labs, who said that Bill, who's a cousin of Dr. Conrad, is also one of the major investors in their company. While we have been trying for months to get his approval for a go ahead on our patent application, Bill has been busy filching our work for his own gain!"

A long silence followed in which Wally Steen stood up and walked to the windows, then back again. He propped himself on the edge of his desk, looking from Alan to Herman with a deep furrow between his brows. Finally, he reached a decision and spoke in an unusually quiet voice. "The ensuing discussion must on no account leave this office, okay?"

"It's understood, Wally," Alan replied and Herman quickly concurred.

"There's an old dictum in navigation that says, 'Use every possible means to check your position.' I just did that and what do I see looming on the horizon? A nasty litigation and a hefty lawsuit for defamation of character filed against The Company by Bill and his associates! Even if you have the evidence, the legal proceedings could drag on for years and we can ill afford such negative publicity against The Company management. Not to mention the tremendous legal expenses!"

"But, Wally, The Company will lose millions in profit!" Alan exclaimed, disbelief in his voice at the president's attitude. "I can read between the lines of our financial statements, you know, and we are aware in R&D that The Company needs a new product to survive. The competition is serious out there. You can't just let go of such sure and easy profits!"

Wally again began to pace restlessly on the thick, sea-green carpet. "Yes, I know, but we have to protect our image! We were always a reputable organization, and we can't have it dashed on the rocks of litigation and petty squabbles."

"Petty squabbles?!" Alan exclaimed with incredulity at such an understatement.

"I know Alan and I would get no significant monetary rewards for our invention, but thzese are millions for The Company!" Herman sprang up, his voice shaking with outrage.

"And there are millions in sunken treasures under the sea, but you have to first invest vast amounts to salvage them. We have a similar situation here. We would have to spend millions on litigation, and I am not prepared to squander The Company profits in this high-risk way!" Wally held up an admonishing finger. "Most importantly, a good CEO will never sully the reputation of The Company's management staff! If you wish to pursue the matter, we'll just have to say it was one of the recently departed or never-to-be-discovered members of your technical troops. You never can tell what one of the many temporary lab assistants would divulge somewhere…by mistake, of course. Get my drift?"

Herman's mouth had dropped open, as he looked in utter disbelief at The Company's top executive.

Alan compressed his lips, his eyes blazed when he eventually spoke. "I will not allow our technical staff to be the scapegoats for your crooked manager! Sooner or later, someone will figure it out too. If Bill Gambill stays on, the truth is bound to come out. Our scientists are no fools!"

Wally Steen shrugged impatiently. "Rumors are always cruising around this place. It adds spice to the otherwise boring lives of all those bookworms down in the research labs. But dealing with Bill is my business. If I choose to keep him on and deny any knowledge of this matter, or if I ask him to leave, only I will decide and you shall soon see by his actions from which direction the 'puff is coming.'"

"**Y**es, Alan, I decided to cut my loses and move on in life," Bill Gambill grimaced, a shifty look in his eyes. He clapped Alan Hawk on the shoulder in a flippant gesture of nonexistent comradeship as they paused in their walk toward the main lobby.

It was Friday. The afternoon following the sudden official announcement that Dr. Bill Gambill was leaving for a prestigious position as President of a small but successful company called Concord Laboratories, Incorporated. Seeing the self-satisfied look in the VP's eyes, Alan's ire rose once more. He could not help thinking that after all their efforts, he and Herman were left with nothing–even compelled to keep quiet–while their flippant CEO safeguarded his own ranks and permitted this brazen executive to get away scot-free with the lucrative profits of all their bench-work and intellectual labors.

Alan suppressed the urge to flatten the man. He knew this was his last chance to find out whether Wally Steen had at least asked Bill to "walk the plank." A cynical spark lit up his eye as he asked the departing VP, "Come clean, Bill. I should think your gains far outweigh your loses, especially since you picked such an . . . *opportune* moment to leave?"

Alan had the immense satisfaction of seeing Bill's protruding ears turn scarlet. From the wary look he flashed at him, it was obvious he had been forced to jump overboard. Well, well, thought Alan, who would have thought it? The wretched man seems to have a guilty conscience after all!

Bill attempted a casual laugh. "Opportune? Yes, I guess it is, isn't it?" He resumed his brisk walk along the corridor toward the exit in the main lobby ahead. "You could become a manager too, you know, Alan, instead of pursuing your unprofitable, academic hobby," he continued. "As an executive you'd have a much better chance to move up and get more for yourself out of this short-sighted Company."

"Short-sighted perhaps, but I should think you can be very grateful for all the far-reaching benefits you were allowed to get away with," Alan said, a sardonic twist to his lips.

Bill Gambill suddenly threw back his head and guffawed. The security guard in the lobby looked up from his novel, curious what the departing VP found so funny.

"Yeah, sure!" Bill said. "You R&D guys have yet to learn that loyalty and gratefulness are the sentiments of fools and losers! Here's my final bit of advice, Alan. When you see an opportunity, don't hesitate... just grab and run!"

Alan reluctantly shook Bill's proffered hand in parting. He watched, with resigned cynicism, as the villainous ex–'vice' president, a smug smirk on his face, sped away in his bright red Porsche with all his loot and the incredibly generous golden boot.

EPISODE TWO

POWER LOOK

Power Look, by the Book,
Perfect fit, with borrowed wit,
On the go, what a show!
But alas, poor young ass,
A minor detail he must learn,
That popinjay from wise discern,
What MBA forgot to teach,
"If the beard were all, the goat could preach!"

There were never enough polished and reflective surfaces in which the Junior Technologies Acquisitions Manager, Mr. Sandy Sanders, could glimpse his most up-to-date managerial "Power Look" reflection.

Even better than his bedroom mirror or his gold convertible's windows were the large front entrance doors of The Company main lobby. In the darkened glass he could admire what was, in his opinion, the image of an ambitious, young executive, well on his way up the corporate ladder only a year after starting his first full-time job.

This Monday morning he felt particularly confident and pleased with himself. He had memorized several new sayings from the *Power Talk* tape, to which he diligently listened on his drive to work every morning, and his new executive wardrobe had been delivered over the weekend by his influential uncle's personal menswear advisor.

Every detail of Sandy's new wardrobe had been meticulously planned. As the advisor had proudly said, "In my exclusive collection of custom gentlemen's clothing, you will never see the bag, drag or sag of the cheap, off-the-rack suits! One cut, one fit is my motto! When you wear my designer outfits, sir, you will make a truly *powerful* statement!"

Sandy Sanders firmly believed every word, and his heartbeat accelerated as he strode with a deliberate, slow gait toward the approaching image of himself reflected in the glass front doors of The Company.

"If you dress like a king, you don't yap like a dog!" Sandy recalled one of his favorite sayings as he admired the flawless cut of the gray, pinstriped suit, which fit his tall, slim frame to perfection. The plain ochre pocket square matched the ochre hues in his silk polka dot tie, which hung like the obligatory plumb line on the pale yellow backdrop of his made-to-measure silk shirt. Seams were pressed, shoes were tasseled and polished and the fragrance of 'I-Man' aftershave, recommended by his barber as the latest "Power Cologne", constantly reminded him of his aspirations.

Sandy stopped briefly by the entrance doors. He glanced again at his new watch—with hands, of course, the electronic type were just too cheap—and then at the reflection of his ultimate "Power Props", the onyx and diamond executive ring and the monogrammed black, executive attaché case in his right hand. It felt very light, for inside were only a blank notepad, a calculator, a leather folder and a Mont Blanc fountain pen and ballpoint, but Sandy was certain that given time and promotions he would soon have more to fill it.

Yes, he was on time and everything looked just fine for his meeting with the vice president of R&D, Mr. Phil Fox. His immediate boss, Dr. Pierre Perr, was on one of his travels, probably at that very moment somewhere over the Pacific winging his way to Australia. Sandy felt an incredible sense of freedom to call the shots in the field of the "Power Game".

Flashing his badge and a smile, whiter than nature intended, at the female guard on duty in the main lobby, he thoroughly enjoyed the appreciative look in her eyes. This gave him an impulsive idea. He glanced at his watch. Yes, he still had a half-hour to spare, enough time to make a detour through the research laboratories.

He was confident that today the two Ph.D.s, not much older than himself, who never showed him sufficient respect, would surely be impressed and would realize who matters and is in charge here in The Company. After all, they did have to report their progress on the collaborative project with Hong, Incorporated, to Pierre Perr, and since Pierre was away, that left only him! He was their big boss now!

"Good morning! How are we doing today? Okay? Very good! As I always say, 'The dogs may bark, but the caravan goes on!'" He quoted the ancient saying he had just this morning appropriated as his own words of wisdom. "So carry on, guys!"

Striding masterfully along the corridors he repeated the string of meaningless phrases in an authoritarian, condescending tone he had finally mastered after many hours of tedious practice with his tape recorder.

He practiced this verbal, managerial superficiality on anyone who happened to pass by along the R&D corridors, over the cubicle walls, through any open office door and even at the much-surprised young woman, wheeling her cartload of daily mail.

"Caravans and barking dogs?!" she murmured, casting a puzzled look after him. "What does he think this is, a doggoned circus?"

In front of the Chemistry Synthesis Laboratory he stopped. Sandy unbuttoned his jacket to give himself a more casual appearance and to better show off his particularly fine gold belt buckle. He opened the door and sauntered inside, placing the attaché case in a conspicuous position on a laboratory bench for all to see its superior quality.

Sandy quickly slipped his hands inside his trouser pockets, where they felt most comfortable in a laboratory environment, at least, ever since he had almost failed his college microbiology B.S. exams. But he preferred to forget those unpleasant years. Thank God! That was all behind him! These days he felt more than adequately qualified with his 'Certificate of Achievement' from an expensive management short course that believed in awarding degrees in exchange for a tendency to show potential managerial skills rather than any actual realization of such attributes. He was confident he could manage anything that came his way.

"A positive attitude; that's what'll get you ahead," he was often told by the course lecturers. "It's all you need for a prosperous career in management!"

With this attitude forever etched in his self-satisfied mind, Sandy stood in the middle of the laboratory and greeted the two scientists.

"Hi! Shang, Bridgett! How are we doing, this morning? Business as usual? As I always say, 'The business of America is business'."

"Oh, yes, and so did our thirtieth U.S. President, Calvin Coolidge!" Dr. Shang Wong murmured, directing a crooked smile and a wink at his colleague. Dr. Bridgett Cohen held back her laughter. They had often joked over what they termed as "Sandy's parroted wisdoms of the day."

Sandy could not understand what these two scientists found so amusing. He tried out a much-practiced condescending look and added in a supercilious tone, "Well, it's good to see you both so busy. That's great. In fact, dynamite!"

He awaited the effect of his words but was again frustrated as Bridgett just looked up at him from her experiment with a slightly distracted frown. Removing her safety goggles, she said, "Well, Sandy, as you can see we're very busy and short-handed. Since you always claim to be a scientist, how about putting on a lab coat and giving us a hand, instead of just standing around looking pretty?"

Her challenging, teasing look flustered Sandy. Pretty?! How come she was not in the least impressed by his managerial manner of speech and his authoritarian "Power Look" ?

"No way!" Sandy quickly dismissed her words with a wave of his manicured hand. "When I quit micro, I said my motto is 'big bucks' not more 'micro bugs'!" He chuckled at his own witticism. "And I assure you I make more of the 'big bucks' now than you two, slaving away in here with all your straight A's and Ph.D.s!" He could not refrain from reminding them of his privileged, exorbitantly remunerated managerial position. "As I always say, it's no use if you can pee a 'straight A' when you're bound for the top, all you need's a 'straight aim'!"

Bridgett came close to him and with narrowed eyes and a frown peered at a point on Sandy's chest. "Say, Sandy, what's that?" she asked pointing to his tie.

Sudden panic colored Sandy's cheeks. Oh, no! There couldn't be a spot on his brand-new tie from breakfast?

He worriedly squinted down his nose to inspect his tie. "Where? I can't see anything!"

Sandy failed to notice the gleam of mischief in Bridgett's eyes as she winked at the equally amused Shang Wong.

"Where, Bridgett?"

Bridgett straightened her features. "Oh, it's really nothing…my mistake. It's just one of the polka dots catching the light. That yellow color looks exactly like dried egg yolk."

Sandy frowned uncertainly. "No! It doesn't, does it?"

"Not if you look at it from this angle," Shang joined them, bending his head sideways, "but looking straight on, and since it is morning, I wouldn't be at all surprised if someone else made the same mistake as Bridgett."

Bridgett fought hard to hold back the laughter bubbling up inside her as Sandy quickly buttoned up his jacket and changed the subject. "By the way, I'm flying out to Korea in two days for a discussion with the technical bods and executive bosses of Hong Corporation's R&D departments. I'll let those guys know what we have achieved on our collaborative project and inspect what they have done this far…if anything at all!"

"Hmm…," Shang responded to his bragging with a dubious look. "And who else is going with you?"

"Oh, just a select management team. Two excellent project managers from Development, who will check how the manufacturing of the films is progressing on which your…hmm…I mean *our* materials will be coated, and the senior manager from Reagents Production, who wants to see if their Reagents facility is up to scratch. I will, of course, present our research data to the top executive managers," Sandy rattled off, full of self-importance.

"But why do the managers from Development and Reagents want to go over there when we haven't even completed our research? Besides, according to the patent lawyers, nobody is supposed to talk about our recent results outside our own Research department?" questioned Shang.

"Oh, the managers on our team are not just anybody, you know? They're well on top of it!" Sandy waved off this legal regulation. "I gave them the copies of your current reports so they will be able to make the necessary business decisions."

Bridgett was not happy with Sandy's obvious lack of appreciation of confidential materials. She also seriously questioned the abilities of the three managers to absorb the necessary technical details and know-how from a couple of summary reports. They had more than clearly displayed their miserable understanding of chemistry in every one of the several previous meetings the scientists had with them. It was bad enough trying to explain organic chemistry synthesis to Sandy, whose limited training was in microbiology.

To her knowledge, none of them had as yet taken the time to ask any of the researchers intimately involved in this project for a briefing.

"Are Pierre Perr and Gus Ferst coming along?" She hoped Sandy's well-informed boss and their Senior Project Leader, Dr. Gus Ferst, would head this auspicious Company delegation.

"No, Pierre's off to Australia and Phil Fox and I decided there's no need for a detail-oriented scientist like Gus to come along and confuse our business issues."

"But if you are going to present our data to the scientists over there, don't you think we should be present to discuss their progress on the mono-molecular coating procedure they are developing with our synthetic material for the sensor films?" Bridgett objected.

"Don't fuss, Bridgett! You just stay where you belong, behind the bench, and leave the management to us. What d'you think, I can't handle this bit of chemistry? It's simple! I'll be well prepared for the discussion with those Korean guys. I'll pull the necessary reports from the computer network and extract the relevant data for my presentation. I'm qualified enough, and I am deputizing for Pierre Perr as the External Liaison Officer for this project. So you see, all you need to do is to keep your noses to the bench, guys, and as I always say, 'Make haste slowly'!"

"And so did the Romans," Bridgett countered with a grimace.

"Anyway, I must be off! I've a meeting with Phil Fox about all sorts of business things. Business is business!" Sandy picked up his attaché case and turned toward the door. As an afterthought he called out over his shoulder, "I'll give your regards, Shang, to all your Korean folk!"

"Don't bother!" Dr. Wong replied. "My Taiwanese ancestors never set foot in Korea!"

"I can't believe that. How come you all look the same?" Sandy chuckled.

"Since everything looks the same to you, Sandy," Shang replied with a cynical twist of his lips, "be careful what you transcribe from our reports. I think Bridgett is right. We really should sit down together before you leave. I hope you'll see that we have synthesized another–"

"I know! I know! There's no need to instruct me. I've got many more important things to do," Sandy replied and with a glance at his watch hurriedly left the laboratory.

Shang shook his head. "Of course, he knows it all," he said in a sarcastic tone. "Everything's the same to him…Oriental faces and all our formulas!"

"I just hope he doesn't screw up our successful collaboration with the research team over there," Bridgett said, turning her attention back to the chromatography columns.

▲

Sandy's meeting with Phil Fox went very well. His "Power Apparel" was immediately noticed and praised by the vice president, after which Sandy became very confident and was able to assure the VP how well qualified and prepared he was for this trip to Korea.

"I'll take with me the extracts of all the pertinent data, which might be of interest to the Korean guys. You know, those two scientists, Shang Wong and Bridgett Cohen, always enter both their experimental data and their excessively detailed reports into our newly installed R&D computer network to which Pierre and I have access. So, I'm all set, Phil. Everything is under my control!" Sandy assured with careless confidence.

He took a letter of invitation from his attaché case and handed it to Phil Fox. "My uncle said he would be pleased if you could come to play a game at his golf club at the end of the week."

Phil Fox eagerly accepted the invitation to play at the exclusive lakeside golf course.

They spent the rest of their meeting discussing a novel Company concept for off-site management meetings to which Phil Fox now invited Sandy.

"I've decided, and Wally agrees with me, that our hard-working management team needs to be able to relax once in a while, away from it all. So every quarter, we'll have an informal get-together, a Spirit of Executive Togetherness, a SET day, to foster better working relations within The Company."

"Where?" Sandy interjected with great enthusiasm. Oh, boy! To be a part of the right set! Then, somewhat anxiously, he inquired, "How do you define informal?"

"Oh, the meeting will be somewhere by the sea with a great golf facility, of course! It will be business, but a casual affair.… I've a particularly fine pair of suspenders I've been dying to show off!" Phil Fox joked with the young, up-and-coming manager.

Sandy was thrilled and to top it all on his return to the office his custom tailor and clothing advisor called the very moment he stepped through the door, to inform Sandy that he had just received a consignment of particularly fine "Power Suspenders" and matching ties. Would he be interested?

An aspiring manager must be able to take a hint and accept the "Signal," Sandy recalled reading in a book brimming with managerial advice. Now no one could say he could not understand the "Code." He quickly asked about the possibility of acquiring some for the SET day, a casual outfit including suspenders but not too loud since it would not be wise to outshine the VP himself.

"Of course, sir, I understand perfectly," his personal advisor replied with practiced diplomacy that made Sandy feel so very important. "I have just the right items for your special needs. The latest "Power Statement" in many companies at the moment are lime green suspenders with subtle pink patterns. You'll be the envy of all the managers. If you could come over as soon as possible, you can have first pick from the selection of patterns, sir."

Sandy immediately canceled all appointments for the day. He had to make his selection now, in time for this important offsite get-together. But just as he was about to leave the secretary called after him that there was an urgent overseas telephone call waiting on the line.

"Damn!" Sandy exclaimed trying to think of an excuse.

"It's from France. Dr. Besansone from Beauchamp International," Pierre Perr's efficient gray-haired secretary said with a scolding look from behind her glasses, as she noticed that Sandy was about to escape.

"You had better take it, Sandy, or Dr. Perr will hear about it and he'll be very upset!" she said with a stern tone. The vainly vacant expression in Sandy's green eyes annoyed Fiona. "I'll transfer the call to your office telephone."

Sandy grimaced and reluctantly returned to his office. He vaguely recalled hearing Pierre Perr's explanation about some sort of a license agreement he was engaged in with Beauchamp International. He must have some notes somewhere, but where had he put them? Sandy impatiently rummaged through the piles of letters, notes and forms stacked up on his desk, which at the best of times looked as if a hurricane had just blown over it. No luck. He gave up and tried hard to remember what exactly this deal was about and what they now wanted? Oh, well, it can't be helped, Sandy thought and glancing again at his watch, picked up the receiver starting off with the only French words he could muster and mangle.

"Bone jurrr, Dr. Bee...san...cent," he mumbled, imitating a nasal tone he thought will improve his French. Oh drat, he thought, these Europeans had impossible names! "Are you calling about your agreement with us?"

"Oui..., yes, the...agreemont regarding the license for the antipodies...."

Sandy screwed up his face in complete lack of understanding. "Your what? Anti...what?"

"We 'ave to be certain if The Company has decided to take the license for the antipodies...."

"The what? License for what? No, we don't have any such license...."

"You don't 'ave the interest?"

Sandy could not figure out what that man with the damn thick French accent was trying to say. He bluffed. "No, we don't!"

"Are you certain? Dr. Perr agreed ve must 'ave your ansver or else ve vill go vidth the antipody...."

"Anti...what?" Sandy interjected, frustrated that this conversation was dragging on so long. What if someone snatched those all-important "Power Suspenders" before he could get to them?

"Anti...bodies...for immunoassays...."

Sandy removed the receiver from his ear to take a hasty look at his watch once more. Get on with it! When he replaced it, all he heard was something about the Germans.

"Yes, yes, we know you're anti-German bodies. Who isn't over there!" Sandy replied with a laugh.

"I'm sorry, I do not understand!" the puzzled voice of Dr. Besansone came over. "So can I take it ve can go vith the German Concern?"

"Of course, you can show concern! We're all for good relations here at The Company. You just go with those Germans, we don't mind!"

"Thank you and goodbye!" the Frenchman finished abruptly.

"Aw-ru-var!" Sandy returned and sighed with relief as he dropped the receiver. That went well...without a hitch and now for the appropriate "Power Look"!

Sandy dashed out, noting happily that the secretary was engaged in a telephone conversation.

When Sandy returned late the following day, very pleased with all his selections of "Power Paraphernalia", he hastily searched through the network files for all of Dr. Shang Wong's and Dr. Bridgett Cohen's reports.

He scanned over the chemical formulas in the reports listed under the filename, Hong, Inc. Venture, and compared them to the scientists' latest entries. He nodded at the screen, interpreting the data to himself. It didn't look like they had made any noteworthy progress, apart from adding some ring-like drawings here and there to the basic molecule. They were writing the formulas now in a slightly different way, but as far as he could see these were not significantly different. Obviously, they also neglected to add these changes into the Hong, Inc. files. Well, he had been asked to present their latest data, so he quickly copied all the formulas and drawings of the molecular structures. He made notes of the summary text from the latest reports, incorporating them into the text for handouts and overheads, which Dr. Perr had asked the secretary to prepare, should he have time to deliver the presentation in Korea.

Sandy was satisfied he was now thoroughly prepared for his important mission overseas.

Several hours later, after settling comfortably in the business class compartment and sipping free champagne, he complained to his fellow managers about the slapdash manner in which those scientists were recording their results into the documentation network files.

"Can you imagine, they are so absentminded, or perhaps just lazy, they did not even enter their latest data and formulas into the Korean file. Their last entry was more than two months old!"

"That's why they need a manager like you, Sandy, to manage and check up on them. Why, all their research would be quite useless if we left them to their haphazard ways," the Chief Development Manager nodded importantly over the rim of his champagne glass.

"A manager's ability to grasp the overall concept, Sandy, is the most important part of any project," added the Reagents Manufacturing representative. "And The Company wouldn't be where it is now without such young experts, like you, Sandy. You're so highly technically qualified. Real management talent!"

They all raised their glasses in complete accord.

Sandy leaned back in his window seat looking down onto the scattered clouds and the sea far below. Already feeling light-headed from all the champagne, he let his imagination run free. Even the President of The Company was under him now, he chuckled to himself.

This taste of business luxury appealed to him and he day-dreamed it must be even better to fly first class, once one reaches the top of the managerial ladder. Sandy Sanders was sure he was well on his way there.

━━━━━▲━━━━━

It was not long into the guided tour of the R&D and manu-facturing facilities at the Hong Corporation when the Korean staff made a startling discovery. The representatives from The Company were certainly not their eagerly awaited American counterparts with whom they had looked forward to sharing the results of their own research. It was not only the plethora of general questions and the vague interest of The Company's representatives, but also their vacillating responses to all the technical questions the Hong Corpo-ration scientists asked, which led them to the conclusion that these men could not possibly be the scientists they had expected.

Although the visitors were full of smiles, the interests of The Company's delegation would have been much better satisfied by the tourist bureau than by the technical staff of the Hong Corpora-tion.

"What's the name again of that shoppers' bargain paradise in Seoul?" asked the Chief Development Manager as they sat down around the conference table in preparation for Sandy's presenta-tion.

"Itaewon," was the polite reply.

"Oh, yes, my wife's very much interested in those fancy green vases and that white Korean jade," the Senior Development Man-ager told the politely smiling scientist next to him. "She said I should not show my face back home without some of these art treasures."

"I love to haggle and give those guys a tough time!" laughed the Senior Reagents Manager, who was becoming very bored with this business trip. He needed more excitement.

"Yes, you can get very good bargains on many beautiful items," the Korean director of research replied. "Now, shall we...?"

"Tell me, Dr. Kim," interjected Sandy eagerly, "where's that place where they tailor those made-to-measure suits and monogrammed shirts? I was told they are ready in one day and delivered to the hotel? You know we are here for only two more days!"

Dr. Kim nodded, the polite smile now gone as he directed an apologetic look across the table at Professor Park, the top chemistry consultant from Seoul National University. "I'm sure my secretary, Mrs. Choi, will be glad to advise you later. Now, if it is...convenient for you gentlemen, we would very much appreciate listening to your presentation, Mr. Sanders."

Sandy pulled an undiplomatic grimace and handed out the printed copies of the overheads. He began in a monotonous voice and galloped though his script.

"As you can see," he said, pointing to his fifth overhead, "we have now synthesized sufficient amounts of the sensitizer material. We have an eighty percent yield, which you can have for the coating of the film, and as you can see these most recent results show the basic structure of the sensitizer molecule...."

Professor Park, who was eyeing the projected molecular structure with a puzzled and skeptical expression on his face, suddenly raised a commanding finger. "Ah...one minute, please, Mr. Sanders! The molecule on the overhead is not of correct structure. This structure cannot adhere to our film material!"

Sandy blinked in absolute incomprehension. "What d'you mean?"

"I mean a molecule with hydrophilic carboxyl end ring structure will have strong tendency to remain in aqueous solution, not form a monolayer on hydrophobic film material."

Dr. Kim and his research team exchanged a flurry of Korean words and chemical structures were rapidly drawn and discussed. In front of the blank, puzzled faces of The Company representatives, they quickly formed a consensus and Dr. Kim explained to The Company delegation.

"Gentlemen, I must agree. This is an incorrect compound. There must be some mistake. You see, the ring structure...."

Sandy flushed. Glancing toward his companions, he received only helpless shrugs and insouciant looks. He decided he was not going to take the grilling from these Korean yahoos without protest!

"Look here, Dr. Keen," he interrupted in aggressive self-defense, carelessly mispronouncing the research director's last name, "these are our latest results. Don't confuse the issues with technical details. If our scientists reported to us that this compound coats films, it coats films!"

"But, Mr. Sanders, " Professor Park attempted to explain, "we only wish to point out that this molecular form is not hydrophobic enough to bind...."

"Professor Park, may I add," interjected one of the Korean scientists with a respectful bow, "it says on the bottom of overhead 'tensile strength'...ah...the molecule we need must give 'tactile strength.'" He quickly scanned through several pages of Sandy's handout. "It might give tensile strength if applied to polymer listed on page fifteen in summary of report."

"But report summary on page fifteen," added one of his colleagues, "is not in agreement with summary statement on page seven, which we got from Dr. Perr's report to us on his last visit."

Sandy began to sweat as a lively discussion, partly in English and partly in Korean, circulated again around the table with hurriedly scribbled formulas, molecular structures and mathematical equations being exchanged. The other three Company managers stifled disinterested jet-lagged yawns and whispered among themselves. They all agreed this trip was a waste of time, since they didn't understand the chemistry and they couldn't contribute to any of this pure scientific gibberish. In fact, they did not understand why Phil Fox had insisted they fly over here in the first place.

The Senior Reagents Manager beckoned to Sandy, who bent down, hoping to hear a brilliant solution to this misunderstanding. "If you can't answer those damn technical questions, why didn't you bring one of our chemists along? They made the worthless compound; they should take the heat."

"What? Take them along, when they can't even get their chemistry right?" Sandy exclaimed. "But I'll see to it they get the heat when I get back!"

Dr. Kim finally stopped the debate of his team and turned to Sandy. "Mr. Sanders, it would appear there is some mix-up. Dr. Perr and you have reported on two different molecular structures with very different properties. Can you explain, please?"

Sandy could not. He swallowed uncomfortably as the light of realization dawned on him. Could he possibly be to blame?

The scarlet "Power Tie" now matched the color of his face as he stubbornly persisted. "I'm sure you have made some mistake. Our scientists know what they are doing and I suggest you consult an expert on at least an equal technical level who can explain this to you!"

"I think we need to think more about this before we sign the extension of the contract," Dr. Kim decided and the meeting was thus brought to a prompt end.

Dr. Kim, himself a scientist, was very annoyed. The specially invited senior consultant of the Hong Corporation, Professor Park, an internationally reputed authority on chemical synthesis, had just been thoughtlessly insulted. Dr. Kim apologized profusely to him, then stood up, bowed and the whole Korean team left the conference room.

The Company representatives were left to Dr. Kim's secretary, where they happily obtained all the shopping information, which was of primary interest to them.

The following day, Dr. Kim made an overseas telephone call complaining to his friend, Dr. Gus Ferst, about the dilettante delegation The Company had sent that nearly ruined their most promising collaborative project.

Dr. Bridgett Cohen and Dr. Shang Wong were discussing results with their project leader, Dr. Gus Ferst, when the laboratory telephone rang. They continued their debate while Gus answered the call, but the frequent mention of Sandy Sander's name drew their attention. The expression on Gus's face changed from disbelief to surprised outrage and he concluded the conversation with a sincere apology. When he replaced the receiver, he turned to the two researchers, curiously awaiting an explanation.

"Damn! That idiotic, ignoramus almost screwed up our entire Korean project!" He briefly repeated what happened to the two flabbergasted scientists. "Sandy told Dr. Kim before he left that you two gave him the wrong reports. I can't believe it!"

With a great deal of feeling, Bridgett and Shang told their project leader the true story.

Later that day, when Dr. Pierre Perr returned early from his successful business trip to Australia, Dr. Gus Ferst informed him of the critical situation precipitated by Sandy.

"The blasted fool. And that's not the only disaster he caused with his silly posturing as a technical manager!" Pierre said angrily. "I think we should see Phil Fox immediately."

▲

"Nice to see you again, Pierre, Gus," Phil Fox greeted cordially as they entered his spacious office. He closed the door and hurriedly retreated behind his large mahogany desk. The expression in his pale blue eyes was blurred by the bright daylight reflecting in his glasses. "You said you wanted to discuss something about Sandy Sanders? A fine up-and-coming manager, isn't he? I read the copy of his Korean presentation. It's a brilliant, smashing summary. None of your scientists could do better!"

"A fine young bungler!" Pierre Perr replied in his disconcertingly straightforward manner.

"Have a seat, Pierre...and Gus," Phil Fox offered. Pierre's imposing stature, his sophisticated elegance and confident cosmopolitan bearing, which served him well in the international technology acquisitions arena, always irked Phil Fox. His expertise in both management and chemistry intimidated the R&D vice president. Phil both admired and envied Pierre Perr's immaculate attire, the stripped suits, the silk shirts and the unobtrusive, color-matched silk ties. Phil Fox found it difficult to deal with Pierre sitting down, never mind when he towered over his desk. "Now, what's all this paranoiac exaggeration? I just said that Sandy is a great asset to The Company. An outstanding prospect!"

"In which case, Phil," Pierre Perr said in his mellow baritone voice, "you obviously are not aware that Sandy's slapdash incompetence just cost us a lucrative deal with Beauchamp in France? Everything was arranged to our advantage. I left explicit instructions with him, which he apparently mislaid, probably between his damn "Power Ties". All he needed to say was, 'Yes, we are interested and will sign the license agreement.' Instead, he told the French company representative we have no interest whatsoever in their method and they are free to make the contract with a German company! I will not tolerate such incompetence in my department, Phil!"

Phil Fox moved his hand over his mouth in a gesture of embarrassment. "That may well be true, Pierre, but you don't have to be so hard on the young man. We all make mistakes sometimes. Just because Sandy doesn't have a Ph.D.—I should say two, which you have in…chemistry and business administration from an expensive university—doesn't mean he has no management talent!"

Pierre Perr mentally dismissed the vice president's acrid comment on his educational background. He had by now grown accustomed to such derogatory remarks and knew well that his degrees and indisputable qualifications always irritated the rest of The Company upper management staff. Without a thought for The Company's reputation and benefits, they had far too often jealously blocked his promotion. He joined The Company because he liked The Company's goals presented to him on paper, but he was slowly getting tired of this lack of appreciation of his endeavors. He had received several job offers from other companies and some were becoming increasingly attractive.

"That all depends on one's definition of management standards," Pierre replied dryly.

"Phil, Sandy also almost lost us the contract with Hong Corporation," interjected Gus Ferst.

"I'm glad you mentioned it, Gus. That's what I wanted to talk to you about anyway," Phil quickly changed the subject, eager to avoid further direct confrontation with Pierre Perr. "Sandy complained to me on his return last night from Korea about the terrible mess your two scientists have in their documentation network. It was impossible for him to sort out the pertinent information from their records, which caused him great embarrassment at the Hong meeting."

"Don't blame my research staff, Phil, for Sandy's inability to grasp even the most basic chemistry on the research project. He stupidly thought he was qualified to present the correct data to the Korean scientists in place of an expert!" Gus Ferst responded angrily. "I can vouch for Dr. Cohen's and Dr. Wong's scientific competence and excellent record-keeping, but if Sandy doesn't understand—"

"Well, that's hardly Sandy's fault!" Phil defended in a voice that began to squeak. He stabbed an accusing finger at his floor to indicate the location of the research department below. "It's your scientists' job down there to educate a manager about all aspects of their project. They have to make sure he knows everything that's necessary to represent them. He has to know as much as they know!"

"That's impossible, Phil! All of my people are specialists in their field of research. They have more experience than Sandy could assimilate in fifty years, assuming he has the capacity to do so! If I may suggest, management should quit wasting the research staff's valuable time by hiring nincompoops like Sandy to manage technical projects. It is time The Company stopped shaming itself overseas and allowed the chemists and other researchers from behind the bench, who are naturally most qualified, to talk about the technical issues and thus expertly represent The Company in all such ventures."

Phil Fox shook his head. "That's not The Company policy. You see, Gus, you research people don't understand a thing about business. Great Scott!" He stood up abruptly to signify their discussion was at the end. "We can't have technical people without any business sense running around the world, confusing all the issues with their detailed, technical jargon. What kind of company will everyone think we are?" His expression was one of total shock at such a preposterous idea. "No, guys, I have decided that if you are so picky, Pierre, I will take Sandy off your hands. He obviously needs a more understanding mentor. I will assign him to our new Corporate Buddy program, where he can interface with more senior managers who will gladly teach him the ropes so he can grow and move up in our organization." He stopped and with all the authority of his position added, "Sandy was hired because in my opinion, and that of the rest of our executive management, he is a bright, up-and-coming young man…, a budding executive in all respects. He has just the right image to present The Company's corporate culture to our shareholders and to our Board of Directors. And that's what matters!"

"And 'if the beard were all, the goat could preach'!" Pierre Perr said sarcastically as he turned to leave with an angry frown.

Dr. Gus Ferst chuckled at this pointedly truthful sally. He was satisfied that at least they would not have to deal with Sandy Sanders on his project any longer.

For Dr. Pierre Perr, the attitude of the vice president of R&D had helped him to make up his mind. That very day, he would accept a long-standing offer from a competitor company, whose corporate culture saw beyond their managers' "Power Look".

EPISODE THREE

THE MEETING MASTER

Minutes of the meetings
He detailed bit by bit,
On megabytes of memory
From hours to years of shit!

The Polymer Amplified Smart Sensor, or PASS, project was right on schedule. The Company R&D staff were brimming with enthusiasm. This was the kind of project that spontaneously sparked the fires of a collaborative spirit among the research scientists in the various divisions within the extensive R&D departments.

"Well, we've nailed it this time. A sure money-spinner!" Dr. Frank Chung, robotics specialist and PASS project leader, laughed, his dark eyes glittering with pride behind gold-rimmed glasses. "The best project, from invention to product all done here, something very rare at The Company in recent years!"

"You bet!" agreed Jake Vern, electronics engineer and Dr. George Trent, head of the Polymer Chemistry department, nodded, a satisfied smile on his face.

They had just handed in the completed and signed disclosure proposal with all the technical data required for the patent application and sent it to the Legal department for further processing.

"What a clincher! The first phase of the evaluation study was an outstanding success," George enthused for the umpteenth time, knowing his colleagues didn't mind hearing it yet again. "Top management will finally see how worthwhile it is to invest in research."

"Let's go for lunch and celebrate!"

Jake's invitation was accepted with alacrity and the three researchers soon made their way toward the exit in the main R&D lobby. But before they had passed the guard they were stopped by Anne Stavros, Frank Chung's technical assistant, who motioned to them to look at the bulletin board, which she was reading with a puzzled frown.

"Do you know about this?" she said pointing with her plump finger to a chart which showed a sort of an organizational tree. "It's just been posted. Nobody said we have a new PASS project manager. How long did you know that, Frank?"

Dr. Chung shook his head. He stepped closer to the board and peered shortsightedly at the notice. As usual, no one had informed him of any impending organizational changes.

"Let's see," Jake, from his six-foot height, looked over Frank's head, while George maneuvered his thin shoulders between them to catch a glimpse of this unexpected announcement.

"Well?" he finally turned to his colleagues. "Did either of you two have any idea about this?"

"Shit!" George swore with uncharacteristic anger. "They've done it again! There's no need for a project manager on PASS!"

"As if it isn't enough we have to deal with an R&D vice president who's a technical ignoramus," Jake added scornfully. "And now we'll have to report to an ass of a manager posturing as a scientist! Damn, it happens every time in The Company. I've seen it before." He groaned.

"But why so suddenly?" Frank queried. "I was discussing organizational problems just a week ago with Phil Fox during our PASS review meeting, and he wholly agreed with me there's no need for an additional manager on this project. He said he wants to make a new start and he wants technical staff involvement."

"He just made a new start," Jake commented dryly. "And here is more proof that you should never believe what our CEO and his executive staff say. Heavens! Frank, you've been around for more than ten years and you're still so naïve."

Frank smiled ruefully. "I'm an optimist. At forty-six I still like to believe there are some guys in management who really mean what they say." He smiled crookedly, shrugged and asked, "Any of you know this guy?"

"Jerry Jott? Doesn't ring a bell. Must be new to R&D," George Trent replied with a thoughtful frown.

"Well, we'll get to know him soon enough," Jake said with a sarcastic shrug, turning his back to the notice board. "Like herpes, project managers have a habit of bursting on the scene just when you think you've gotten rid of them!"

*J*ake's prediction came true the very next day when the three researchers received a note from Jerry Jott informing them he was the Senior Project Manager in charge of the PASS project. He added that he had just been transferred from The Company's North American Sensors Engineering Division.

"I remember hearing this Division was closed down because of low productivity," Jake commented with a satirical gleam in his eyes as the three researchers rode the elevator up to the second floor of the R&D administrative building.

"Yes, but surely you can't put all the blame on one individual," Dr. Trent said, trying to meet the new man without prejudice.

"Not all the blame, but he did state that he was the senior manager in charge of operations up there…." Jake left his sentence unfinished as the elevator door opened.

They walked in silence toward the end of the long, carpeted corridor where the office of the new project manager was located. The sunshine penetrated through the open office door into the corridor and they had their first glimpse of their new manager sitting at the computer and typing with vigor.

Frank knocked on the open door, but Jerry Jott only nodded curtly, his head topped with a thick crop of smooth salt-and-pepper hair. His eyes remained fixed to the screen and he just continued typing.

The three researchers looked at each other with perplexed amusement as they waited in silence in front of the open door for more than five minutes, until Jake finally had enough and clearing his throat spoke out.

"Mr. Jott, if you are so busy, would you rather postpone our meeting to a more convenient time?"

Jerry Jott finished the sentence he was typing, then saved and exited the file. The tinkle of a clock chime could be heard from the computer screen as he finally swung around to face the three scientists, inspecting them with a pair of expressionless, pale blue eyes.

"You were early," he rebuked them, like a teacher talking to naughty schoolboys. The weak smile he directed at them was pleasant enough, but it did not reach his eyes. Was it just superficially genuine or genuinely superficial? The researchers could not quite decide.

Noticing their solemn faces, Jerry Jott stood up and in formal greeting extended his hand, adorned with a large diamond signet ring and a heavy, gold chain bracelet.

The scientists introduced themselves; Jerry Jott indicated to them to sit down at a round conference table in the corner of his office.

"I have to tell you from the beginning that I value punctuality above all else. I mean that you will have to get your timing exact…to the minute," he said, still smiling as he closed the office door and took his place at the table, where a portable word processor was ready for him to take notes on the meeting.

"I was assigned to this PASS project to get your research moving efficiently and without any delays. The R&D deadlines set by management must be met, and I will see that what needs to be done, really does get done!"

"And so it has been, up to now," Jake retorted grimly. He looked with a cynical smile at the row of books displayed on the shelves all dealing with various aspects of management techniques and advice on efficiency of management. "You won't need those methods on this project. Our work is on time…."

"Even ahead of schedule," interjected Frank.

"And moving along without a hitch!" completed George.

"Well, as your project manager, that's what I am here to decide," came the autocratic reply. "You must present and explain all the results to me and tell me all your ideas about the project. I'll get you organized so you can improve your research productivity!"

Frank handed Jerry the summary of the recent project review. "This project was only recently reviewed and Phil Fox gave us his blessing to continue as we did until now."

Jerry extended his lips into an all-knowing, supercilious smile that was beginning to irk the three scientists. He flicked through the pages of the report. "Of course, Phil is in favor of the project, but he doesn't have time to look into all the finicky technical details…."

"We were not exactly swamping him," interpolated Jake, recalling the last project review for which they had racked their brains for suitable non-technical examples and golf-related terminology to make the project more understandable and palatable to Phil Fox. They felt they had succeeded very well.

"That's what all researchers believe. I know, I've been around guys like you long enough and sooner or later you all run into some kind of communication problem, and that's what I'm here for–to facilitate, communicate and delegate!"

He sat back with a self-important look, as if waiting for a round of applause.

While his words inspired an instant bout of indigestion in his listeners, which no amount of antacid could cure, a smugly contented expression slipped across Jerry Jott's face. He interpreted the researchers' silence as acknowledgment of his indisputable communication skills.

"Now that you know my role, let me give you my meeting schedule." He handed to each of them a detailed timetable for the following month.

Frank, George and Jake looked at it in surprised disbelief: A meeting was scheduled for each day the first two weeks and every other day thereafter.

"Well, I can see you'll be very busy. You must have been assigned to manage several projects," George said with a sigh of relief. The light of hope that this man would be too busy to bother them flickered also in the eyes of his two colleagues.

"Oh, heavens no!" Jerry shook his head. "Don't worry, I have only one project to look after, and that is *our* PASS project!"

The three researchers looked at each other. They didn't worry. They were panic-stricken, appalled, dismayed!

"Good God!" Jake could not hold back his emotions any longer. "You can't be serious about this schedule?!"

Jerry's affronted expression clearly showed he was in complete earnest. "Oh, but I am! We have to put together an organizational plan, build a computer network for the project, raise company-wide awareness of PASS...."

Dr. George Trent had enough. "And how do you expect this project to progress with so many distractions? Research isn't conducted in meetings. It's carried out by planning experiments and by many hours of concentrated effort and hard work in the labs. I hope you don't think we will have time to attend all these meetings!"

The project manager's pale blue eyes surveyed the three project leaders with uncompromising frigidity. "Then, you'll just have to schedule your lab time to fit in with all of my meetings. Phil Fox expects it of the project leaders. If you need help to work out your personal timetables we can set up a meeting to discuss it!"

---

*T*hree months passed, The PASS project received no promised increase in research funds and no requested additional technical personnel, and yet upper management constantly commended the project for its outstanding progress.

Frank fell into a sickening despondency. He and his colleagues tried hard to find time to carry out their research work as before, but nearly every experiment was cut short by one type of meeting or another. There was no end in sight to the meeting chain reaction. Meetings multiplied exponentially and it was generally agreed among the three increasingly frustrated scientists that Jerry Jott was surely a godsend for all The Company's competitors, who monitored the progress of the development of any new Company product.

He organized off-site meetings in local hotels, restaurants or nearby parks, on-site meetings that rotated around every one of the twenty meeting rooms in the R&D facility and in offices that Frank and his colleagues did not even know existed.

There were review meetings to discuss data from five years ago, when the project first started, and meetings to discuss the future; meetings to decide whether the correct decisions were made and meetings to amend the decisions. There were day-to day, month-to-month and year-to-date strategic planning meetings and meetings to follow up on the strategies. There were biweekly lab meetings to discuss experiments in progress, weekly group meetings to discuss the results, bimonthly report meetings to evaluate the monthly progress and meetings to present data to lower-, middle- and upper-level managers. All these had to be edited and censored for complexity of scientific language by Jerry Jott, until they eventually ranged from cartoon strips to complete scientific nonsense.

Frank's protests, Jake's sarcasm, and George's threats to quit were all given passive hearings, but resulted in no changes in any schedules.

"Don't you have anything better to do than complain all the time?!" Jerry asked during one of his daily lab inspection tours. He brought his fist down hard on the lab bench. "You will do as I say! I am the project manager!" He drew a steadying breath and gave a wan smile at the shocked scientists. "You must let me worry for you. We're doing excellent work! Upper-management's thrilled, enthusiastic about the project. They're abreast of it now, and you should feel good about yourselves. Without *my* positive attitude, *our* project would never have gotten anywhere!"

He then decided that maybe the researchers needed something more tangible to appreciate what team spirit meant on a project. He called a "fun" meeting, which included all the people on the project from the technical lab assistants to the project scientists. All research activities stopped for two days.

"We need some way to identify with the project. A sort of PASS project logo. I want all of you to think about it and bring me your ideas by this afternoon. Do you want badges, pullovers, T-shirts, mugs, ties, or scarves? And let me know your color preferences."

"We have an important experiment planned for this afternoon," Frank protested angrily.

"It can wait!" snapped Jerry Jott. "We will have a design meeting tomorrow morning."

"I don't see any logical reason for this meeting to ruin my experiment. The samples must be analyzed tomorrow or they will go off!" Jake raised his voice.

"Look, Jake! When your manager says the meeting is important, you all have to attend. And that's final! I'm sure you can find some way to prevent your samples from going off."

"But there is no way!" Frank exclaimed.

Jerry Jott brought his fists down onto the tabletop with a loud bang. "I don't want to hear any more objections! As the lab project leader, Frank, you have much to learn about how to motivate your people! And I expect to see you all here tomorrow!"

Two weeks later, Jerry Jott called an impromptu meeting to distribute his selection of green and navy pullovers and T-shirts, mugs and badges. He was clearly miffed when Frank, Jake, and George did not show any great enthusiasm for, what he termed, "the incentive goodies for the troops."

"Give us more money for lab equipment instead!" Jake objected. "As I've told you repeatedly, we need a flow cell adapter on the old spectrophotometer to automate and speed up the measurement process!"

Jerry Jott shook his head. "I can see we will have to have a meeting to talk about your attitude. You're always too negative. Everything is just fine!"

"But the project is getting nowhere!" Frank protested in dismay. "We're not making any real scientific progress with all these damn meeting distractions!"

"You let me and the rest of upper-management decide on that! It's meetings and communication that make a project work!" Jerry Jott responded with his favorite phrase and returned to his incessant note-taking and typing.

The constant sound of Jerry Jott's tapping on the keyboard of his ever-present portable computer drove Frank, George, and Jake to distraction. Wherever Jerry went there always followed a detailed and scientifically mangled trail of minutes of the meeting, which the researchers respectfully filed for janitorial disposal.

By the beginning of the fourth quarter, it was obvious to nearly everyone in the research department that the PASS project was suffering from meeting asphyxiation and the life and vigor that drove a successful research project team had been extinguished. Then the inevitable finally happened.

Phil Fox drew up a new budget. The PASS project was canceled as showing no promised product. Jerry Jott complained about the lack of new ideas and cooperation from the technical personnel.

"I can't understand it," he told Phil Fox on the golf course at a program management off-site meeting. "I tried to get those research characters organized and improve their productivity, but they're so damn stubborn! Can you imagine, they had no appreciation for the PASS project logo and perks I arranged." He gave a deeply puzzled look. "My methods were very successful in manufacturing. Everyone on the production floor loved it! I had them running around like well-trained pigeons, just as the popular management books advise, readily responding to all I said. If you ask me, those research guys don't belong in a well-managed company like this. I can't see why The Company invests in them at all?"

Phil Fox leaned on his golf stick. "Hmm…I never understood those eccentrics myself. With all this to enjoy in life," he waved his golf-stick over the greens, "why would anyone opt for bench work? I mean, I know The Company has to have some patsy to hold to the R&D grindstone, but still…." He paused to eye the direction of the next hole. "You are sure you motivated them enough?"

"Damn sure I did! I praised them, I encouraged them, I set up meetings and meetings…."

Phil Fox putted successfully. He beamed. "Well, maybe canceling the project will teach them a lesson to be more cooperative when they are transferred to the next one. We've heard too much of PASS in the last year anyway. We can all do with a breather." He chuckled. "I think, I'll pass on PASS!"

The Company executive officers, advised by their technical middle-managers, all flippantly agreed to pass on PASS.

Patent filing for the PASS sensor was discontinued, but Frank, Jake, and George would never forget that two years later a competitor firm successfully delivered a slightly modified version of their Polymer Amplified Smart Sensor.

The only moment of satisfaction they shared about the aborted PASS project was an anonymous note that appeared one morning, shortly after the demise of the project. It was distributed by electronic mail to all participants of the PASS project and was attached to The Company's bulletin, which announced that Jerry Jott had been promoted to a higher managerial position in another division in The Company. It simply stated:

> ## Eulogy on
> ## PASS Management
>
> *Gone forever, Project PASS,*
> *Stifled, warped and mangled,*
> *Drowned in Management Morass,*
> *Jerry-rigged and strangled!*

Although a lot of guesswork went around, the author ensured that it originated from the Central Data Processing department and was thus not traceable.

EPISODE FOUR

WITH OUR GRATEFUL THANKS

Your splendid work deserves a mention,
How profitable is your invention!
And just to show we are impressed
That you really did your best,
All our Managerial Ranks,
Wish to send their Grateful Thanks:
So for your patent, here's a Cent,
On your vacation to be spent?
And though the Major Dividend
With Company Bonus for us is meant,
We hope you, too, are well content!

It was the same kind of balmy July evening, under the soothing light of a full moon, that four years ago had created the stimulating atmosphere for the birth of Dr. Chad Brunswick's novel idea. The solution to a nagging design problem had suddenly flashed through his mind. It seemed so natural and exciting once it presented itself after many months of contemplation, calculation, and deep cogitation that Dr. Chad Brunswick could not help laughing out loud at the Man in the Moon. The illusory silver face seemed to share his joy at the time and appeared to encourage and urge him to write up the invention disclosure for the patent application late into that very night.

How long it now seemed since he had felt such an all-consuming enthusiasm. He felt lucky that his wife, who was a scientist at the university, understood the engrossing interest that had driven him to work twelve-hour days, getting up at three o'clock almost every morning and spending many weekends in the laboratory. Without any hidden motivation other than to see the fulfillment of his novel idea, he soon initiated a new line of research on the Fiber Optic Circuit, or FOC, project, which he planned would take about four years to reach its zenith. With FOC now in its fifth year, Chad looked back with pleasure for he had completed the task long before the preset deadline and FOC had succeeded beyond his wildest expectations.

The first year the FOC system was introduced it had enjoyed tremendous success and proved to be the most ingenious, unique, and essential component in all the new generation, high-sensitivity instruments, which The Company had on the market. In the first year alone the FOC system earned The Company ten million dollars in profits. Yet, why did Dr. Chad Brunswick feel the need to seek out again that familiar face in the sky on this July evening? Was it merely an anticlimax or was it some other problem that had been nagging at him?

Chad settled down in his favorite garden chair. His wife's eyes from across the table and the stoic Man in the Moon both now seemed to be asking him the very same question that had also taken shape in his own subconscious.

"Well, Chad, was it all worth it?" his wife finally voiced his own thoughts.

Chad looked uncertainly at the plastic presentation box she had placed on the table, which contained a brand new "cent" and an Inventors Recognition Certificate, on whose yellow background the plain black words declared: "The Company recognizes Chad Bronswack, Ph.D., for his outstanding contribution to the Fiber Optic Circuit design patent US567432."

"After so many years with The Company, you'd think they could have made the effort to at least spell your name correctly!" his wife commented dryly.

"Wally can't spell," Chad replied.

"I'll bet he can when he writes himself a handsome bonus check from the profits on your FOC invention!" His wife paused for a moment long enough for the chirping of a cricket to intrude on their conversation, before adding, "I'll ask you again, Chad, was this worth all the hard work?"

Chad looked up at the moon in whose clear, chimerical incandescence images of past events appeared before his eyes.

"I don't know…when I think back over the past five years at The Company, the first thing that comes to mind is…."

"*…A*lthough we haven't yet attained the projected level of stability and sensitivity," Chad explained and pointed to the diagram displayed on the overhead projector screen.

"Are you saying we have a serious problem?" interrupted the FOC project manager, Mr. Dick Planke, with aggressive and somewhat hostile fervor.

"No, I didn't say any such thing, Dick," replied Chad with a startled glance at the three other participants of the FOC Task Force meeting.

"I can read between the lines, Chad! You can't bamboozle me, you know. I've been with The Company for more than fifteen years, and I've seen many projects come and go because of sloppy design problems!"

"But Chad just said," interjected Tom, the electronics engineer, "that there are no problems!"

Dick Planke shook his large head that to Chad appeared to take on the expression of a stubborn ox. "Then why don't we have any positive results after two years of your research?"

"Come on, Dick," exclaimed another indignant voice. Ted had been involved in this project since its early days. "You know very well this project has made tremendous strides forward since its beginning."

"Yes, we have built the breadboard and it's functioning well. We've already evaluated the system extensively," added John, a senior design engineer.

"Then, why do we still have problems?" Dick persisted. "I'm not at all in favor of this FOC system design. In my opinion, this will turn out to be a lemon and we'll never reach our goal!"

Chad wanted to tell him to quit including himself in the project accomplishment goals. His scientific contribution was about as significant as a spurious electrical discharge, but Dick Planke was the assigned project manager, highly regarded by Phil Fox, vice president of R&D, for his outstanding golf stroke. In the VP's opinion this also qualified him for the position of Chief Engineering Projects Manager.

Chad knew it would be useless to speak his mind to someone who habitually viewed every research challenge as a problem. "My calculations show that the required level of sensitivity will easily be reached with a straightforward modification in the design on which John, Tom, and Ted agreed and have already started to work."

Dick grimaced. "No, no! I believe we should validate those calculations of yours before we go any further with this project."

"Look, Dick, we were hired for our technical expertise. Now, either you trust us to know our science or The Company shouldn't do any research and development!" Chad exclaimed. "I can't see why you suddenly think we need to validate our well-proven research work?"

The obstinate look in Dick's eyes hardened. "Because *I* am the manager in charge of this project—*you* are my troops!" He pointed a commanding finger at the scientist. "And if I say I want a validation, you will do as I say and hand over your data, right now!"

"Okay, Dick, I'll distribute the algorithms and design modifications to the appropriate members of our technical staff," Chad conceded with an angry frown, knowing that his opposition would bring a tirade of insubordination charges on his and his colleagues' heads. He wished for nothing more at that moment than to return to his work unhampered by Dick Planke's autocratic and unprofessional interference.

"No, I don't think that will be necessary," Dick Planke said with a supercilious expression. "I will take a look at them myself."

Surprise and disbelief were evident on Chad's open face. He well recalled the last meeting when Dick had more than demonstrated his lack of mathematical competence. Dick Planke must have also remembered that occasion, but he persisted with a defiant look. "I did do higher math in school, you know, and your math is very straightforward!"

With a cynical smile on his lips, Chad nodded his consent. "Be my guest!" he said, went to his office and returned, handing him copies of pages covered with equations and complex design drawings.

------------------------------▲------------------------------

Six months sped by and in the excitement of his research, Chad almost forgot he had given Dick Planke the mathematical and engineering package.

The project progressed very well and the specifications were met with respect to sensitivity, dynamic measurement range, and stability. The FOC research team was ready to incorporate the design into an instrument system to test the boost in sensitivity expected from the novel fiber optic circuit.

Then one day, Dick Planke walked into the lab and announced in his ponderous voice, "I just want to inform you that my initial evaluation has shown some inconsistency in your math and I decided to send your math package for outside validation to just the right expert."

Chad sighed in frustration. "Who is this expert of yours? What are his qualifications?"

"If I chose him he's qualified," replied Dick with a smirk. He paused on noticing the flash of anger in Chad's eyes. "Okay, Chad, if you must know, it's Mike Ray."

Chad and the three engineers exchanged disbelieving glances. Mike Ray had been the worst technical assistant Chad had ever had and he remembered being most surprised to hear that Mike

Ray had become a freelance engineering consultant after leaving The Company.

"You must be kidding, Dick!" Chad exclaimed. "That man couldn't do first-grade algebra, never mind validate these complex, applied physics calculations!"

Dick Planke dismissed this argument with a shrug. "I wouldn't be so big-headed, Chad, if I were you! I know you guys in R&D think you're the cleverest, but I'm the manager here, and I can cancel this project faster than you can say algebra! All this FOC stuff of yours may well be good for nothing and besides, Phil Fox knows all about this arrangement and fully agrees."

"Did Phil also review the math?" Chad asked in surprise, brushing aside the personal insults.

"He doesn't need to," Dick replied. "He trusts the experts I select!"

▲

Several months of intensive work continued on the FOC research project. Chad and his colleagues decided that for the sake of progress on the project, it would be best to ignore the frequent insults to their scientific competence flung at them by their project manager.

When Mike Ray's evaluation statement was finally sent to The Company, neither Chad nor his coworkers were given the courtesy or opportunity of reviewing it before copies were circulated to all levels of management by Dick Planke. Thus, it happened that two weeks following the distribution, when the FOC research team called a meeting of the R&D technical staff and managers to demonstrate their highly successful breadboard instrument, the managerial staff was conspicuous by its absence.

"I can't understand this lack of Company interest," Chad said, after demonstrating the outstanding increase in instrument sensitivity, which had excited all the technical R&D representatives.

"And where's Dick?" Tom wondered aloud, scanning for his face in the slowly dispersing research staff crowd. "His secretary assured me he would be available."

"And we stressed the importance of this demo in the memo we circulated," added Ted, picking up a spare copy to convince himself that the words "An Important Success in the Development of the High Sensitivity Fiber Optic Circuit System" were printed in bold and double-underlined as they had requested. He shook his head in frustration and turned to help Chad pack the precious instrument.

It was at that moment that John rushed into the lab, breathing quickly and looking very upset. "You guys won't believe what I just heard!"

Three pairs of curious, bespectacled eyes focused on him as he rapidly continued, "I talked to Roger Voss, over in development–"

"The newly hired Instrument Development Systems Manager, Mr. Roger Voss?" asked Chad.

"Yes, and when I asked him if he was coming to our FOC demo, he practically laughed in my face, saying he had read Mike's validation document that Dick Planke had circulated to management for further comment. He told me he had better things to do than waste his time on a crappy idea that clearly had no sound math foundation."

Chad felt his blood pressure soar as John handed him a copy of the mathematical evaluation Roger Voss had provided. He put on his reading glasses and barely holding his rage in check, read through the document while his colleagues discussed the dreadful implications.

"Did you tell Roger Voss about Dick's attitude?" Tom asked.

"You bet I did!" John said. "And I didn't spare any shots!"

"Of all the conceited, idiotic managers I've had to deal with in twenty years here at The Company," said Tom, "Dick Planke…thick as two short planks…beats them all in rotten management practices!"

"Well, what did that fool, Mike Ray, have to say?" asked Ted, trying to catch a glimpse of the validation report over Chad's shoulder.

"Here, have a look for yourself, " Chad replied with icy disdain. "I've seen enough!"

He stood up and walked with a determined air toward the door.

"Chad, what are going to do?" Tom called after him with significant anxiety.

"What I should have done many months ago!"

▲

"I'm sorry, Dr. Brunswick," Phil Fox's gray-haired, petite secretary said, "but Mr. Fox is busy at the moment."

"Is he alone?" Chad persisted, glancing at the closed door, behind which he could hear a repetitive clicking sound.

"Well, yes, but he's still busy and he doesn't wish to be disturbed."

"I said this is urgent and I intend to see him *now*!" Chad demanded. The determined, irate expression on his face made the secretary jump. Her eyes grew wide as Chad simply advanced past her desk to the oak office double doors and knocking briefly entered the vice president's sanctum.

Phil Fox was startled. He swore as he looked up from his mini-golf course, putter in hand, annoyed that the golf ball had missed its hole and was rolling over the green carpet and under his table.

"Mr. Fox, I'm so sorry," the secretary called from behind Chad, "but he insisted...."

Phil Fox swung his golf stick casually and set it aside. "Close the door, June, please. Chad, what brings you up here in such a state?"

"This idiotic evaluation of the FOC project, which Dick Planke circulated throughout The Company management, without even telling me or letting me look at it first! You must have seen it?"

"Oh, yes, I remember," Phil said. He took the report from Chad and flicked carelessly through the pages. "It's not very complimentary is it?"

"It's the biggest load of crap I've ever seen!" Chad exclaimed. "All Mike Ray did was to substitute my math symbols for his own and then he proceeded in his usual incompetent way to make glaring mistakes in mathematical logic throughout the entire package! If you'll let me show you, Phil—"

Phil rapidly retreated behind his solid mahogany desk and sat down in his high-backed, leather chair. "No, no, Chad, you don't have to. I really do believe you," he said with the same alacrity with which he had accepted Mike Ray's negative statements only a week ago. "If you say there's been a mistake, I take your word!"

"In which case, would you please remove Dick Planke from this project immediately? His atrocious management style resulted in blacklisting of the FOC project so none of the managers turned up for our demo today!"

Phil Fox cleared his throat uncomfortably. "Hold on, Chad. I can't—"

"Yes, you can!"

"Let me look into it, Chad…I'll see what I can do. But tell me, how is your project coming along, anyway?" The vice president of R&D attempted to placate the irate senior researcher.

Chad put aside his personal frustrations with Dick Planke and took up the offer to talk about what truly mattered to him.

"Would you like to round up several of your systems managers and come down for a demo? I think you'll be impressed with what we have to show you. In my opinion, Phil, we are ready to start manufacturing the FOC system and upgrading the present instruments in the field."

What the second FOC demonstration lacked in technical questions, it more than made up for in management politics. It was, therefore, an unmitigated Company success.

Since Phil Fox had arranged the meeting on behalf of Dr. Chad Brunswick, everyone invited turned up promptly. It was indeed an unusual event as Phil Fox rarely set foot in the R&D departments and his face was less well-known to most of the research staff than those of the janitors. Chad and his colleagues looked on with a mixture of amusement and cynicism as the negative opinions of the managers underwent a complete transformation.

"Dynamite project!"

"What potential! It could immediately boost profits!"

"Fantastic! I haven't seen such a brilliant invention since I joined The Company!"

Dick Planke quickly followed suit. His face flushed, he vigorously nodded his wholehearted approval.

"We moved this project along all the way from its conception!" he boasted several times during the demonstration. "I remember when it was nothing more than a few scribbles on the whiteboard and look how we forged it into a real project! And you know, the last time I saw it was two weeks ago. It's *amazing* how much progress can be made in such a short time since that junk of a report from Mike Ray crossed my desk! Incredible! I swear I hardly recognize the project!"

Chad refrained from commenting on Dick Planke's effusive words of praise and his liberal use of the managerial "we." He schooled himself to a state of impartial observation of the political maneuvering around his invention.

"Yes, Dick, that report wasn't worth the paper it was written on," stated Roger Voss, the latest addition to the overstaffed managerial echelon. It was obvious he wished to assert himself in front of the VP-R&D, and underscore Dick Planke's unsound decision.

Chad swallowed a chuckle as Dick Planke turned scarlet, and Tom, Ted, and John exchanged open, mischievous winks and smiles.

Roger Voss's barbed remark, however, rebounded off Dick's thick skin. "Absolutely! Trash it! We were almost led right down a blind alley!" He checked the expression on his boss's face. Phil Fox nodded. He appeared to have quite forgotten Dick Planke's previous antagonistic views and an emboldened Dick declared, "I'm a firm believer in some healthy controversy to stimulate research productivity!"

"Exactly!" Phil Fox agreed with a meaningful glance at Chad, who calculated the odds and decided it was in the FOC project's best interest to reserve all the biting comments he would have liked to make for his close friends' ears. His cynical sense of humor prevailed and he nearly burst into laughter as Phil added, "Scientific debate always leads to great discoveries! Good job, Dick!"

"Chad, if you would agree I think I should like to start with the transfer of this project over to Development." Roger Voss decided to stake his claim. After all, he had also heard from one of his university consultants that Chad's scientific reputation extended beyond The Company walls. This project was just what he needed to ensure a promotion for himself. It was a sure winner.

"I'm extremely impressed with the technical solution to the electronic sensitivity problem! It's super! Brilliant!" Roger Voss praised. "I think we can contribute greatly to FOC in the Future Development Technologies department and give it the push needed to get it through manufacturing!"

Phil Fox consented and Chad silently predicted that Roger Voss would ride on the crest of the FOC project for a number of years to come.

<hr />

It was at The Company Inventors Recognition Dinner at a local Sheraton hotel that the misunderstanding arose, which afforded Dr. Angela Brunswick, Dr. Chad Brunswick's wife, a glimpse into the *high esteem* with which The Company regarded her husband's research achievements.

Dolly Planke, the effervescent third wife of Dick Planke, whose current passionate interest centered wholly around exercise programs and health foods, overheard Angela tell Dr. Greschwin and his wife by the buffet table she was working in "aerodynamics."

"Oh, how fascinating!" Dolly Planke interrupted in her high-pitched voice. "You must tell me all about this new program. I haven't ever heard of it before, but aerodynamics sounds like a cool way to get it all out of your system!"

"Well, yes, I suppose it is. I've never really thought of it in that way before," replied Dr. Angela Brunswick, both surprised and pleased that someone should take a keen interest in such a specialized field. "Though I must admit, I have always found it to be very exciting."

"It must be!" Dolly continued blithely, peroxide blonde curls bobbing about her mature baby face. "How long have you been practicing it?"

"Almost fifteen years."

"Wow!" Dolly squeaked. "It's been around so long? I can't believe I've missed it, and you look so fit, too."

Dr. Angela Brunswick laughed at the most unusual compliment she had ever received. "Thank you. I guess it does keep me on my toes!"

"Gosh! But I'll bet it makes you too fit all over too! Tell me, what exactly does it involve?"

In her enthusiasm, Dolly was completely unaware of the puzzled looks directed at her by Dr. and Mrs. Greschwin and Chad Brunswick, who had stopped their debate to listen to this confusing conversation.

"I think one could define it most simply as the study of the dynamics of the forces acting on bodies in motion through the air," replied Angela.

Dolly's long lashes fluttered. Her small tip-tilted nose and pouting mouth and the awed expression in her large, round, brown eyes gave her an oddly infantile look.

"Gosh! Wow! Gee!" Dolly squeaked and after a thoughtful pause added, "It must be great for the body to have all those forces acting on it! I wonder if the health club Dick and I just joined offers such a program? It's expensive enough. You know, membership for life is eighty thousand dollars and that doesn't include facials and body massages, but with all the fat bonuses Dick's been getting recently for his hard work on this FOC project, we decided to go for it!" She beamed happily, blissfully unaware of the discrepancies in The Company compensation policy.

"I think, Dolly, we're talking at cross purposes," Dr. Wayne Greschwin pointed out with an amused glance at the other members of the party, who had also realized Dolly's misunderstanding. "We were discussing physics!"

"Yes, Wayne, I know. You're definitely among the good-looking inventors here tonight, so what else would we be discussing?" Dolly persisted with a coquettish look. "Angela and I are both interested in physiques. And I specially admire the tall muscular type, like my hubby!" She burst into high-pitched laughter.

"Angela is a professor of physics at the university," Chad explained.

The smile on Dolly's face froze. "Physics? You mean all that math and stuff, not anything like aerobics...aerobic dynamics?"

Angela nodded and with a half-smile confirmed. "Physics."

Dolly's eyes grew big as saucers and she dissolved into laughter. "Oh, gosh! How does your husband stand it? You're much too clever!"

Angela, who was about to give her honest opinion on such a remark, was saved a reply as Wally Steen, president of The Company, stepped up to the microphone on the speaker's rostrum at the front of the room. He tapped the microphone for attention. The invited Company employees, drinks in hand, turned from the buffet table.

"Good evening, everyone! I hope you are enjoying The Company Inventors Recognition Dinner." He paused to hear the murmurs of agreement. "Each year, The Company applauds and gives special recognition for the outstanding achievements of our scientists and inventors, whose patents are keeping this great ship of ours steaming ahead at full speed into the golden horizons!" He paused again for the obligatory applause, loudest from his managerial staff. He then read out the names of the ten scientists to be awarded.

The first to receive the Recognition Certificate and award was Dr. Chad Brunswick. Wally Steen shook the inventor's hand, bestowed on him a broad, sailor's smile and reiterated the same words of congratulation he had used every year for the past ten years at this one and only Company social occasion for R&D staff.

"Well done! Great job! Let's keep those patents drifting in with the tide in the coming year too!"

"Enjoying The Company dog and pony show?" one of Chad's long-time colleagues, who would also be awarded this evening, commented to Angela Brunswick.

"Congratulations, Leo!" she wished in a whisper.

"Forget it, Angela!" Leo grimaced. "I'm sick and tired of The Company's recognition. This is the last patent I've filed for The Company. I've decided it isn't worth bothering anymore."

"You can't seriously mean it, Leo?"

"Oh, but I do! One of these days I'll get a breakthrough that'll take me from here to my own business. Many engineers I've known over the years have wised up, got an idea on the job, not written it down in their patent notebooks and left to work on it elsewhere." He gave a twisted smile. "It's not ethical, but the Legal department would spend more money trying to prove the idea was conceived here than it's worth!" He pointed to a stocky man at the far end of the room. "Do you see that jerk over there? I've had to report to that manager for the past five years and whenever I propose a new idea he says, 'I don't give a damn, Leo, it's not in my work objectives!' So, why should I care? He still gets the bonus, and I get barely three to five percent increase in salary, just enough to cover inflation."

Angela understood his frustration and quipped, "You could be famous with your inventions some day!"

"I'd rather have infamy! Inventors get forgotten!" He suddenly broke into a smile.

"Now, if I found a way to vaporize our worthless management with my invention, I'd go down in history and have the grateful thanks of everyone in R&D!"

Wally Steen called out Leo's name and with a wink in parting the disillusioned twenty-year veteran researcher strode toward the podium to collect his Company reward.

Dolly Planke, who had been hovering nearby watching the proceedings with vacant interest, stepped up to Angela. "You must be as proud of your husband tonight as I am of mine."

"Yes, very much so! " Angela replied with a smile.

"They both did so much work to bring this FOC project to a product," Dolly continued blithely. "You will be joining us for The Company cruise of the Greek Islands next month, won't you?"

Angela Brunswick took a sip of wine to give herself time to recover from this revelation.

"The Greek Islands?" she asked, wishing to hear more about this exclusive perk, which she guessed must be related somehow to her husband's invention.

"Oh, yes, Wally's hired a big yacht and we'll be flying to Greece, then sailing all around the Islands, viewing all those Greek ruins and a guide will stuff us with all that great history. It's a great team-building, stress-control adventure, says Dick. And boy, does he need it after all the work he put into the project from its very conception!" She cast a questioning look at Angela. "I'm sure you and your husband must have been invited? After all, Dick said the cruise is to celebrate the first year of outstanding Company profits the FOC project raked in!"

"Yes, maybe he was," Angela feigned ignorance. "Scientists are so absent-minded."

Dolly tittered. "And with the two of you in science, I wouldn't be surprised if you don't both forget that Chad is the great mind and brilliant inventor of the FOC system, as Roger Voss told me earlier this evening."

"No, Dolly, we don't forget it...even if The Company does!" Angela said as Chad joined them, The Company award in hand.

Dolly's surprise at Angela's comment was distracted by the arrival of Dick Planke and Roger Voss.

"Well done, Chad!" they both shook hands with the inventor.

"That was a long haul," Roger said, "but we finally made it!"

"And you've got your patent, Chad!" Dick said, a hint of jealousy in his voice.

"The Company's patent. As the inventor, I've only applied for the patent in my name," Chad replied and turned to his wife. "Shall we go, dear?" He indicated the departing group of executive officers heading toward the exit door with Wally Steen at the center. "I think the party's over!"

As they waited for the elevator to the car park, Dolly approached them, curiosity evident in her big eyes as she eyed the small blue box in Chad's hand.

"How brainy you must be to think of such an invention that brings millions in profit for The Company. I'm dying to see what you got from Wally. Can I take a peek inside that little box?"

Chad and Angela exchanged a meaningful glance and Dick Planke hurriedly interjected, "Dolly, hon, don't bug Chad! It's just a token!"

"By all means, Dolly, take a look," Chad said, ignoring Dick's words and smiling, handing her the box. "You're more than welcome to see how The Company rewards its inventors!"

"I love small boxes," Dolly laughed with childish eagerness. "As you said, Dick, when you bought me this three-carat diamond ring last month, right out of the blue...." She raised her hand to show off the large solitaire in its heavy gold setting.

"Never mind what I said, hon," Dick tried to prevent Dolly disclosing too much about their financial situation. But Dolly was irrepressible.

"Oh, but you were so cleverly witty, hon," Dolly persisted. "You said, 'Small box, big bonus.' Now, let's see, Dr. Chad, how big your bonus is!"

"Did you hear, Chad," Roger Voss interjected quickly, as they all watched Dolly open the box. "Next year, The Company has decided to give a five-hundred-dollar check to the patent holder and if there are several co-inventors, each will get three-hundred dollars!"

Chad nodded. He had heard talk that the Legal department had recommended that "the cent," or the "peppercorn," awarded to inventors was no longer considered appropriate in these changing times, but it still awaited Wally Steen's approval.

Dolly opened the lid and raised the box to her eyes. Disappointment was evident in her voice as she exclaimed with fake enthusiasm, "Oh, how...how...nice!"

She closed the box and returned it to Chad, when suddenly her face brightened as a thought struck her. "I guess it is only a token of The Company's appreciation, isn't it?"

"Yes, the *only token*," Chad replied dryly.

Roger Voss cleared his throat. "You did get a release from Legal to publish your paper on FOC, didn't you?"

Chad nodded.

"Well, then, you'll get your recognition outside The Company too," added Roger, not without a tinge of envy.

"By the way, I was invited to give a plenary presentation on the FOC system at a meeting in Paris, France, this September," Chad said, with a questioning glance at his project manager.

Dick Planke frowned. "Two months is somewhat short notice to approve a trip overseas. Let me see first, Chad, how much we can spare from the department travel budget for such a technical spree!"

Chad compressed his lips and they walked in silence to the car park. As Chad and his wife stopped by their old Chevrolet, Dick Planke hurriedly took his leave.

"Well, that was a nice outing. We'll say good night for now!"

"I'm pleased to have met you, Angela," Roger Voss extended his hand. "And I'll see you in three weeks time, Chad. Management's now off to an off-site planning meet!"

"On the high seas!" Dolly beamed at Angela. "Look forward to seeing you!"

"Come along, hon, we haven't got all night!" Dick was getting impatient with his wife's silly disclosures, but Dolly resisted her husband's tugging hand. She leaned closer to Angela, saying in a confidential manner, "I'd be so proud if my hubby was clever enough to get that shiny cent! You can always have it framed, but you can't frame a bonus check," she giggled. "I spend it much too fast!"

Dick and Roger laughed out loud and Dolly, waving a friendly goodbye, was promptly whisked away.

*A*ngela gave a crocked smile as her husband fell silent after recounting the highlights of the FOC project.

"This evening was an eye-opener for me," she said. "I'll never forget driving out of that parking lot at the Sheraton, following Dick's brand new white Mercedes with personalized number plates that read "FOC 1" and then later on the freeway following Roger's new Lexus with plates that proclaimed "Rogs FOC"! And you, the actual inventor, get nothing but a miserable *token cent* for your hard work…no bonus checks, no Company cruises, not even the funds for a conference as the invited speaker! Do you know what a bonus check would mean to us? We still have a mortgage over our heads and two very bright kids to get through college!" She paused to draw breath. "All you have to show for all your hard work is a superficial thank you, an unframed piece of paper and a blasted cent! What else do you have to take with you from The Company?"

Chad smiled grimly. A resolute gleam sprang up in his eyes. "Well, my love, the old Romans used to say, *Omnea mea mecum porto!*" He tapped his temple.

"Everything I own I carry with me?" Angela translated with a frown. "Your knowledge, love, of course!" she exclaimed on a laugh as sudden understanding dawned on her. "So you have finally decided to take up the offer from TechnoChem?"

"By the end of this week, The Company will have my letter of resignation!"

THE STATUS CHAIR

Its swivel leg is on four wheels,
You won't believe how soft it feels,
Padded, molded by design,
For Managers of Level Nine!
But you are just a Level Four,
So keep your feet outside my door,
And don't you ever, ever dare,
To park your ass on this, MY CHAIR!

Dr. Andrew Bradford was very pleased with the results of his efforts. He flexed his fingers, which hurt after judiciously applying a screwdriver to the four shiny screws on the backrest of the perfectly suited chair he had discovered in the corridor. Tilting it forward and upright, then manipulating the armrests to a lower, more comfortable position, the only adjustment he had to make was to the seat height. The tight height control lever finally yielded after a generous application of lubricating oil and the chair became a perfect match for use at the newly arrived prototype instrument.

Andrew had been assigned to evaluate the performance of this instrument, one of his very first projects since the start of his employment at The Company two weeks ago.

With a satisfied feeling of achievement, he lowered his tall, lanky body onto the well-cushioned seat, his long legs bent comfortably as he sat down and with a murmur of sheer contentment, fired up the optics unit. Lights flashed and the instrument came to life with whirring tones that sent a quiver of anticipation and excitement through the most recent research member of the Electro-Optics Engineering department.

Gee whiz! Doing development work in industry is real great, he thought, recalling the difficult time he had during the past year at the university as a "post-doc" struggling to get a grant approved for research on a similar instrument system.

Engrossed in making a selection of the equipment settings on the control panel, Andrew Bradford paid no attention to the commotion in the corridor outside the laboratory. Suddenly, the laboratory door was flung open with a crash. Andrew leaned back to look around the corner at who could be in such a hurry. He saw his boss, Dr. Greg Green, accompanied by a tall, corpulent man and casually noted that this man, whom he could not recall having met before, appeared to be suffering from high blood pressure. His narrowed blue eyes were bloodshot and his flabby cheeks glowed with heightened color.

Andrew turned his attention back to the instrument.

"But I tell you, Greg, it didn't just disappear!" the disgruntled, low voice of the corpulent man intruded into Andrew's thoughts as the two men advanced into the laboratory.

"I know, Udo. Calm down, will you?" Andrew's supervisor replied. "What makes you think it's here in the first place?"

"Because someone, whose name I shall not divulge, said they saw one of your people *steal it*!"

"Come on, Udo, you can't go around accusing people of theft!" replied Greg. "If they did, they must have just borrowed it and I'm sure they'll return it, if you tell them politely it's yours!"

Greg attempted to calm him down with a jocular laugh, but Udo obviously did not find any humor in the situation.

"The hell I will! Some junior pipsqueak dares to take one of *my chairs* and I have to be polite?!" Udo's irate voice reverberated through the laboratory where all conversation had suddenly ceased.

Andrew, now distracted, stopped to listen and again peeped around the corner. Udo's back was turned to him and he saw that his boss looked very uncomfortable. Behind him, several researchers and their lab assistants tried to hide their amusement and surreptitiously grimaced and winked at each other.

A sudden bleep from the display panel drew Andrew's attention back to his experiment. With a carefree shrug, he concentrated on the dials.

"There it is!" Udo suddenly yelled.

Andrew smiled to himself. That should make him happy, he thought, focusing on the flickering numbers on the liquid crystal display panel.

"You!" Udo bellowed again.

Andrew frowned with annoyance at this persistent distraction, but continued to record the numbers from the instrument display panel.

"Hey, you! Do you hear me?!"

Andrew glanced up as a shadow fell over his notebook. To his surprise, the man named Udo was towering over him, his face contorted with anger, outrage, and indignation as he started to shake Andrew's chair. He shouted, "You! You stole it! Get off my chair!"

As Andrew quickly began to rise, Udo furiously pulled the chair from underneath him. The young scientist grabbed the lab bench to keep himself from falling. Was the man crazy?

"What have you done to my chair?" Udo roared. "Just look at it! You've ruined it, and you took it without my permission! How dare you!"

Andrew felt a flush of embarrassment creep up his clean-shaven face. His ears burnt. All eyes in the laboratory were focused on him. And in front his new boss too. Oh, shit! He hadn't meant any harm!

"I...I...I'm sorry, but this chair was standing in the corridor for the past week and no one claimed it, so I assumed–" Andrew stammered apologetically.

At the university no one ever took such exception for borrowing a miserable chair. His professor even gave his chair for spare parts to fix a homemade optics bench!

"This chair was in the corridor because my office was being refurbished and this type of chair, according to personnel rules, cannot be used by someone as junior as you!"

"I'm sorry, as I said I didn't mean any harm. There was no chair available for my new instrument here and since this chair wasn't being used by anyone, I just assumed...."

"You *assumed*, did you? Well, in our Company you never assume—*you ask*! And you don't just take a Level Nine manager's chair for lab work! I can see you'll have to learn a helluva lot about The Company regulations and managerial rights! Greg, this young man surely deserves a reprimand!"

Andrew was speechless. But as he gazed at Udo, a sudden inkling that he had seen this man somewhere before began to emerge from the recesses of Andrew's memory banks. Yes, he had seen this irate, flushed face once before! But where was it?

An ass? Of course! Yes, those "ass's ears"! Despite his acute discomfort, Andrew's eyes lit up. Boy, was he glad he had visited the barber to shave off his beard and cut short his long hair before joining The Company! His lips began to tremble with mirth as in a flash he recalled in his mind's eye, the incident he had witnessed at the university a year ago when this "important" Company manager had visited his Prof.'s laboratory.

"The Company is interested in our instrument design," Professor Pringle had told Andrew with a satisfied smile early that morning over a cup of steaming coffee.

"Any possibility for funding our research?" Andrew asked hopefully.

Professor Pringle shrugged. "Who knows? I've had dealings with those industry guys before and most of the time we are on the giving end."

"To paraphrase old Caesar, *Veni, vidi, swipeee?*" Andrew chuckled and Professor Pringle nodded, a cynical light in his eyes. "Don't we have a confidentiality agreement with The Company?"

"We do," said the Prof., taking a business card from his pocket. He added, "But it often works both ways. They also need new ideas or consultation on design theory. I must admit I'm looking forward to it this time. According to the letter I received, we may have a whole lot to offer in which The Company is interested."

Professor Pringle handed him the impressive gold-embossed business card. "Mr. Hess, The Company representative, is coming today to discuss the algorithm with us and to see our research equipment design and function. As you see, Andrew, he is the Chief Program Manager of the Electro-Optics Engineering department. He told me over the phone that he has over thirty years of technical management experience."

The Prof. took a sip of coffee and looking over the rim of the mug said hopefully, "If all goes well, this time next year we could even buy a shredder to shred our grant application forms!"

Two hours later than expected, The Company representative arrived. Andrew noted that the Prof., a man known for his calm, patient and kind nature, waved aside this lack of punctuality and cordially greeted The Company man, inviting him into his office adjacent to the lab. Since the door remained open, Andrew overheard, without intent, a surprising snatch of their conversation.

"…Yes, if you're interested in funding for your research, you're talking to the right man. I'm in charge of the funds and I can allocate them, as I see fit, for any outside projects, like yours. The amount is negotiable, but I'm sure we can come to an agreement that will ensure enough for your work, yourself and…for my efforts and approval as well. I could get you a cool million. As I say to all our outside consultants, it's a 'give and take' relationship…a confidential agreement between the two of us, of course!"

Andrew now listened unashamedly. He could not believe his ears! The man was obviously proposing that he should get a kickback out of The Company outside research funds! If he did this with several outside consultants, he must be quite rich by now, Andrew speculated. He was curious how Professor Pringle, known for his philosophy on honest, clean living, would respond to such a blatantly dishonest proposal.

He heard the rustling of some papers and after a pause, the Prof.'s even reply. "Half a million dollars is just what I envisioned would be sufficient for the development of our optics modulator, and our university and your Company lawyers can draw up an agreement for any potential patent rights. I myself do not accept any…rewards and I think it is best that we now go into the lab to see our breadboard instrument."

Soon afterwards, The Company man, his face very flushed, followed Professor Pringle into the laboratory.

Andrew, sporting a newly grown beard, tied-back long hair and attired in the typical university uniform of well-worn jeans and sweatshirt, looked up expectantly from his work behind the bench. His welcoming smile faded for the expression on his Prof.'s face was far from congenial, while the corpulent manager, attired in a starched white shirt, pin-striped navy suit and polished snake-skin shoes, appeared to be highly annoyed.

"So, you're saying that based solely on those math formulas you just showed me back there," the manager waved his hand vaguely in the direction of the Prof.'s office, "that thingamadoger will fly?" The tone of his voice appeared to have changed from the condescending, facile manner he had used in the Prof.'s office to a derogatory antagonism.

"Yes, that, thingamadoger, as you call it–the Electro-Optics Detector Modulator, EODM–is already airborne," Professor Pringle replied with a half-smile. He always discouraged loose scientific language in his students. "And, yes, it is based on the algorithm The Company is interested in and it has been extensively evaluated by my post-doc, Andrew…."

The Company manager ignored the young man behind the bench. He snapped his eyes and with a wave of his ring-covered hand said, "Huh! University student evaluation methods don't generally wash well in industry, you know. You will have to let me be the judge of how useful it is to The Company after you turn on that thingamabob!"

Andrew stood by and watched with bated breath as Professor Pringle compressed his lips and switched on their department's pride and joy. He gradually calmed down as he gave the requested demonstration.

"Does it always respond so slowly?" The Company man asked. "I can already see that we will have to work on your design–if we decide to take a license on this instrument."

Andrew looked up in surprise. Though the electronics was home built, the instrument was, nonetheless, designed around the most up-to-date technology. There were no detector-modulators with faster responses available anywhere in the world!

"What? But this is a nanosecond response scale," Professor Pringle replied with obvious astonishment. "It is a unique, rapid response modulator! Scientists from around the world have visited our lab to be able to carry out measurements on this instrument and confirm some of their own research."

The Company man cleared his throat, looking around skeptically. He withdrew a lizard-skin notebook from his inside jacket pocket and Monte Blanc fountain pen and began jotting down some notes. "Practicing science is all very well, but I still have to be convinced that the theory behind all this razzle dazzle is sound!"

Professor Pringle nodded his willingness to explain his favorite theoretical aspect of the research. He quickly stepped up to the whiteboard.

With a red marker pen he expertly wrote down several equations with the quickness of long-term familiarity. The Company man sat down on a lab chair and supported his flabby chin on his right hand. His small eyes followed the Prof.'s writing skeptically.

"Hold on a minute!" he suddenly exclaimed, raising a thick finger and pointing to the last of the five equations. "What does that 'z' thingamajig over there mean?"

"It is the vector parameter. As you can see, here," the Prof. pointed out the symbols in the first equation, "the end result of this primary equation here is expressed by the 'z' term."

"Oh? I don't see how you can multiply that 'z' with the inverse of 'p' in the third equation, to get to the nanosecond rate."

"As I just said," the Professor replied patiently, "the solution is derived from the primary equation, which is based on the Gerome-Wilson principles of time-related signal modulation."

"But I don't think you can base your algorithm on that! There must be some mistake somewhere!"

Andrew could not believe his ears. Was this man an electro-optics engineer or not? Every first-year student in the Prof.'s class knew that you had to use the Gerome-Wilson principles in time-signal modulation calculations.

Professor Pringle's face took on a look of patient sufferance, the kind of expression Andrew had seen often when the Prof. was faced with a particularly slow student. "Let me explain the basic Gerome-Wilson principles first," he said and began to write the lecture notes from his first year tutorial classes.

"I don't need any of your lecture stuff!" The Company man interjected aggressively. "It's too general—"

"If you'll let me continue I can show you that it does apply to our conditions here. It is an essential parameter in the algorithm, which I used in the design of the modulator, which your scientists told me The Company would like to develop," the Prof. said with an uncharacteristic edge to his voice.

The manager waved aside the offer with impatience. "I know all that!" he said, a sneer on his lips. "What I say is, how can you suddenly introduce that doodad over there—"

"You mean, the 'g' coefficient?" the Prof. asked, irritation at such extremely lax scientific language beginning to show in his tone.

"Yes, that 'g' you stuck in there without any reason, just to show the nanosecond response of your modulator."

"Look, Mr. Hess, if you will not allow me to explain the basic premises, step by step, how can we discuss the results? You did come here for consultation, didn't you?"

"Go ahead, consult, but first you'll have to convince me that modulator breadboard gadget of yours really does what you claim!"

"Once you understand the Gerome-Wilson principles it will become obvious to you!" Professor Pringle replied and began to write furiously on the whiteboard, explaining the principles whether the man wanted to listen or not.

The manager's eyes snapped into slits and with heightened color he appeared to listen.

"Did I make myself clear now?" the Prof. asked.

To Andrew it was crystal clear.

"Let's just say that you might be right, but I'll have to think it over when I get back. In my opinion you've based the algorithm on incorrect premises and I can't see how your modulation can have nanosecond responses!"

"But we have just demonstrated it to you!" the Professor raised his voice. "And believe me, I have discussed the theory behind this with my colleagues in depth. It is theoretically sound! If you will let me explain–"

"No need to repeat yourself. Your fancy breadboard looks fine, but your theory won't hold a photon!"

"Neither will your muddled understanding!" Professor Pringle finally lost his temper.

Never had Andrew seen this gentle, calm man so irate. "This theory," the Prof. continued, "has been published in peer reviewed international journals. And if you can't or won't take the time to understand it, I can't help you! You came here for a consultation and possible collaboration, so take it or leave it! I don't give a damn!"

The Company man turned scarlet. "Who do you think you are? A puffed-up, hotshot university Prof.? Your consultation cost The Company a lot and it isn't worth shit! I say your assumptions are flawed…fraudulent!"

Andrew held his breath in anticipation of the professor's response.

"The only fraudulent assumption around here is that you know anything about this subject! You'd flunk the most basic, first-year exam! So, get out of my lab, you ignorant jackass!" Professor Pringle retorted, controlling himself with a visible effort and aiming a shaking arm at the laboratory door. "And you can take your consultation fee back to The Company and stick it in your jackass's ear! I never want to see you again. And you can report back that I wouldn't want to waste my breath consulting for The Company, which entrusts its management to such a technical ignoramus! I will have no difficulty finding a more appreciative company elsewhere!"

Scowling furiously, Udo Hess strode out of the laboratory in such a hurry, he almost collided with Andrew. Professor Pringle slammed the door shut behind him saying, "And this moron even tried to bribe me! He asked for a kickback from the development grant! God help The Company with such corrupt managers!"

In less than two weeks, the professor found funding from an overseas company.

▲

"Well, Greg, are you going to take this…from this…?" Udo's voice trembled with rage.

On a sudden daring impulse, Andrew completed, a mischievous twinkle in his eyes, "This ignorant jackass?"

Udo Hess froze for an instant and turned to scrutinize Andrew suspiciously. The clean-shaven face of the young scientist seemed vaguely familiar, but he could not quite place him. The words he used must be just a coincidence, Udo Hess figured, wiping several drops of perspiration from his forehead.

"Yes," Udo continued, "that's a good description of you, young man! You've got a great deal to learn! Don't think that just because you've got a high-flown college degree, you know it all! You know nothing at all about The Company culture and the kind of behavior management expects of its technical people!"

"And what has that got to do with your damn chair?" Andrew's boss, Dr. Green said with an exasperated sigh. Winking at Andrew, he added, "Andrew, please, restore that chair to its original condition and take it back to Mr. Hess's office."

Udo nodded importantly and on his way out glanced back at Andrew with a thoughtful frown.

An hour later, Andrew stepped into Dr. Green's office. Even though the door was closed, Greg Green lowered his voice.

"A word of advice, young man, you'd better never mention Professor Pringle's name to Udo Hess. I am aware of the way Udo botched our chances for the Electro-Optics Detector Modulator in his usual self-serving way. I was the one who proposed we finance Professor Pringle's instrument development project."

Andrew looked at his project leader in surprise. "So why didn't you come along when Udo Hess visited Prof. Pringle's lab?"

Greg leaned back in his chair. "One thing you'll soon learn around here is that management makes all the business decisions even when they should be based on technical merit."

"But how can The Company tolerate such waste and vice and still hope to survive? It lost both an outstanding consultant and an excellent product?" Andrew queried in the tones of the keen, yet inexperienced employee.

"On the laurels of our past, successful products. The Company coasts along on management that's so well greased, all technical input doesn't have a chance of sticking!" He laughed at Andrew's surprise. "But I never said that, you understand?"

Andrew understood. He nodded thoughtfully and began his Company growing process with mounting doubts about his initial, idealistic enthusiasm for industrial research.

"Now, let's forget about all this nonsense and discuss the results of your experiment," Greg said. With a wry smile and a distinctly cynical tone in his voice he added, "By the way, Andrew, don't you ever, ever dare to park your ass on a *Status Chair*!"

FROM COMMOTION TO PROMOTION

Blustering like high speed gales,
When in science talks of sales,
But to salesmen never fails
To relate tall science tales!

A Jack is he of every trade,
In every field he's sure to wade,
Impresses all with his charade,
And for his show he's highly paid!

With such a Manager galore,
No need for Experts anymore!

*L*oud booming laughter announced to all within several corridor lengths of the meeting room that the Project Manager of the Materials and Devices Research Project, Dr. Dan Nuthing, had returned from one of his frequent business trips overseas.

As was his usual habit, he immediately called together the six members of his group–four senior scientists and two technical assistants–to discuss their progress in his absence. It did not bother him that the two technical assistants, Kim and Betsy, doodled in irritation that they had to waste their time in unproductive meetings listening to their supervisors educating the project manager when so much lab work still had to be done. They sighed and grimaced to each other during the brief summary Dr. Janice Palovsky and Dr. Albert Lim presented.

Neither did he pay any attention to the frustrated glances Dr. Helen Afiyet and Dr. Mark Kane shot in his direction as the two assistants began a sniggering susurrus in the middle of their presentation.

He had long ago brushed aside what he termed as the scientists' arrogant suggestions that their technical assistants would be more gainfully employed carrying out routine work in the laboratory. When the two assistants echoed their agreement with this proposal, Dan Nuthing had promptly rejected their request. He now looked on them with misguided sympathy, deciding that their bosses must have definitely intimidated them.

Dr. Nuthing was a great believer in a general business education policy for all employees, which he expounded at length given only a wisp of encouragement.

"A good manager," his opinion was often aired and heard by all along the corridors, "brings everyone together and gets everyone involved at all levels. There should be none of this I'm-better-than-you-are business, because we are all the same, of exactly the same value, on this and every project. We all contribute equally!"

The four researchers frequently wished he would extend his generous ideas of equality to the area of compensation. His egalitarian ideas rapidly dwindled when it came to technical personnel requests for funds to attend essential scientific conferences, especially those overseas. He was particularly tight-fisted in response to any request for an overdue salary adjustment, yet his self-serving generosity reappeared with surprising swiftness whenever he saw the opportunity to take credit for contributing to the project's advancement.

"We did it this time!" he announced jovially just prior to his recent trip to a marketing meeting in Honolulu. Stopping in the laboratory doorway, for he rarely ventured further inside either in mind or body, he turned to the vice president of R&D with great deference in his voice for the high position.

"You see, Mr. Fox, we are making brilliant discoveries in here and we all contribute in our way. I must say that without my management's hoopla and cajoling, these guys would still be playing with putty!"

What he called "hoopla and cajoling" he now implemented once again at this progress meeting. Raising his hand in a timeout football referee gesture, he brought Dr. Mark Kane's summary to an abrupt end. He was beginning to feel distinctly lonely for the familiar sound of his own voice.

"Hold it! I can see you've all been working hard. I'm impressed! Well done!" He suppressed a yawn that underscored the superficial nature of his encomium. "As I pointed out to you all before my departure," he continued, conveniently forgetting he had asked them not to bother with the synthesis of all that "organic crap," "your newly synthesized Compound Z is clearly a breakthrough! I hope you all realize its enormous potential and its immediate application in increasing the resistance of The Company's best-selling Plastison product!"

The four researchers glanced at each other, frustration and ire mirrored in their eyes. What had they been telling this man since his assignment as project manager to this project six months ago and for the umpteenth time during this past half-hour? Was he sitting on his ears or was he wholly ignorant of the basic technical understanding required to manage a synthetic organic chemistry project? Surely not! After all, the man even had a Ph.D.!

This had puzzled the scientists for quite a while after Dan Nuthing became the project manager, until one day, Dan had boasted about his doctoral thesis in botany completed some twenty years ago and never practiced. When he realized he had no interest in this field of research, he had decided to take a couple of management courses and here he was now, ready to take on any research project as a "technical" manager.

Janice Palovsky recalled these facts now in her mind as she looked on the ebullience of Dan Nuthing's spouting. She silently fumed. He was a typical "counterfeit" scientist.

The scientists in R&D had often questioned how upper management could consistently produce such mismatched project managers–or was this actually regarded as great managerial skill? And why couldn't they have entrusted this position to the technical project leader, Dr. Helen Afiyet, who was a most knowledgeable chemist with a sound business sense and excellent communication skills?

Instead, they had to tolerate this pompous loudmouth for whom every technical script had to be prepared word for word each time he reported to upper-management on their project's progress.

Progress? Janice smoldered. How could they even hope to progress, when so much of their research time was wasted in tutoring a manager, whose only talent would have rivaled a top secret scrambling device, for nothing they told him ever quite retained its correct technical meaning. Did they think managing a research project was just a numbers game? It required more than a glancing acquaintance with general science!

Increasing the resistance, indeed! Dr. Janice Palovsky felt her blood pressure soar. Surely they had each just stressed repeatedly that the value of Compound Z was in *lowering* the resistance, thereby increasing the electromagnetic flux through Plastison! That was the quintessence of the invention. An increase in resistance, as Dan Nuthing had said, would have meant overheating Plastison and reduced efficacy. In other words, a useless product!

"I think you mean a reduction in the resistance, Dan," Janice forced herself to correct him in a polite, yet firm voice.

Dr. Nuthing shrugged his broad shoulders and smoothly gave his verbal accelerator an extra kick down. "Increase, decrease just different sides of the same wire!" He gave a stentorian laugh. "Conductivity depends on resistance and an increase in one can lead to a decrease in the other, so reduced flow through Plastison results in lowered efficacy and Compound Z will naturally increase all these beneficial effects!" He paused to see how his bluff had affected the scientists with a self-satisfied and defiant expression. "You do understand, don't you?"

Janice frowned. What kind of verbal garbage was that?!

"Come on, Jan," Dan continued. "It's not all that difficult to follow!" He bared his large teeth as Janice shook her head. "Gee, guys! You're all supposed to have a brain. Put them to work! Do I have to explain everything to you again?"

"I thought we were explaining our results to you–perfectly

clearly!" Dr. Helen Afiyet interrupted and pointed to the data displayed on her projection overhead.

"You don't *explain* to me, Helen," Dan replied, a sharp edge to his voice, "you *report* your results to me, and it seems I'm the one doing all the explaining around here!"

He glanced at the two technical assistants for approval. "Don't you agree, Betsy, Kim?"

"Oh, yes! Absolutely!" Kim and Betsy assured with falsely ingratiating smiles and cast mildly apologetic looks at their supervisors. After all, Dan Nuthing was the project manager and could do more for their promotions than the powerless researchers.

Kim quickly decided now was her opportunity to ensure her prospects for advancement. She knew well that Dan Nuthing's words did not exactly make any technical sense but nonetheless added, "That's brilliant, Dr. Nuthing!" She always addressed the managers by whatever titles they might have or aspire to. "I've never had it explained to me quite like that before!"

She earned a kick under the table from Betsy for her obsequious behavior and looked down to avoid the annoyed glances from her supervisors.

Dan Nuthing's ego was flattered. Dr. Mark Kane exhaled loudly to relieve some of his tension. Dan misunderstood. "Don't worry, Mark, you can do it too! It's all a matter of presentation! I can tell you a lot about that. When I was in Technical Sales I always first explained the benefits of a product to the customer so that he thought he had really understood all along, and then it would sell itself! The technical nitty-gritty will all be irrelevant when I sell this Compound Z to upper-management."

"Upper-management?" exclaimed Janice in surprise.

"But we aren't that far! We've only just started a stability evaluation of Compound Z," Albert protested.

"We're far from ready to release it!" Helen added firmly.

Dan waved his hand and whistled to stop their protests. "Whoa, guys! *I'm* here to decide when we're ready and *I* have decided that we are! Today was just a dry run and from now on we'll pretty up this Compound Z, add some pizzazz and before you know it, it'll be the talk of The Company! Our President, Mr. Wally Steen himself asked me the other day how things were getting on, and this, I can tell you, is what we in management, call visibility! All the way up to the very top!"

The meeting proved to be only the first in a long series in which Dan Nuthing's major contribution was in the selection of often garish, boldly contrasting colors for the overheads. The researchers' suggestions for a more subtle, scientific presentation scheme only triggered flippant jokes and were promptly brushed aside.

Dan Nuthing's enthusiasm for the project was gaining momentum with each passing day. He finally had something worthwhile to do at work and like a steamroller he pulverized every suggestion that happened to stand in his way or did not coincide with his plan of action. Visibility was his motto and where else could he be assured of that than by informing his old friends in the Technical Sales and Marketing departments.

"Hey! Joe! How're you doin' today!" he roared warmly into the telephone.

"What's up, Dan? Robby's here with me—"

"Well, put me on the speaker! What I've got to say is for all the world to hear!"

"Dan!" greeted Robby's hoarse voice. "We haven't heard from you since you switched to R&D. Made any great inventions yet?"

Dan did not need any better prompting. "Takes time, you know! R&D requires a whole different way of thinking. It's not just sweet-talking the customers like you guys do, you know!"

"Watch it, big mouth!" his friends laughed with a teasing threat. "What did you do for ten years over here? Sweet-talked all the female customers!"

"Come on, Joe! Let's leave my divorce out of this! I've regained my creativity since I broke out of the noose and, boy, did we come up with a great new compound over here in my group!"

"Such as?" A skeptical tone was evident in Robby's question.

"Such as Compound Z that'll blow the socks off the current Plastison market. Even Wally's all excited."

"Do you see much of him then?" Joe seemed impressed.

"Do I? The hell I do! Almost every couple of days since we invented Compound Z," he exaggerated. "And Phil Fox's behaving more like a bloodhound urging us to get it presented to upper-management!" Sounds of approval from his friends spurred Dan on. "I tell you, we work like the blazes here, slogging away night and day in the lab. I've got to be on my toes all the time, swishing the managerial whip over the researchers' heads, making sure they stay on track and they don't forget to see the forest for the trees! You know how easily those research guys get themselves into blind alleys!" He gave a hearty bombastic laugh. "But that's research for you–all in a typical R&D day's work!"

"We all remember the stories you told us about your days as a researcher and we always knew a scientist like you was wasted in Sales, Dan! They should give a guy like you the Nobel Prize for the work you're doing in R&D!" Robby interjected. "But frankly, I don't know how you can stand it with those R&D guys. I stay well clear of those departments. They always make me feel like I didn't do my homework, if I don't know the blasted formulas of their pet compounds I'm selling!" The three friends guffawed loudly.

"Yeah, well, even Phil intimated they're a pain in his neck most of the time! Just thinking of them, he told me last time, ruins his golf swing!" He paused for the answering laughter and bragged, "But they aren't difficult to handle if you can lead them and stay on top of their research efforts!"

Dan Nuthing had clearly come close to the upper ranks, Robby thought. You never knew when such acquaintance would prove useful. "Tell us, how soon will you be able to get us involved in a marketing evaluation on that "Z " thing?" he asked, eager to jump onto the bandwagon.

"Pretty soon, I should imagine," Dan promised, very much in his element. "I've got to give this big review presentation to upper-management. And, of course, our patent application must be completed." He paused briefly to make a note to tell the Legal department that his name should be appended to the patent application. "I'll arrange a meeting with you guys later. I just thought I'd let you know in advance. You know, for old times' sake–I haven't forgotten you. I may be a scientist now, but my heart's still with marketing!"

"You sure are a fine bridge!" Joe tried to ingratiate himself. "Any chance of an invite to your great review meet?"

"Yeah, good idea! I'll simply tell Phil you're interested!"

As Dan replaced the receiver, he thought hard for a plausible reason with which he could convince Phil Fox. He decided that since Phil Fox had been nicknamed "bean counter" in R&D, he must have a keen understanding of marketing issues and probably would not object.

Now, what else could he do to move further into the limelight? He recalled Kim mentioning that the four researchers were compiling technical data to publish their results. At the meeting next day, he therefore demanded they submit to him a comprehensive written review of all data on Compound Z.

"Apart from the latest results of the evaluation, we've already completed it," Dr. Helen Afiyet started to explain, but Dan Nuthing raised a silencing finger.

"That's what you think! Until I've had a chance to review your script, you're not even walking. You're crawling!" He laughed loudly and patted Dr. Helen Afiyet's shoulders in a gesture that was at the same time condescending and avuncular.

Two days later, he received the hundred-page project review document. Dan Nuthing grimaced with obvious displeasure as he scanned the authors' names. He said nothing, but frantically tried over the next two weeks to turn their sentences around until the original meaning was wholly mangled beyond scientific comprehension.

The four scientists fought back to salvage their work from destruction, but they soon realized it was impossible to convince Dan that his editing made no sense. Tactful comments on his incorrect interpretation of the scientific facts only resulted in veiled accusations of insubordination against their project manager's wishes.

"You've all got serious ego problems!" Dan Nuthing accused the researchers the day after his contributions had been deleted. "Stop wasting your time on my grammar, turning my words around here and there. I have a great deal of experience in writing executive reviews!"

Frustrated that Dan had failed to see it was not the grammar but the technical content of his contributions to which the researchers objected, they decided the situation warranted some surreptitious measures. Working late one evening, after Dan had left, they altered the text back to its original, technically correct version and used words familiar to Dan. They gained some small pleasure from the fact that Dan Nuthing did not even notice when he re-read the review, clearly believing he had indeed contributed significantly.

This fact he emphasized at the final group meeting. "I believe we are almost ready to present and circulate this project review document, except…for minor additions here and there." He tapped the authors' names on the cover page of the review document and continued in the light-hearted, benevolent tone of a dictator, who would tolerate no opposition, "I mean, such as your obvious oversight in omitting to add my name to the authors listed here! And I'll make sure this omission is also corrected on our patent application."

The four researchers meekly submitted. They knew it would be futile to oppose him.

"I wouldn't say anything," Dan added, "but you can't deny I did contribute. And all we have to do now is get it bound and distributed to those who count in The Company. I'll find the best person for this job. The review has got to impress…that's what'll sell at the upcoming presentation!" He beamed at them like a benefactor. "And don't worry, guys, I'll make sure your names get some exposure too!"

"We will be present at the review anyway, won't we?" Dr. Albert Lim asked.

Dan Nuthing hesitated. "Well, that depends on how upper management feels and what we decide to discuss. If it's just business-related matters, you're not expected to be involved–"

"But the presentation overheads are all technical," Janice Palovsky objected.

If you could still call the presentation technical, Dr. Helen Afiyet thought cynically, recalling how much they had to simplify it.

Dan directed a surprised look at Janice. "Of course they are! And as a technical man, I can more than take care of all the technical aspects from now on!" He paused and on an after-thought added, "But we'll see. Maybe you can be in on that part of the review–if you insist!"

The researchers did. Dan Nuthing, feeling somewhat cornered, put on an affronted expression. "Okay, let me see if Phil Fox has no objections. But, if you do attend, I don't want to hear a squeak out of any of you. Keep your mouths shut and let me deal with upper management. You don't want to screw up this project's prospects, do you?"

He had no idea what serious misgivings the four researchers had about the future of their project in his hands.

In the meanwhile, Dan planned further tactics to impress upper management. By an extraordinary stroke of good luck, he encountered just the perfect person: Lady Luck herself, who claimed to have all the right connections.

▲

All day long, wags her tongue,
Drops a name, plays the game,
Knowledge base, a sorry case,
All declare, there's nothing there,
Ruins all, techs take the fall,
Creates commotion, gets promotion!

It had been a long day for Dona Trivi, B.S. chemist. She took off her white lab coat and sat down behind her desk with an exhausted sigh and a martyred expression on her thin, pointed face. Anyone entering her well-appointed office at four that afternoon would have been convinced she had spent a tiring day in the research laboratory.

Yet, first impressions can be deceiving. The fact that she did not have a simple cubicle office, like the majority of other more senior and higher qualified scientists in R&D, but had been granted a spacious office with a view should have given even the most casual visitor some pause for thought.

A cursory inquiry would also have revealed that the white lab coat was only a temporary measure for additional warmth since the air-conditioning unit in the R&D building had been set too low that day. Then, on closer observation, it would have become more than obvious that from her precipitously high-heeled shoes to her inch-long carmine nails, she was as much at odds with serious laboratory work as ballet slippers were for mountaineering.

So how did she accomplish any research in R&D? Her boss, the Analytical Evaluations project leader, had three technical assistants assigned to her who carried out all of her lab work, wrote her reports and obtained instructions from the other senior researchers in the department when data of any value were required.

And what personal accomplishments entitled her to such a privileged position in R&D, despite her assistant-level qualifications? She had long ago proven herself useful, to quote her own job description, as "Interdepartmental Liaison Officer." In other words, "The Company Gossip Monger"!

Dona sighed again. She had tried every wile possible to weasel some more information out of Dr. Mark Kane on Compound Z, for her boss had heard a rumor that a review meeting was to be scheduled. She had been wholly unsuccessful and was beginning to suffer a severe bout of depression.

Like a parrot drenched in a torrent of its own words, she curled up for comfort on her perch, a high-backed chair, another special favor granted on the excuse that she had a bad back.

What could she do to get at the information? She glanced at one of the many photographs of her eight-year-old son. Her husband had divorced her several years ago for her excessive expenditures, and she now used her single parent status as a ploy to gain pity from management and as a lead to an exchange of personal and work-related information. This time, however, her ploy had not worked at all. She nervously wondered if she was losing her touch or were these scientist types, like her ex-husband, just incomprehensible to her?

Absently, she chewed one of her artificial nails. What she needed was a man with prospects. She frowned as she re-read one of the sexually explicit one-liners strategically pasted to the walls: *Don't mock me, unfrock me!* And not even these had been able to get her any kind of significant date in the last year!

Her frustrated musings were brought to a halt as her telephone rang.

"Dona!" a female voice sounded eagerly. It was Nancy, one of her assistants, hoping to ingratiate herself to the person responsible for her end-of-year review. "Dona, I think you might be interested in a bit of scuttlebutt I just heard!"

"Yes, yes, what is it?" Dona's high-pitched, edgy voice replied, as she tugged impatiently at the tight red curls that dangled loosely about her face.

"It's about the Compound Z project."

Dona's dark, beady eyes flashed with sudden interest. "What about it?"

"Well, Kim—you know, one of the project assistants working at the moment for Mark Kane—"

"I know all that! What did she say?"

"Okay! She said that Dr. Dan Nuthing—"

"Dan Nuthing!" Dona could not help a squeal of eagerness. She had seen him around and heard all about his exciting reputation in management circles as a brilliant scientist and outstanding project manager. If only she could get close to him.

"Yes, Dr. Nuthing, himself," Nancy continued in a hushed voice, "will be giving this real important review to upper-management and is trying to round up as many big company wheels as he can. He's also looking for a quick way to get his project review flashily bound for distribution!"

"Thanks, Nancy! You're in for a raise!" Dona replaced the telephone with a bang, her flippant promise forgotten in the euphoria she was feeling.

She jumped up from her chair, her low spirits soaring on a geyser of hope. First thing this evening she had to get to the beauty salon. Her son could fix his own dinner; Mama had more important things in mind. Her nails had to be redone, her hair, her face—maybe she would even have a full body massage after the aerobics class. She would help Dan Nuthing if it was the last thing she would do! A man with such a reputation...oh boy!...a manager with at least a five-figure salary, a great bod and all those managerial benefits to match!

*D*ressed for success in a new scarlet suit with yellow lapels and cuffs, high-heeled shoes dyed to match and an enormous yellow bow pinned to her frizzy, red hair, Dona Trivi walked into Dan Nuthing's office. Her dangling earrings swayed provocatively as she introduced herself and boldly offered her services on the binding of the review or anything else Dr. Nuthing had in mind.

"I hope you don't mind my interfering like this," Dona said with a broad, ingratiating smile, "but I do know Jack Sintex very well. You know, he's the manager in charge of the Printing and Binding Service, and I heard you're interested in getting this wonderful review of yours through the mill ASAP!"

Dona's calculating eyes, outlined with layers of green and purple eye shadow beneath plucked, arched brows, never betrayed for an instant her eagerness.

She sat down and crossed her long, slim legs revealing a pair of very sharp, bony knees. She was tall and thin, without much of any feminine curves, but then she knew there wasn't a trendy, flashy outfit, which would not drape itself about her as comfortably as on any coat-hanger.

To Dan Nuthing's eyes Dona Trivi looked like a fashion model. "I'd love your help! Where have you been all this time? How come we haven't met before, sugar?" Dan boomed and laughed excitedly.

Dona tittered, emitting a series of short nasal gasps. She was ecstatic.

"You haven't been looking in the right places, Dan! With your mind always so busy, inventing all kinds of clever things and managing those research bods…well, I'm not surprised you don't have time to look around. But I've been here all along, and now I've come to lend a little hand!"

She extended the bony, claw-like appendage, which to Dan appeared elegant, delicate and in need of protection. He leaned forward and instantly gripped her hand in his large clasp.

"It's a deal, lovely!"

Dona beamed and held his eyes. They were a brownish-green. The very color of her checkbook!

"And I also happened to hear you were looking for a quick way to distribute your review."

"Well, how did you…?" Dan marveled, keenly surveying her provocatively shaking leg.

"I have my connections in The Company," Dona said mysteriously to enhance her aura of self-importance. In a lowered, confidential tone, she added, "Phil often lets a kitten out of the bag over lunch."

"Oh, yes," Dan replied, impressed by Dona's connections with the VP of R&D. Not to be outdone, he hurriedly added, "But Wally only allows an occasional meow in the ear of a good friend!"

Dona's eyebrows rose higher. Was he an intimate friend of The Company president? "You know Wally Steen well?"

"Sure! He and I go back a long way….all the way to my days in Technical Sales," Dan replied, forgetting to add that their feet had only occasionally shared The Company booth at an exhibit here and there. "We both ensured our Gemtech product line sold millions!"

Dona tittered. "You're so clever and versatile! I'll bet Wally used his sailor's charm, though. He really turned it on when he invited me for a tour of his yacht this summer!"

Her eyes darted across Dan's face and noted with pleasure that he was impressed. Her white lies sounded plausible. She skipped over the fact that she had driven to the marina, sought out Wally's yacht, waited for him to appear and begged to come aboard. "I also know all the guys on the program management team. And I could help round them up, if you like."

"I'm sure you don't need to round 'em up…just give 'em your sweet smile and they'll come running!"

Dan and Dona stood up and he placed his arm around her shoulders. She quickly snuggled up to him. Her heavy, cloying perfume, which brought on allergic reactions in many employees as it always lingered along the corridors, like the scent of a long departed skunk, now enveloped itself around Dan. He breathed it in deeply and his head swam with amorous sensations.

"Say, big guy, don't get any fancy ideas!" she giggled and with a mock-bashful look, pushed him away playfully. She gave way to her nasal laugh. "What do I get for all my help?"

"How'd you like to come to the big review?" Dan offered. She had such a network, all he had to do was tap into the lines.

"Sounds great to me!" Her eyes gleamed with sparks of avarice. "But Phil may not think that's enough."

"What d'you mean, babe?"

"I mean, my three techs are in limbo at the moment. If I don't give them a project to work on soon, I may lose them. Can't you use my technical expertise on your Compound Z project?" Her eyes darted to the impressive technical review lying on Dan's desk. If only she could be associated with it too!

Dan understood perfectly. In fact, he was feeling very miffed. That morning, he had a most upsetting discussion with the researchers and patent attorney. That pipsqueak from Legal had dared to take the researchers' side! He had even had the nerve to tell Dan that legally his contribution as project manager was not sufficient to warrant adding his name to that of the inventors on the patent application!

"In legal terms, an inventor is defined as the person who comes up with the idea from scratch, not someone who just manages the project," the attorney had said.

"But it's part of my job description that I don't just manage the project! As the project manager, I approve their experimental plans, I report on the project's progress to upper-management and I lead our progress review meetings. So you can see, my contribution is invaluable to the project!" Dan Nuthing had protested.

The four researchers had not said a word in support of his claim to the patent application and the legal representative shook his head and with an authoritative stroke erased his name.

From that moment on Dr. Nuthing developed serious doubts about the feasibility and value of the project. Perhaps that Compound Z invention was not so perfect, after all, and Dona might be just the right person to help him deflate those scientists' egos.

"Yes, that would be perfect!" Dan said. "After all, you are part of the Analytical Evaluations group. Who could ask for a better expert? Besides, I don't trust those four presumptuous scientists in my group to conduct an impartial evaluation of their pet compound. We'll get the protocols from them and you can re-do the short-term stability testing over the next two weeks before the review." He shook his head. "Who knows what you may find! Good or bad, it'll mean sure exposure at the meeting and I could do with such a bright chemist's support!"

With grave misgivings, Dr. Helen Afiyet and her colleagues agreed to collaborate on the additional evaluation with Dona Trivi's group.

Dr. Albert Lim swore beneath his breath as the researchers left Dan Nuthing's office. "The way he put it," Albert said to his equally annoyed colleagues, "if we don't agree, he'll make sure it'll look like we cooked the test data!"

"And may God help us if we hand over the protocols into Dona's hands," Dr. Janice Palovsky said, recalling the reputation of Dona and her group for careless work practices. "Have they ever done anything but a plethora of incoherent, negative evaluations of any project to cross their lab door?"

"Down here in the research labs we all know that," Dr. Helen Afiyet interjected. "But our management's propensity for avoiding direct contact with research personnel and preferring Dona's foolish claptrap reports and opinions has always swayed their judgment in her favor!"

Dr. Mark Kane chuckled and to relieve the tense atmosphere, he lightly rapped his head with his knuckles. "I'm convinced, if you knocked on her head it'd echo in there!"

"I didn't know sound travels in a vacuum!" bantered Albert Lim as they parted, smiling despite their frustrations.

Predictions sometimes do come true. Especially when they are unpleasant. Dona Trivi, backed by Dan Nuthing, refused any advice from the researchers on how Compound Z should be handled. She firmly insisted that her technical assistants should not take any instructions from the scientists to prevent, as she put it, "...meddling or bias—you never know what those researchers will do to ensure they get visibility!"

Horrified, the four scientists looked on as Dona Trivi's techs flagrantly disregarded and misused their meticulous protocols. Every time they passed Dona's laboratory they saw their precious, light-sensitive samples lying on top of dirty, messy benches, exposed directly to overhead lighting for long periods of time. Instruments were not calibrated properly, samples were diluted into trace metal contaminated tap water instead of the required triple distilled deionized water and many other such malpractices.

Meanwhile, Dona's direct supervisor on the Analytical Evaluations project approved her initiative in taking on such an important task.

At the end of ten days, the four researchers and their technical assistants were not in the least surprised to hear that Dona Trivi was already very busy fulfilling her job description. Dashing along the corridors from one program manager's office to another, she informed them with zeal of her negative results and her highly competent group's inability to reproduce the researchers' "blown-up" claims of Compound Z's stability.

Dr. Dan Nuthing refused to listen to the researchers' protests.

He incorporated Dona Trivi's negative report into the written review to give a measure of balance to the project, as he put it, and added her name to the front cover, just in time for the project review meeting.

Dona's self-professed expertise in uncovering a serious flaw in Compound Z rapidly spread throughout middle-management. She was soon viewed as "an aggressive, independent scientist with all the right attributes for promotion and acceptance into managerial ranks".

Nuthing Dan was in fine fettle,
Puffing steam to prove his mettle,
His head grew to an August size
Before the VP's very eyes,
And on he puffed with all his might
And suddenly grew very light....
Then, what did Dr. Nuthing do?
Not much...
As hot air rises, he was promoted too!

The review meeting notice was sent to all Company VIPs as Dr. Dan Nuthing instructed. Managers from the middle through the upper echelons of R&D, Marketing and Sales, and Manufacturing congregated at the appointed hour in the R&D conference room adjacent to Phil Fox's office.

Most had turned up because of the strategic location, hoping for a couple of words with their R&D VP. They all carried copies of the project review tucked under their arms, in most cases merely to give the impression that they had indeed read it and were ready to pass judgment.

The project scientists were simply informed by Dan Nuthing that the program management review committee had decided that since they would be discussing business matters at the same time, their presence was not required. They would be more than adequately represented by their own project manager.

While the four scientists took the day off from work to discuss their future prospects in The Company, Dr. Dan Nuthing and Ms. Dona Trivi were intent on establishing theirs. In a spectacular show of salesmanship and exaggerated technical confidence, they stood side by side in front of the gathered managerial staff, flipping through the overheads prepared by the researchers–subsequently modified and mangled by Dr. Nuthing–and very superficially interpreted the technical data, which they assumed they understood.

Together they presented the expected image of managerial efficiency, clad in dark, tailored "Power Suits". Dona peered through a pair of gold-rimmed, plain glass spectacles. Her pained expression suggested to most of the members of the Review Committee that she possessed an indefinable aura of scientific competence. To the few who did not admire such attributes in a female, her strategically located lapel badge, with a picture of her beloved son, engendered just the right measure of sympathy for her single-parent status. She conveniently brushed aside the fact that her "ex" had a successful medical practice and he paid more than a sufficient amount to cover both the pleasure of being rid of her, as well as far more than the legally required amount of child support. Though she always complained that he was miserly, she chose to ignore the fact that she frittered away most of the child support on designer fashions.

Her staccato tone with its nervous, near hysterical tremble was most appreciated by Phil Fox. He disliked women who sounded too confident. He smiled encouragingly with undisguised admiration.

Dona and Dan, their heads swollen with importance, finally sat down to a round of appreciative nods to await the verdict on Compound Z.

Phil Fox spoke up. "Excellent presentation. Outstanding review!" He glanced at his watch. "It's almost lunch time. Let's make a decision, folks, before we break. Give me your opinions and feelings on whether we should spend any future funds on this project."

"We can't just get rid of it. It does appear to have some promise! Let's have a word with the researchers before we decide," the Development Project Manager, Jeff Hovalsky, suggested. He quite liked Dr. Janice Palovsky. After all, like himself, she was of Polish extraction.

"I see no need to drag them into our business discussion," Phil Fox said, impatiently glancing at his watch. "I'm satisfied with the presentation as it is!"

"But from their review here," interjected the VP of Sales and Marketing, who seemed to have at least read the report summary, "it appears this Compound Z could bring in a significant profit, if we stick with it. It may be worth doing a market survey."

"Mike, but didn't you hear the results of Dona's group's careful evaluation?" objected Joe, Dan Nuthing's old friend from the Sales division. He gave a derisive sneer. "This Z compound clearly doesn't have the required stability for shipping! I think those research guys are bananas!"

"Come on, Joe!" protested Dr. Mike Vander, the VP of Future Development Technologies. "I'm sure they could find a way to improve the stability. Even bananas can be preserved for shipping!"

"Yeah, but at what cost?" Joe questioned immediately, triggering a round of understanding murmurs and nods.

"You've hit a hole in one there!" Phil Fox exclaimed, recalling his lunch-hour appointment to play a round of golf at the local club. He was pleased that someone had at least raised such a valid objection to spending more money on research that didn't promise any immediate profit as far as he could see. "What do you think, Al? Is it worth pursuing this elusive "Z", from a legal standpoint?"

The recently hired patent attorney squirmed under the weight of the decision suddenly thrown into his lap. His boss had already berated him for his treatment of Dr. Nuthing's claim to the patent application and he now had no wish to be held responsible for any further decisions dealing with this project.

He cleared his throat and kept his eyes on the VP's face for a sense of direction. "There were some queries from the patent examiner…but, if the compound were determined to be sufficiently novel, it should be patented." He paused. Noticing a twinge of displeasure in the VP's eyes, he diplomatically reversed his opinion, as expected of an astute attorney with a Company career ahead of him. "But who knows how many more questions the patent office will want to have cleared. I think it might take up a great deal of legal expenses to provide all the data and legal replies…."

"Money, which would be better spent on that litigation we have going at present, right?" Phil Fox prompted and the attorney, seeing in his mind's eye the piles of paperwork waiting on his desk, nodded in relief, sensing this additional burden would soon be removed.

"Alright, then, I'm satisfied! I can see we're unanimous that at present we cannot spend more on this research project," Phil Fox decided and no one objected. Turning to Dan and Dona, he added,

"I'm grateful for your assessment, Dona. You've saved The Company a significant amount of money. There comes a point when you've just got to trust your best scientists!"

Dona adjusted her glasses, nervously shook her crossed leg and accepted the compliment with a broad smile and a flirtatious glance at Dan Nuthing.

Dan expanded his chest and drew himself up to his full, bulky height. "An honest evaluation is all we were looking for and Dona really gave us that. Negative or not, the results speak for themselves!"

Dona suddenly tittered. Her nasal gasps became the cynosure of attention. "I was just thinking–Compound Z just got a "zero" rating!"

Amidst hearty laughter at her incredible wit, the final decision was made to slow down the project and eventually phase it out. The patent application was to be withdrawn and the research team was to be reassigned to another project that would give a faster return on investment.

▲

Several months after his laudable contribution to the downfall of the Compound Z project, Dr. Nuthing's voice could still be heard booming down the R&D hallways. He had been promoted to Principle Project Director in Engineering Development, enjoyed a huge increase in salary, a company car and various other Company confidential benefits, given to a manager at his elevated level.

Mrs. Dona Trivi-Nuthing was welcomed into The Company managerial ranks and on the basis of her "outstanding scientific ability" was promoted to the position vacated by her new husband, Dr. Dan Nuthing. When this news was given to the four frustrated inventors of Compound Z, they promptly handed in their resignations. Mrs. Trivi-Nuthing shrugged her angular shoulders on the day the scientists left The Company.

"I'm glad to see the last of them! I'll just have to hire new Ph.D.s with a better attitude!" she told Phil Fox, her words tumbling out with a much-admired aggressivity. "Dan says it was a mistake to let the technical staff hire them in the first place. It's time we managers with the right people skills did the interviewing for the R&D staff!"

The vice president of R&D was in complete agreement and Dona was entrusted with her first assignment as Project Manager.

In R&D, however, more than one senior member of the technical staff was yet again appalled by this myopic management decision.

"Typical!" commented one veteran scientist to his equally vexed and frustrated colleagues behind closed laboratory doors. "That's the problem with our management here. How can someone whose technical knowledge is way below the bench hire someone whose expertise is expected to reach far above the bench? She can't even conceive of the extent or lack of the applicant's abilities!"

His friend gave a cynical grimace. "It's no wonder our already meager R&D resources are squandered on so many 'good guys' with big political smiles and no technical know-how, who are all preoccupied with ambitious plans to escape lab work and join the useless managerial ranks, ASAP!"

The Compound Z project was soon forgotten and relegated to the long list of aborted Company projects, until one day Betsy, one of the Compound Z technical assistants, rushed into the laboratory excitedly waving the latest issue of the *Chemistry and Engineering Industry News*.

"Just listen to this!" she laughed excitedly and read aloud: "*Afiyet, Incorporated* has just announced a merger with the multinational chemical company *Luminex Industries*. Afiyet Inc. has already had enormous success with its invention Compound Zeta, and it will now be marketed globally.

"At a recent interview the Executive Vice President of Afiyet Inc., Dr. Janice Palovsky, confirmed that the original work on Compound Zeta was carried out at The Company. She said, 'Management released the patent rights due to a lack of Company interest in further research and development of a compound they considered would not yield a quick profit.' When scientists were asked about the secret for their success, Dr. Mark Kane and Dr. Albert Lim, vice presidents in charge of Manufacturing and Marketing, said, 'We believed in our product.' President/CEO of Afiyet Inc., Dr. Helen

Afiyet, added, 'The technical personnel, who have worked on the product from its conception, also make the crucial management decisions in our own company. We all wear many hats here and all the hats fit perfectly!' It would appear that more than one company could take a cue from Afiyet Inc.'s hatter!"

The scientists listening to the report were both pleased and disappointed at the same time. The article circulated around The Company like wildfire. However, when challenged, the Nuthings brushed it aside at the monthly program management meeting.

"What can anyone do?" Dona shrugged and paraphrased the latest management books she had just read. "In management we can never win. When we lead well, the troops believe they did it all, and when they make a mess, we take the blame," she sighed and shook her head. "With the best of intentions you can never rely on your techs to do a good job! It was their sloppy work that cost this Company the project. I think it'll have to be my unpleasant duty as the newly appointed project manager to hand them their pink slip bonuses!"

"And well deserved, too!" Dan added, to the general agreement of the managers, who were only too eager to forget their own roles in the dismissal of the prickly project. "I wouldn't be at all surprised," Dan continued vociferously, "if those research guys didn't mix in some samples that were already no good, knowing all along that if The Company discontinued the project and gave them a release, they could go out there and make it on their own! Hell, I always suspected that R&D foursome was a devious lot! Just look at the way they put their own interests before those of The Company!"

THE DOUGHNUT DEAL

Teamwork Spirit, how you're disguised!
But R&D had you well analyzed,
You're a farce and impure, not '200⁰ Proof',
Diluted, you're naught, but a
Management Spoof!

The Company veterans had to delve deep into their memory banks to recall the last time there was an off-site meeting for its R&D research staff. In fact, even the exact site was in dispute, for some remembered a local beach resort and others thought it might have been at a lodge in the mountains. All agreed at least twenty years had passed since the great event. Had the program management committee finally decided to include technical personnel in the decision making and planning processes that would influence future R&D research directions?

The invitation memo, signed by Mr. Phil Fox, vice president of R&D, proclaimed that "teamwork planning" was the motto for this meeting.

119

Dr. Jennifer Adams and her colleagues, Dr. Dave Bradley and Dr. Paul Liu, read their copies of the memo with incredulity tinged with hope and enthusiasm.

"Great! It's about time! I've been in R&D for six years and I'm beginning to think, feel, and stink like a mushroom behind this bench! The last conference I was allowed to go to was to a town an hour's drive away because it happened to be directly on the project subject I was working on!" Dave's freckled face beamed over Paul's cubicle wall.

Paul nodded in agreement, but his words belied his own anticipation. "Well, don't get too excited. This one's only a four-hour drive away. At least it seems we might get an opportunity to contribute to program management's R&D planning. We'll sure give them our input!"

"You bet we will! And I just can't wait to sample what it's like at a managerial off-site meet! Look, it says, here, in this resort brochure that there's a swimming pool, tennis courts, and a golf course. Pity I had to sell my sticks to pay off my Ph.D. tuition fees," he reflected.

Paul's interest was captured. "Those adobe-style accommodations look great!"

Jennifer stood up from behind her desk and stepped on tiptoe to look at her colleagues over the cubicle office wall. "Hey, guys, don't get carried away! Remember, this is a meeting for technical staff not management, and we've been invited to attend mainly to give presentations on our research work."

She smiled at the startled expressions and added in a lowered voice, "If you ask me, it's only because our project managers can't answer questions on any technical details!"

"Who cares!" Dave shrugged. "At least we will indulge in sumptuous breakfasts, lavish lunches, and extravagant dinners!"

"And doughnuts of every kind!" interjected Paul, tall, thin and always hungry. "The kind filled with fresh cream and smothered in chocolate. John, the new manager over in Applications, said they had that kind each day at their program management meet in Florida!"

Jennifer joined in their laughter. "I guess I could forget to count calories for such a gourmet feast!"

The three colleagues car-pooled to the Desert Cliffs resort. Its location, they soon found out, was not so much secluded as well hidden. Perhaps undiscovered would have been a kinder description, lying as it did in the embrace of a somewhat barren range of boulder-strewn, craggy mountains. Jennifer was not the only one to notice that the pictures in the glossy brochure advertising the resort must have been taken in more lucrative years. With growing dismay they observed the rust-covered iron railing that bordered the hotel premises, the peeling paint on the adobe buildings and the golfing greens that were far from verdant.

Yet, the car park was full and in the simple, Mexican-style decorated interior of the main lobby, there was a lively crowd of The Company's technical staff, chatting and laughing in an informal atmosphere, mingling with several retired couples enjoying a modest vacation.

"Well, Jenny, take your pick!" greeted Dr. Wayne Greschwin, a jovial man, in his late fifties, one of The Company's R&D veterans.

He laughed at her puzzled expression and the other scientists, who had already registered, called out, "With whom will you share?"

"Share?" Jennifer asked with a frown, glancing at the equally puzzled expressions on the faces of her two colleagues. Then an uneasy realization dawned. "You can't be serious."

Paul's flash of enlightenment came at the same time. "Do you mean we have to share rooms?"

"What?!" exclaimed Dave indignantly, the color of his face beginning to match his red hair. "When the hell have our managers ever had to share a room at their off-site meetings?"

Dr. Wayne Greschwin, Dr. Alan Hawk and the other assembled veteran scientists chuckled. "But we're only technocrats—or hadn't you realized it yet?"

"And according to this belated memo," interjected Dr. Harry Potts, waving the offending sheet of paper in the air, "which you'll get when you register, they over-booked the rooms. Our response was obviously too enthusiastic!"

"Bullshit!" Dave exclaimed, the annoyance evident on his face. "They just can't count beyond ten!"

"Wrong, young man!" Dr. Greschwin patted Dave on the back. "They can count, alright, when it's in their money clip!"

"Come on, guys!" Jennifer smiled to calm her colleagues' temper. "Let's make the best of it! At least we're lucky to be at an off-site meeting. Barbara, will you share?" she asked the only other female participant.

"Sure!" Dr. Barbara Wang immediately agreed. "I'm only too glad you are here. We are a rare species at this meeting, the only women scientists and," with a laugh she turned to the group of male colleagues, "we expect respect and extra special treatment!"

"We all promise, don't we guys?" Paul called out and their male colleagues unanimously agreed that the two ladies could have first pick of the largest doughnuts.

———————————▲———————————

*T*he afternoon introductory session was a brief welcome by Dr. Wayne Greschwin, who had to stand in at the last minute for the vice president of R&D, Phil Fox. For some undisclosed personal reasons, Mr. Fox could not come on time to give the opening speech at the Technical-Management Exchange Symposium at the Desert Cliffs.

The scientific program was, therefore, pushed forward in the schedule, which suited the fifty invited R&D scientists very well, for they enjoyed sharing technical information and discussing their scientific progress. The Company management staff members were conspicuous by their absence, though. This would not have upset any of the research staff if it were not for the colorful banner Phil Fox had composed, which decorated the front wall of the meeting room.

"*Technical-Management Exchange Symposium*" it read in big bold, purple letters on a yellow background, "*Symposium Charter: A Novel Approach to Technology-Driven Program Management with a Frank and Open Exchange of Technical Thinking and Management Planning: Teamwork Spirit–The Company Goal!*"

"So, where's the other half of The Company team?" questioned more than just Jennifer during the late afternoon break. "And I was advised by Dr. Nigel Jansen to tone down my presentation to make it more understandable to our managers!"

"Well, you at least had the foresight to take along your technical overheads," Paul said, cringing at the bitter taste of the over-brewed coffee.

"Everyone enjoyed your presentation, Jenny. It was excellent!" Dr. Greschwin interjected.

"In which case, would you mind, Wayne, if I junk most of my overheads and just draw some of them freestyle?" asked Dave. "Bob Fraser, my new project manager, insisted I take out all the formulas, molecular structures and equations. He says it makes my overheads too busy and such technically detailed stuff won't go down well!"

Dr. Wayne Greschwin, who was in charge of the scientific aspects of the meeting, compressed his lips. "Bob would say that wouldn't he? But since none of them are here to get confused, go ahead. Just remember, Dave, this is meant to be a technical information meeting, until tomorrow at least, when the program management staff will join us."

"But where are they?" Jennifer asked again. "I understood they are interested and are eager to at least lend an ear to our presentations."

"So they said!" Wayne Greschwin shrugged and walked away in an obviously evasive manner that led Jennifer and her three colleagues to guess this Company veteran scientist knew more than he was willing to disclose.

Paul turned his attention to some "comfort" food. His disappointed, hungry expression was mirrored on many other faces as they surveyed the side table on which the refreshments were laid out. The gourmet fare consisted of nothing more than a jug of hot water, one variety of tea bag, a pot of coffee with a nondairy creamer, and a few tepid cans of Coca-Cola.

"What I'd like to know is, what happened to all the doughnuts?"

The scientific session finished for an hour break at seven but by that time, since it was early December, it was dark outside and any recreational activities were out of the question. There was just enough time for a shower in the musty-smelling rooms before dinner.

"I enjoyed the sessions, but I swear, I'm starved!" Dave said as Jennifer, Barbara and Paul walked briskly back to the dining room along the poorly lit walkways.

Paul rubbed his stomach. "I hope they give us something substantial, or I'm driving out of here to the first restaurant I can find!"

"You won't find any around here," Barbara chuckled. "You're not the first to suggest a trip to a decent eatery, but this place is so out of the way, it's a two-hour drive to the nearest town!"

"And Barbara and I are still waiting for our first choice of promised doughnuts!" Jennifer persisted.

"Well, you can have an extra helping of dessert," Paul suggested, "after which we can all go for an early morning hike into the mountains tomorrow!"

The receptionist in the main lobby catching these last words smiled and interjected, "I'm afraid I wouldn't recommend that, sir! The rattlers and coyotes are out this time of the year and we even had a mountain lion sighting a week ago!"

"Great!" exclaimed Dave with heavy sarcasm. "Is the bar open at least?"

"Certainly, sir. It's down the corridor," replied the receptionist, a sympathetic look in her eyes. "All the people from The Company are already there, and drinks are free on The Company account."

"What? Really?" chorused the surprised group.

The receptionist frowned and checked some papers on her desk. "Oh, excuse me. My mistake! Tomorrow, drinks will be on The Company, you just have to show your manager's hotel pass, but," she queried, "I suppose you're not managers, are you?"

She received an affronted look from the four scientists and Jennifer's reply, "You guessed right! It shows doesn't it?" made her laugh.

After The Company technical staff warmed themselves with predinner drinks for which they had to pay, a very lively group entered the dining room. They even found amusement in the meager menu, which they sarcastically decided must have been specially ordered for the technical staff's good health. It consisted of a simple dinner salad with green cheese dressing, three varieties of pizza and a watermelon and banana fruit salad. The two decorative strawberries, everyone present agreed, should go to the most under-represented staff members, the only two female participants.

"Things have got to shape up tomorrow," declared Paul hopefully, as they parted that evening. "After all, teamwork is our goal!"

*B*reakfast was in perfect keeping with the previous evening's dinner. It consisted of some leftover fruit salad, a rubbery Danish pastry with blueberry jam filling, butter, and the usual selection of coffee or tea. After some initial grumbling, the technical staff consumed it resignedly, accustomed as they were to making do with a meager R&D budget, and brushed aside thoughts of material sustenance for far more stimulating scientific discussions. In fact, many of the paper napkins were covered with formulas and patentable ideas by the end of the eight o'clock breakfast hour when Dr. Wayne Greschwin, who was to chair the morning session, stood up. He wondered if the participants would like to continue their informal discussions for the rest of the morning.

"Phil Fox phoned in to say that he and the program management team will be arriving later than planned for the technical-strategic planning session, some time after lunch. We will then meet for the official dinner with our president, Mr. Walter Steen, at seven. He will be giving a speech on," Wayne Greschwin put on his glasses to read the faxed memo, "the ETT program: Efficient Teamwork Technology."

The expression of momentary puzzlement on his face was voiced by one of the researchers, "What on earth is that?"

"Don't ask me, ask Wally!" Wayne's reply triggered general laughter and all agreed that since the presentations were finished yesterday, they would prefer a morning of informal discussions.

"Well, shall we go outside? It's a beautiful morning!" Jennifer proposed to her friends, packing away her formula covered napkin.

"Maybe I should staple this into my patent notebook…idea conceived at Desert Cliffs…."

"Yes, witnessed and understood by Drs. Stale Danish and Weak Tea!" Dave quipped.

"But where did Dr. Doughnut go?!" Paul remarked.

At that moment Barbara came around the corner and beckoned conspiratorially. "Listen! Listen, guys! I just called our department secretary to find out if the chemicals I ordered arrived. She said the whole program management team flew down here last night. In The Company executive jet, of course, from an off-site meet in Canada. They are now staying at a resort not more than a forty-minute drive from here!"

The colleagues glanced at each other. "Shall we…?" Dave raised his brows. His friends immediately understood his mischievous question.

"Why not! Let's drop in on them!" Jennifer chuckled.

"Where there are managers, there's sure to be…," Paul began and they all finished in chorus, "Doughnuts!"

———————▲———————

*T*he four scientists looked around in disbelief.

"Are you sure this is the right place?" wondered Dave as he raised his hand to shield his eyes from the glare of the water in the large ornamental pond.

"What a magnificent setting!" exclaimed Jennifer, admiring the rolling, manicured lawns and golfing greens. A lush garden with classic Greek statues and urns brimming with a profusion of exotic floral displays wreathed the glistening white walls of the spectacular hotel.

"The Hyatt Oasis Resort, that's the name Joan gave me. They should be somewhere in here!" Barbara said.

They made their way back to the lavish, marble hotel lobby, where water fountains played and streams cascaded amid hanging plants and exotic flowers.

To the surprise of the four scientists, the hotel receptionist knew The Company management team well. They had apparently stayed here before and they soon made their way along the hushed, thickly carpeted corridors glowing in shades of Adam green and white and lined with artifacts from the Greco-Roman period.

"Apollo Room…Hercules Room…Ceres Room…." They read the signposts on the way to the conference rooms.

"Atlas Room!" Paul halted their search in a low voice. "They're in there!"

They hesitated for the first time, uncertain that they really wished to confront their deceitful managers, when the door of the conference room burst open and cut off any chance of a speedy retreat.

Quickly they stepped into the shadows behind a huge potted palm, and feeling somewhat ridiculous, they hoped to be inconspicuous. Phil Fox's characteristic voice, which always reminded Jennifer of a high-pitched duck call, filled the silence of the corridor. It sounded clearly above the boisterous masculine tones of the fifteen other members of The Company program management team, as they hurried through the open double doors of the Atlas Room.

"…and I'd say we've just got enough time for another round of golf before we tee off for the Tech-Symposium," Phil was saying.

"Oh, God! Not that hell hole!" brayed Bob Fraser, the VP of Systems Management. "If there's a decent hole on those greens, there's bound to be a gopher in it!"

They all found raucous humor in his comment and Phil Fox patted Bob's broad shoulders. "As I always say, the art of good management, folks," Phil Fox's high-pitched quack interjected, "is to train those technical pigeons…I mean gophers…down there to retrieve our balls while we play in the big league rounds that put The Company on course!"

"Which course?" asked another member of the exclusive program management team. "St. Andrews would suit me just fine!"

"How'd you guess, Jerry?" Phil replied as the casually attired group rounded the corner. "I've that in mind for our fourth quarter off-site meet! My wife's Scottish and she proposed it!"

"But how will our technocrats make it?" asked a vaguely concerned voice, trailing the crowd.

"If those behind-the-benchers can come up with an invention to build a raft and sail after us...."

Phil Fox's voice faded in the distance, leaving only the echo of lingering laughter that left a bitter aftertaste in the mouths of the four eavesdroppers. There was no need for words. The look in their eyes reflected the hurt and outrage they felt.

"Good heavens! What do our pompous managers think they are? The owners of The Company?" exclaimed Jennifer. "They always talk about us as 'the employees' and never include themselves!"

"Damn it, you're right, Jenny!" Paul concurred angrily. "Managers are employees like everyone else at The Company. Calling us pigeons! They're the ones with the bird brains and most of them don't even have an accredited MBA. They're not even qualified for their jobs! Why they think they have some God-given right to such perks, I'll never know!"

"Well, I'm going to see if their 'royal highnesses' left anything in there for the 'gophers,'" Dave said defiantly and led the way into the Atlas Room.

They stopped short just inside the doorway. It was not only the sight of the huge silver trays still laden with a profuse selection of cheeses, salamis, lobster and shrimp, vegetable and fruit salads, petite fours, and the long-awaited doughnuts that brought their progress to an abrupt halt. Standing at the foot of the table, a cream-filled éclair about to enter his mouth, was the President of The Company, Mr. Walter "Wally" Steen. He looked up in surprise and then beamed his seafarer's welcoming smile. His navy yachting jacket, white pants and blue and white sneakers more than hinted at his hobby.

"Come in! Come aboard one and all!" he put down his éclair on a plate, wiped his fingers on a napkin, then beckoned and came toward them. "I remember you, Jennifer, a very clever scientist!" He held out his large hand in greeting, shook hands and turned to the others. "Barbara...Dave and...Paul? Right! It would be a sad day when a captain couldn't remember the names of his crew!" He showed-off his unique talent for memorizing faces and names, even though he had met them only once at an R&D product launch in-house celebration. "So what brings you all here? You're late for Phil's meeting, you know!"

"Yes, we…just happened to be in the neighborhood and…," Jennifer began.

"And we decided to have a look around…," added Paul, his eyes on the managers' fare.

"Well, what a coincidence!" chuckled Wally Steen, correctly interpreting his hungry look. His sailors were also always hungry. "Come along, help yourselves!" he invited heartily. "Have a doughnut, there's plenty left and I sure don't like to see good food go to waste!"

He seemed to enjoy the way in which Paul and Dave pounced on the food, piling their plates high with every item available. Jennifer and Barbara restrained themselves and each took only a couple of shrimp sandwiches. "Tell me," Wally Steen spoke as the scientists seated themselves on either side of him, "how's the meet going down in Desert Cliffs?"

"Technically, very well," Jennifer replied with reserve.

"Yes, it's real worthwhile to have a technical get-together," added Dave after swallowing a mouthful of bread and salami.

The four young scientists exchanged questioning glances. Should they air their feelings? This was their chance, but for what? Would they be classified as "troublemakers" or "constructive contributors"?

Paul suddenly suffered a bout of indigestion. He pushed his plate aside. "The Desert Cliffs symposium's meant to bring technical and managerial staff closer together. How on earth can that happen when we went through the entire technical symposium without a single staff member from the program management team being present? Management's here, we're over there!"

Wally Steen leaned back and waved his hand like the sails on his yacht. "Well, what would you suggest? That the whole of R&D stay here?" he raised his bushy brows high on his wrinkled, suntanned forehead in utter disbelief. "Heavens! You see, that's the problem with you technical people, you've got no appreciation for the budget! Isn't it enough that R&D guzzles our profits at an alarming rate?" He paused for breath, a moment of voluntary amnesia erasing the fact that a minuscule percentage of The Company's overall budget supported research projects. "Besides, all that's irrelevant! Program management staff members know everything they need to know about what's going on. They're an excellent team! Outstanding! Superb! Hand-picked by Phil himself, and you'll get your chance this afternoon to meet them personally and contribute to The Company strategic plans."

He stood up, somewhat uncomfortable in the silence that greeted his words. "I'm real glad to have had the opportunity for such an excellent discussion!"

The scientists' lack of reply did not bother him. He quickly returned to his usual off-hand manner. "Well, I'll be off then!"

The four members of The Company technical staff stood up and silently shook hands with their elusive Company president.

"We will see you this evening for dinner and at the planning session?" asked Barbara boldly.

"Umm…no, I'm afraid I won't be able to make it," Wally Steen shook his head with apparent regret. Then, showing a flash of white teeth added, "I'll be in the International Pacific Coast Executive Regatta early tomorrow morning. Confidentially, The Company's expanding toward China! Besides, Desert Cliffs," he shuddered and grinned, "the name alone makes me feel shipwrecked!" He hurried out and glanced back at the door for a brief wave. "See, you all! Make some great plans, folks. I'll be looking out for your novel ideas!"

"Let's go!" Paul grimaced in disgust.

"Hey! Don't you want to take any doughnuts?!" Dave asked, grabbing one on his way out.

"I lost my appetite!"

▲

*P*hil Fox appeared in front of his technical staff audience in old jeans, a crew-neck pullover and a crisp white lab coat with a pair of laboratory safety goggles dangling around his neck.

The rest of the program management staff had also discarded their Dior, Gucci and Ralph Lauren casual wear, which they had worn in the Hyatt resort, for the kind of cheap, casual clothing in keeping with their perceptions of the technical personnel dress code. However, their disguise was not perfect, for they hadn't replaced their gold Rolex watches, executive diamond rings and heavy link bracelets, their Mont Blanc fountain pens and leather, monogrammed folders, which The Company supplied exclusively to employees at the appropriate managerial levels. This slight oversight was, indeed, whispered in Phil Fox's ear by one of his more astute managers shortly after their arrival—but Phil's last name was not Fox for nothing!

Standing beside the microphone, he proudly showed off the laboratory coat, which he had last worn more than twenty years ago in his B.S. biology course, and which he had kept over the years to prove his long-renounced intention to become a scientist.

"Welcome, to the Technical-Management Exchange Symposium! As you know, I am a part of the management staff team, but as you can all see, I always was and still am at heart, a technical man!" Phil began his speech.

Loud cheers and enthusiastic applause from his handpicked middle-management, sitting in the first two rows, greeted his words. They all often also regaled the scientific ranks with long-winded anecdotes from their underpaid lives and boring days behind the bench. The sheepish glances, furtively cast backwards at the technical staff by the two previously active scientists who had deserted the technical troops to join the managerial ranks for the sake of greater pay and benefits, did not go unnoticed.

Phil Fox scanned the rows of his technical staff audience for evidence of support in similar vein. His bright grin was answered with forced smiles and quickly subsiding, lukewarm applause. Assuring himself that scientists in general are sadly lacking in any normal sense of humor, he hurriedly launched into the speech he had rehearsed last night before his full-length bedroom mirror at the Hyatt Oasis resort.

"Our Company is entering a new era of product development and strategic planning." He raised a fist to show his resolve. "We believe in quality...quality programming, quality engineering... quality research and development, and quality planning. Our vision for the future involves new ways of thinking, novel approaches to strategic planning!" He paused for effect and to allow such complex managerial terminology to sink into the minds of his technical listeners. "And that is why with Teamwork Spirit—we have come together here at this fine Desert Cliffs resort!"

"Wow! And I thought it was for the gourmet cooking!"

The unexpected comment triggered instant laughter among the technical staff. It was Phil Fox's turn to accept the sally with a forced smile and a pink hue colored his earlobes.

A concerted look of disapproval at this impertinent remark swept across the faces of the program management team.

"We are here to accomplish far more significant tasks than to indulge ourselves!" Phil Fox continued in a voice of a strict authoritarian. He raised his hand. "On you, our scientists, rests the future of The Company. With your ingenious discoveries, inventions, and patents we will get off the ground. We may not be there yet, but we are moving!"

He flung his arms out for emphasis. "These are challenging times. We must keep our competitive advantage in novel product research, in the development of these products and in strategic planning! No matter how many knocks we sustain, we'll always get up to bat! Remember, all of you, Teamwork Spirit and sharing are The Company goals! Together we can make it!" He finished with a flourish to the instant, enthusiastic applause from the two front rows and polite, brief clapping from the R&D staff.

When the plaudit subsided, Phil Fox motioned to a member of his program management staff to begin distributing thick stacks of stapled paper to the rest of the attendees. "The handouts summarize for the technical staff the procedures we have developed for future strategic planning. I advise you to familiarize yourselves with them."

As the general hubbub that accompanied the distribution of these documents subsided, Drs. Jennifer Adams, Barbara Wang, Dave Bradley and Paul Liu flicked through the thirty sheets of paper.

"For pity's sake!" exclaimed Barbara in a hushed voice. "Why all this crap for what should be a straightforward, logical planning session?"

Jennifer shrugged. "Why make it simple when you can complicate it just as easily? What else do the managers have to do for their astronomical wages and bonuses?"

"Look at this!" Paul pointed to a flow diagram on page twenty-nine. "They've already made their plans for the technical objectives!"

"And just take a look at page seven. The project they listed as number one with the most funds is the Microbiology project that's been spinning around for the past five years and still hasn't progressed a single step in any positive direction in all that time!" Dave scoffed.

"Yes, but you know why?" Jennifer leaned closer. "Because Mark over there is on the program management team and he has convinced them it's the era of genetics."

"Genetic engineering, maybe, but that particular project's a dead duck in the long run!" interjected Paul.

"So, what does Mark care?" Dave grimaced. "I heard he doesn't give a damn. If he can pull it out for another five years he's home free for his retirement. But look where they listed our LCD project! The second before last and we've got five patent applications filed on it and we've already started a successful transfer to Development!"

"Those guys are unrealistic and completely of touch!" Jennifer grumbled. "But maybe we'll get a chance for some input?" She was an optimist at heart.

The chatting died down as Phil Fox resumed, "If you have anything to add, write down your proposals in the space provided on the last page and a member from the program management team will contact you before we finalize our plan."

Dr. Wayne Greschwin suddenly stood up. "Phil, I think the meeting here was organized to discuss these program management proposals first," he paused and pointing to the slogan on the banner attached to the wall in front of them, quoted, "'in a frank and open exchange of technical thinking and management planning.' Don't you agree?"

"Sure," Phil conceded. "Which part do you have problems with?"

"All of it, Phil. Every single, damn part of this bullshit!"

Phil's shocked gasp was barely audible amidst the spontaneous applause from the technical ranks. He recovered himself enough to raise his voice, which sounded more than ever like an outraged duck squeak. "Hold on! Okay! But if there's too much disruption of The Company Teamwork Spirit, we'll get nowhere!"

The prediction of the VP of R&D was quite accurate. The debate continued for a full hour and no agreement was evident between program management and R&D staff.

Therefore, Phil Fox summarily announced the end of the session.

"The contributions by the technical staff will be reviewed and assessed by our experienced program management team. Copies of the final version of our strategic plan will be distributed to you all. Thank you everyone for your Teamwork Spirit. We will meet again for dinner!"

Milling around the refreshments, which now surprisingly included decent cups of fresh coffee and plates full of plain doughnuts, it was generally whispered among the disappointed technical staff that few changes, if any, would be made to these predetermined strategic plans. Their prediction proved true a month later.

The expectations of the R&D staff about this joint meeting were completely demolished. Even the doughnuts rapidly disappeared, consumed by the voracious members of the program management team, who crowded around the buffet table, excluding even the most determined R&D scientists.

Dinner that evening, served in the conference room, was a definite improvement over that of the previous evening. Only a handful of the program management team, who could not think of any plausible excuses, such as Phil Fox's golf tournament dinner, stayed behind.

Perhaps that was all for the better, for hanging over the R&D vice president's banner proclaiming The Company charter was a large sheet of paper with the following verse, written with a bold red marker pen:

Technical staff invented the Dough,
But where did all the Doughnuts go?
The Doughnuts were divided,
For it quickly was decided:
Since Teamwork is our goal,
We'll do the usual thing:
Technical staff may share the Hole,
And Managers, the Ring!

Who could have done such a delightfully villainous thing and give such added meaning to Phil Fox's banner? Jennifer and her friends all mirthfully agreed they had never before seen Dr. Paul Liu's eyes dance and sparkle with so much mischievous pleasure.

EPISODE EIGHT

SILICON WOMAN

> From Silicon Valley,
> Among Silicon Chips,
> Came Silicon Woman,
> With Silicon Lips,
> Made Silicon Promise,
> Of Silicon Boobs—
> But there's more in her Brain
> Than just Silicon Tubes!

From the day she joined The Company's R&D department as one of five technical assistants on the Thermal Detectors project, she was known as the "Silicon Woman."

This whimsical nickname was initially coined by one of the mischievous younger technicians when she had just transferred from The Company's recently closed Microchip Development division in the Silicon Valley. It stayed with her since her obviously perfect figure, which she flaunted most skillfully, led to corridor gossip that she must have taken a fair amount of silicon with her from the Valley!

Fanee Teese took all such teasing innuendoes with a laugh and a shrug of her shoulders, which was eyed with open admiration by all her male colleagues, including the Senior Technical Manager, Dr. Frank Stanovsky. As usual, when she entered his office this morning–and he often invited her–Fanee's technical contributions were far from his mind.

"Come on in, Fanee. Have a seat!" he indicated the chair opposite his desk and from behind half-closed eyes minutely surveyed her decollete. His eyes strayed lower as she crossed her legs with deliberate slowness.

Frank Stanovsky nervously blew a cloud of smoke from his large cigar and guiltily turned away from the silver-framed picture of his three sons and sweetly smiling wife. "Fanee, what can I do for you this morning?" he asked.

Fanee recrossed her legs and bent forward to expose more of her tantalizing cleavage, while Frank speculated again on the accuracy of her nickname.

"Well, you've done so much for me already in the past year, allowing me to take time off to attend afternoon classes twice a week," Fanee said in her sensuous, husky voice, a grateful look in her wide sea-green eyes.

"Oh, don't mention it, Fanee. It's the least I can do to help such an...able-bodied and talented employee as yourself!" Frank puffed on his cigar. The family portrait became increasingly obscured in the swirls of blue-gray smoke.

With a coquettish glance and flash of white teeth, Fanee showed that she took no offense to such insinuating remarks. "Thanks, Frank, I appreciate it. I was wondering, since it's coming up to review time, if you could tell me how I can further improve my performance?"

"Oh, I can't say that you need much improvement. But have you talked with Dr. Pamela Westin?" He blew a circle of smoke over his head. "She is your direct supervisor."

Fanee flicked a stray flaxen curl behind her ear that set her large gold earrings tinkling in synchrony with the five bangles on her wrist. "She doesn't talk to me very often," Fanee pouted her heavily frosted pink lips. "I think she's reached the saturation point directing the work of five people. Even though two of them have Ph.D.s, I think she just can't handle more than a handful. I'm left very much to myself and I need some real professional advice and feedback." She paused for Frank to swallow her insinuating words and continued with an ingenuous, "You're the manager on this project and you are such an inspiring leader."

Frank rolled the cigar between his thick fingers, wallowing in her praise. His eyes strayed again to the fulsome contours of her bright orange mini-pullover.

"As far as I can see, you're keeping well east of things…very well, indeed…very well!" He cleared his throat and leaned forward in his chair and extinguishing his cigar, glanced at it as if seeing it for the first time. "Sorry, I forgot to ask if you mind?"

"Not at all!" Fanee reassured. "My part-time job requires a high smoke tolerance!"

"Oh? I didn't know."

"I had to earn money to put myself through college and even now, the money here—I'll be honest—isn't all that great!"

"What do you do, then? Waitress?"

"Doesn't pay enough." Fanee showed a set of pearly-white teeth and her eyes danced mischievously. "Frank, why don't you come and assess my performance for yourself. If you like art and music, you might find some pleasure and bring some of your manager friends along. The restaurant serves an excellent lunch and it's very popular with upper-management, who like to relax for an hour or so over lunch!"

"Where's this place that I've missed?" Frank asked eagerly.

"Only a thirty minute's drive from here, close to the beach. It's called 'Booby's Bar and Grill'."

Frank agreed with alacrity to arrange an off-site lunch meeting with several friends from his group and other departments. Of course, Dr. Pamela Westin, who was the Senior Project Leader, was not invited. The meeting was, after all, meant to discuss "managerial issues" and she was only on the technical staff.

———▲———

"Where is everybody?" Dr. Pamela Westin asked the department secretary a week later. "The place is deserted and it's only ten-thirty. I can't find Frank, Mike, Joe, or any of the managers to sign this urgent capital requisition form. Besides, I had a meeting scheduled with Frank at eleven to discuss the reviews for the group's scientists."

Sandra looked up from her computer. "Frank canceled the meeting just before he left with Mike, Joe, Ed, and Ken for an off-site lunch to discuss the new review procedures."

"But as the technical supervisor, I should also be present at that meeting!" Pamela protested. "Frank assured me that after the mistakes the managers made last time in grading scientists I would have an input this time! Besides, Frank, Joe, and Ed all report to Mike, and Ken, like me, is also a member of the technical review committee. If he is included, why am I excluded?" She frowned in annoyance. "What are these guys up to?"

The secretary raised her brows and said with amusement, "In my crystal computer screen the mists are clearing and I see five men entering 'Booby's Bar and Grill'...."

"What!" Pamela exclaimed. "Isn't that where Fanee works part-time?"

"You mean, wiggles all that silicon over lunchtime!" Sandra chuckled.

Pamela started in disbelief. "You can't mean they went...?"

Sandra laughed. "Don't look so surprised, Pam! I've been a personal secretary for twenty years and if you'd like some advice, you either catch 'em red-handed or they'll never admit their sins! Everybody knows you are an excellent scientist and your technical assistants all like and respect you, but," she paused and with a look of maternal concern added, "to put it bluntly, you're not political enough to compete with our great managers! Take care of your own fanny, or Fanee will take care of it for you!"

Pamela frowned. She had dismissed the gossip that she had heard about Fanee's derisive remarks concerning her project leadership, but it was review time, and if Frank took Fanee's comments seriously, it could influence the review he would give her. Frank's prejudiced opinions regarding female scientists' Company careers were well known.

Pamela had tried to be fair in her assessment of Fanee's technical abilities and the standard of her lab work. She had given her a more than generous review. She knew she could have been much more critical, but she had even been forgiving of the many mistakes Fanee had made by not following her clearly written instructions. Disappointed, she now began to suspect that Fanee must have gone over her head to Frank to seek an undeserved promotion through petty intrigue.

"Did you ever have lunch at Booby's?" Pamela asked the secretary, a determined spark in her eyes. "I need a witness!"

Sandra grinned and pulled on her jacket. "I thought you'd never ask!" She laughed as she picked up her car keys. "Wait until I tell my husband tonight, he'll have a fit!"

―――――――――▲―――――――――

A dim, red light enveloped the two conspirators as they entered 'Booby's Bar and Grill'. The sharp scent of beer mingled with mesquite and cigarette smoke. It was a crowded, popular restaurant, the clamorous atmosphere filled with throbbing, sensual rock music, masculine voices and feminine high-pitched laughter.

Pamela's courage to proceed with this plan faltered. She glanced for support at Sandra, who grinned back her encouragement mixed with mischievous glee.

"Don't worry, Pam!" she chuckled. "Most of the clientele are managers out for a lunchtime high! I've made reservations here before for many of our managers who can afford the place on The Company account!"

The waitress, who was wearing nothing more than a very tight miniskirt and revealing blouse, checked Sandra's reservations and seating preference, while Pam scrutinized the customers. Sandra was right. They were all respectable-looking men and women attired in conventional business suits, seated at tables in booths separated by latticework panels. The booths all lined the walls with a view to the center of the room where a sort of dimly lit stage was visible.

"I asked her to take us to a table close by The Company group," Sandra whispered as they followed the waitress to a booth with a table for two.

Sandra nudged Pam, pointing to a large table through the latticework in the adjacent booth. They clearly saw Frank puffing merrily on his cigar, Mike drinking from a tankard of beer, and Ken and Joe laughing boisterously at some private joke.

Pam sat down, pleased that they could not see her and suddenly felt ridiculous. "If I wasn't so mad at those damn male chauvinists, I'd walk right out! Do you see Fanee anywhere?"

Sandra craned her neck. She shook her head in disapproval and pointed to the door at the right of the bar where a parade of tall women in high-heeled shoes, modeling the latest in erotic, see-through undergarments marched out. A round of appreciative wolf whistles and clapping greeted them as they stopped by each of the booths, turning provocatively with swinging hips and pointing out the special features of the lacy trimmings.

Pam and Sandra watched with disgust the reddened faces and leering expressions of their Company managers ogling the women and taking a keen interest in the lingerie. "I'll bet they wouldn't dare bring that lingerie home to their wives!" Sandra commented dryly.

Then, the music reached a crescendo, the light grew dimmer and a golden cage lit up at the center of the room. Dancing in the cage, in an iridescent G-string bikini wearing the usual array of gold bangles and hoop earrings, was Fanee. For the first time Pam realized the full significance of her artistic name: Fanee Teese!

Watching her expert, sensual gyrations in perfect timing with the pounding rhythm of the stirring music, Pam realized the girl had a talent that would have rivaled the world's greatest belly dancer!

She peeped at The Company men. Frank, his cigar held between his teeth, was drumming the table top with his fingers to the beat of the music, while the other men leered at Fanee's body, joining in with the other diners, cheering and clapping. As the tempo of the music hit a crescendo, Fanee finished her performance with a flourish.

Fanee's artistic skill was rewarded with cheers and a standing ovation as she finally descended from her cage and brazenly sat down on Frank's lap, while his companions looked on with envy.

"Well, Pam, it's now or never!" Sandra urged. "Let's embarrass them!"

Pam stood up and hesitated as she heard the waitress taking their orders.

"Guys, what'll it be? Steak of the day...rare, medium or well-done?"

Frank patted Fanee's backside and chuckled. "I like 'em rare myself, but for your performance I'll give a well done!"

"Is that all the review I get?" Fanee slipped off his knees with a pout.

"Ah, come on, Frank!" Mike protested, trying to turn Fanee's attention to himself. "Don't be such a miser! Anyone who is so versatile and limber must also be a great performer behind the bench!"

"Oh, yeah?" exclaimed Fanee. "I've never tried it behind the bench!"

"But I'll bet her technique's just as admirable in a lab coat!" guffawed Ken. "Only that straight-laced, stick-in-the-mud, Dr. Pamela will most likely not see it that way and give her a fair review!"

"We'll see about that!" Frank boomed. "I'll be the judge of what's a real talent and who deserves the highest merit increase for a great performance!"

Pam had heard enough. Her surprise appearance on the scene had the desired effect. Shock, dismay, and defiance chased each other across their faces. "Pam! What are you…? Sandra?"

Fanee slipped away, murmuring that she had to change.

"Hello, guys! A pleasant, productive lunchtime review meeting, I must say!" Pamela said with sarcasm.

"Didn't you tell me to invite Pam, Frank?" Sandra feigned innocence.

Frank extinguished his cigar. He was annoyed. "No…yes…but not here! You should listen to me next time, Sandra!"

"Come along, join us, Pam, Sandra," Mike laughed and winked at them.

"Sorry, thanks, guys. We had our lunch," Sandra said.

"It's getting late and I've an experiment going!" Pamela added. "But I do expect to be invited to your next review meeting *in-house*, when the topics under discussion will be the *real* performance reviews." She turned to her project manager. "By the way, I'm sure you'll be pleased to know, Frank, I've already written all the reviews for the people in my group, including Fanee's–naturally, I didn't take into account her outstanding performance today!" She paused and added, "Personnel may have a hard time accommodating your judgment of her overall talents!"

Frank laughed at her words, trying to hide his acute embarrassment, but Dr. Pamela Westin could feel his resentment at her interference.

---

*F*anee crossed her legs and accepted her review from Dr. Pamela Westin with a flippant, good-natured smile. "I guess it's fair," she said. "Between you and me, I understand your position. Sandra told me why you came over to 'Booby's'. But you can't blame a girl for trying!"

"Try it somewhere else, Fanee!" Pamela said in her straightforward manner. "You've got talent but not for research work in R&D!"

"I know it, Pam," Fanee laughed. "We all put our best parts forward. You've got your brain and I…well…I've got my bod. So long as those guys in management are susceptible—all's fair in love and work!"

She stopped as Frank knocked on Pamela's cubicle office wall. "I'd like to talk to you, Fanee, after you two finish!"

Fanee eagerly stood up to follow Frank, but turned back on an after-thought. "Did that sleaze ball take it out on you, Pam?" she asked.

"He didn't dare. It would have been too obvious, but I'll either be moving to another department or away from The Company by the end of this year," Pamela replied. She was tired of Frank's smoky management style.

"I wish you luck, Pam. You're okay!" Fanee beamed, winked back at Dr. Pamela Westin and hurried after Frank.

"*I* heard you're off to Marketing under Joe, Fanee," Frank said, nervously lighting his cigar as Fanee closed his office door.

"Not literally!" Fanee beamed and Frank chuckled at her sally. "Joe thinks I'm definitely well suited for the position he has in mind!"

"We could always find a good position for you here in R&D, if you wanted to stay," Frank offered, gazing at her from behind his cigar smoke.

"The salary for any technical position in R&D doesn't compare to the offer I got in Marketing! But thanks anyway, Frank. I'm meeting with Joe now. Maybe someday I'll come back to R&D– through management."

The Silicon Woman made her hip-swinging, sensual way down the R&D corridor for the last time, knowingly turning the heads of all she passed. One of the R&D technical assistants, standing with a group of researchers near the coffee machine, grimaced as Fanee glanced back and winked.

"There she goes, dancing her way up the managerial ladder," he commented dryly, "while two of my friends, with outstanding degrees in Marketing and many years of field experience, who recently applied for the same key position, were rejected. With her in the field," he added with acid amusement, "our customers will probably think silicon is our new product line!"

Amid the caustic laughter, a temporary summer student, peering over his glasses after the shapely object of their discussion, gave a wolf whistle at her retreating figure. A comic, drooling expression on his rotund face and with his hand on his heart, he recited:

> "*Watch out, Salesmen, here comes Fanee,*
> *With sense of timing quite uncanny,*
> *Of Sales she hasn't got a clue,*
> *But knows precisely what to do....*"

He paused, searching for a suitable ending, which Dr. Pamela Westin on a laugh provided:

> "*She jiggles and wiggles, takes every chance,*
> *To soar up the ladder and quickly advance!*"

A TASTE OF THE COMPANY JUSTICE

How much he knows,
He truly is a Whiz!
What ideas he sows—
If only they were his!

Throughout the entire Applied Research Technologies, ART, department, a branch of The Company R&D division, bright banners proclaimed this to be a very special day.

Everyone was invited and expected to attend the potluck lunch in honor of the Senior Vice President, Director of ART, Dr. Victor Paul " V.P." Barron's thirty years with The Company. The lavish celebration had been planned and organized a month in advance by Dr. Barron's devoted, twenty-year personal secretary, Mrs. Loyola Fraise, who suggested that since this was an ethnically diverse department, everyone should bring a taste of his or her "heritage food".

No one dared not to sign up on the list of potluck contributors. It was more than mere rumor that V.P. Barron himself scrutinized it after hours, and Loyola Fraise suggested it would be

147

in everyone's best interests to fulfill their culinary duties and rise to this glorious occasion.

Despite whispered comments among trusted colleagues that they or their spouses had better things to do in the evening than to prepare sushi, curries, sweet and sour pork or bake a Black Forest cake or apple pie, they all dutifully turned up on the day with their creations. The long conference table was soon laden with appetizing samples of international and domestic cuisines.

As the forty department members sampled the variety of dishes, Dr. Heinz Herzog wiped his fingers after eating a particularly sticky bun and murmured in Dr. Albert Tanaka's ear, "Just right for the occasion…sticks to anything, like V.P. himself!"

Dr. Tanaka cast a questioning look at his younger colleague. "I suppose you discussed your new synthesis process with him yesterday?"

"Yes, fool that I am! He insisted on co-authorship, if he is to let it pass through the department Patent Review Committee meeting at the end of this month."

Albert glanced around. He had survived in this department for the past fifteen years because caution was a natural part of his nature. He also knew well that V.P. Barron relied on a well-established network of informers from technical assistants to one or two favorite junior scientists, eager to ingratiate themselves in exchange for a range of minor privileges, which someone in his management position could and did offer. Albert Tanaka waited for Dr. Todd Dean, a current confidant who had just sampled one of V.P.'s rare favors, a business trip overseas to an international conference in France, to step out of hearing range, before replying.

"It's his well-known practice, Heinz," he said with a shrug. Noticing another member of his research team standing nearby, he beckoned to her to join them. "How are you, Tessa?" he asked in a hushed voice, glancing at the pensive look in her gray eyes. "Is there something on your mind? Would you like to talk with me?"

Dr. Tessa Euler nodded. "Yes, please," she whispered, "if you'll have some time later. I just had a meeting with V.P. That's why he's late now and I think he didn't like what I said to him."

"Aha," Dr. Tanaka nodded sagely, "we'll talk after this farce is over." He then politely joined in the clapping as V.P. Barron entered the room. "And here he comes, our Company 'Whiz,'" he added in a voice loud enough for all to hear. Tessa, who had come to know and like her boss well over the last three years at The Company, detected the subtle sarcastic intonation in his words and the exaggerated smile that accompanied the bow he gave in greeting the vice president of ART.

"Congratulations!" everyone called out as V.P. Barron, his head nodding approvingly on its long neck, surveyed his troops and acknowledged the expected adulation with a self-satisfied smile. He held up his hand to stop the applause. If he felt any disappointment that despite The Company-wide announcements only four middle-level managers from adjacent departments had turned up for this great event, his sharp, dark brown eyes never betrayed his emotions.

Loyola Fraise, however, could not contain her annoyance at the way upper- management had ignored the event. She turned to Mary, one of V.P.'s favorite technical assistants. "After the many years V.P. has given The Company, you'd think at least our vice president of R&D, Mr. Phil Fox, would turn up. But I guess his golf's more important than V.P.'s Research department. And in my opinion, Mr. Wally Steen, our president, has never quite appreciated V.P.'s great scientific contributions!"

"If you ask me, they're jealous of the brilliant inventions and theories he always comes up with!" said Mary. She idolized V.P. Barron and in her opinion he was the greatest scholar the technology world had ever known.

Loyola nodded her wholehearted agreement and gazed with adoration as her boss started his speech.

"Thank you all! I must admit when I started my career at The Company as a young scientist, thirty years ago, I looked up at the 'old timers' and thought I'd never get there. Now, I'm standing here and I can't hardly believe I finally caught up with them!"

General laughter greeted his smooth, well-prepared words. His loose, chinless mouth parted in a wide smile, revealing a set of perfect, expensive, white teeth. He spoke with a practiced, polished ease that matched his glib manner, groomed appearance, and elegant designer suit.

"After so many years with The Company," he chuckled, his Adam's apple bobbing up and down above his red bow tie, "I think I've outlived most of the nuts and bolts in this place, except perhaps for The Company foundations!"

At this point, Loyola took her cue and quickly stepped forward. "But, V.P., you are the *very foundation* of The Company research, and we are here to celebrate your *tremendous intellectual achievements* over the past thirty years!"

On the table in front of her, she set up a framed poster. Hidden behind a white silk cloth was an oversized congratulation card and a golden, gift-wrapped box. "These are from your department staff. V.P., accept your new title: 'Dr. Whiz'."

After due applause, she read aloud the prepared encomium:

"*With over seventy patents granted, hundreds of invention disclosures, and countless research ideas that have over the years given invaluable scientific stimulation for all research personnel in your ART department, you and you alone, are our unrecognized Nobel laureate. You are a scholar and true academician, deserving in every way to be named, 'The Company Whiz.'*"

V.P. Barron's chinless face expressed delight at such obvious flattery. Prompted by his secretary, he uncovered the colorful poster. The image of Merlin the Magician with V.P.'s facial features reaped the expected approbation. He then opened the card, glancing quickly over the signatures, while many of the senior and junior researchers exchanged meaningful glances and cynical smiles. They had not realized until now that all their own inventions and scientific discoveries had been inspired by such a superior intellect!

Dr. Albert Tanaka diplomatically shuttered his eyes, an enigmatic smile tugging at the corners of his lips. Dr. Tessa Euler kept a straight face and meditated on the far wall, while Dr. Heinz Herzog was not the only scientist present with an acute migraine headache.

"Oh, what a great card!" V.P. Barron exclaimed, laughing genially, a self-satisfied gleam in his eyes as he surveyed the faces of his subordinates.

"Please, do go ahead and read it, Dr. Barron!" prompted Mary in her excited, ingratiating, high-pitched voice. "Dr. Todd Dean wrote the inscription specially for you!"

V.P. Barron bestowed an approving smile on his current favorite, whose pale, chubby face flushed. "It's just a feeble attempt, V.P.," he stammered, running his hand through his thick blonde locks.

"Well, let's see if it's patentable!" V.P. quipped and after everyone dutifully laughed, he read aloud, "*To The Company Whiz...One of a Kind, The Greatest Mind!*"

V.P.'s ego was clearly satisfied. He proceeded to unwrap the present. "Oh!" he exclaimed, nodding his appreciation. "I've always admired this executive gift item. This gold watch has so many features, which I, by the way, helped to design, and finally I'm on the receiving end!" He pressed a button, triggering a tinkling sound. "The VP alarm! Now, I'll have to be on time for all my meetings!" he joked about his notorious tardiness. "If I can tear myself away from my research musings and remember to set the alarm, but I'm sure Loyola as always will remind me!"

Loyola basked in this praise and Mary quickly initiated a round of brief clapping.

"Now, let me see," V.P. Barron continued, holding up the watch, "I'd say we have just enough time left to finish off all that delicious food, so I won't keep you any longer. Thank you all!" He playfully pressed the alarm button to signify the end of the presentation ceremony.

Obligatory hand-clapping and cheering that expressed sincere admiration from those who knew him only through superficial contact, and forced smiles lacking substance and genuine warmth from those who had come to know him too close for comfort, greeted his witticism.

Half an hour later, as the department members dispersed back to their work, Heinz Herzog joined Tessa Euler and Albert Tanaka as they walked along the corridor back to their offices.

"Oh boy, I didn't realize what a brilliant man, V.P. is!" Dr. Herzog said, his voice loaded with sarcasm. "How much he knows—he truly is a whiz!"

Tessa shook her head and with a wry smile added, "And what ideas he sows!"

"If only they were *his!*" Dr. Tanaka concluded the sally in a dry voice as he and Tessa entered his office and closed the door.

▲

*T*essa took the offered seat opposite Albert Tanaka's chair for his desk faced the wall and did not present a protective barrier.

"Now tell me, what did our big boss say to upset you, Tessa?" Dr. Tanaka leaned back in his chair in a relaxed, open manner.

"He called me in this morning, saying that he wished to discuss my progress on the development of our Sub-attomolar Protein Analysis project."

"And you told him we are making excellent progress?"

"Yes, I did, but that was not what he really wanted to discuss. He didn't even look at the data! What he wanted to talk about was the possible licensing option on my work, which I had brought with me to The Company three years ago. You remember, I told you about my micro-analytical method for detection of lipolytic enzymes? I offered it at that time to V.P. for review on a confidential basis, so that he could advise me on whether The Company would be interested in licensing it and carrying the cost of patenting the invention. He is the executive member of The Company Patent Review Committee."

"Aha...yes, I recall," Albert Tanaka said, "it was your invention and you said your post-doc professor suggested you patent it since the university was not interested in filing a patent?"

"That's right, but I didn't have and still don't have the money to patent it and then continue paying the fees for the upkeep of the patent on a worldwide basis."

Albert Tanaka nodded in agreement. "Ah, yes, it can be very expensive, I know."

"All this time, I've been waiting for a reply, hoping The Company would take out a patent on my behalf and draw up a license agreement. When I gave it to V.P. for evaluation he seemed to agree. He even said that the method had great potential and would contribute greatly to the ongoing enzymes research project within ART," Tessa Euler frowned. "Then, this morning he said that since I have been working in ART where enzyme research is being conducted and I have attended enzyme-related meetings, he can't be certain whether I didn't pick up the idea from somewhere in The Company!"

Albert Tanaka's eyes narrowed and he stroked his nose thoughtfully. "And what did you say?"

"Well, I said I had proof I was working on this project at the university in New Zealand long before I joined The Company. The work was, in fact, a continuation of my Ph.D. thesis. I told him I couldn't see how he could suggest that, when no one here was working on anything remotely related to my micro-analytical method for detection of lipolytic enzymes!" She paused for breath as outrage and anger welled up inside her. "And do you know what he did?"

"No, but I can hazard a guess," Albert Tanaka smiled cynically. "He presented you with The Company invention disclosure form, which outlined some sort of modified version of your invention proposal, with his name as inventor on it and a space for you to add yours, if you wish. Am I far off the mark?"

Tessa could not believe how closely her project leader had described the actual events. It was as if he had been standing right there in V.P.'s office. "It's exactly what happened, Albert! He even said, in his opinion, the method still needs optimization, which is not true at all as the method has been fully optimized and evaluated! He added that we could work on it in ART and The Company itself could patent it in his and my name!"

"Naturally, you would then be awarded the glorious certificate and the generous reward, the 'Inventor's Cent'. You know management still didn't fulfill their promise to us that The Company will increase the inventor's award to a token five hundred dollars!" Albert said dryly.

"But, Albert, how on earth did you know what happened in V.P.'s office? Who told you?"

"Deja vu, Tessa!" Albert leaned forward and in a confidential, lowered tone said, "There's one thing I can say about the man. He's predictable. Since he has always found success with his methods, he has had no reason to change them. A long time ago I read an appropriate verse and I have often thought of it when observing V.P.'s methods. Let me see, roughly translated it said:

What crime is hardest to detect,
Takes years of practice to perfect?
No fingerprints are left behind,
For stealthily he'll pick your mind.
Without acknowledgment or fee,
Your intellectual property
No longer now belongs to you,
And leaves you wondering what to do?
With others' work he makes his name,
On pilfered labors rests his fame!'"

"Exactly! That's V.P. to a tee! Do you mean to say he used the same tactics to pilfer your ideas as well?" Tessa was astonished that V.P. would dare to treat a world-renowned chemist like her supervisor in the same ignominious way.

Albert Tanaka nodded. "On many occasions. It's the price we scientists pay sooner or later for staying in his ART department."

"But what award does he get from all The Company patents apart from his personal prestige? There is no monetary compensation, as you said."

"In his managerial position a substantial bonus check is dependent on his research productivity. But he is merely a shell of a scientist with the heart of an avaricious manager intent on climbing the ladder to the executive top of The Company."

"With all due respect, Albert, why do you allow him to get away with it?"

"Tessa, V.P. may not exactly be loved by upper-management, but he is the only image they have of a manager-scientist. He reports on The Company research to the Board of Directors, is regarded by many managers without science degrees throughout The Company hierarchy as a top-notch scientist, and is a powerful man with an extensive network. If you cross him, you might as well forget any future in The Company and maybe even outside for sooner or later, he will be asked by any new employer for a character reference. Why do you think the ART department has such a high staff turnover?"

Albert Tanaka paused for three shadows to pass by his frosted glass, office door window. Mary's voice receded into the distance before he spoke again. "Few people stay longer than a couple of years in ART. A few other scientists and I stay because research in industry still pays more than academia and we have family expenses and responsibilities to consider. A young scientist, like you, who came over from New Zealand and is now a naturalized American, is still not so much dependent on V.P. for a job. But, of course, I wouldn't like to loose you! You are definitely an asset to my project, and a very talented, knowledgeable chemist. It is difficult to find someone these days, who is still willing to work hard behind the bench instead of setting their sights on a well-paid managerial position."

He looked with concern into Tessa's eyes, "So, what exactly did you say to him this morning?"

Tessa Euler shrugged. Her eyes expressed worry as she realized the full implication of the direct way in which she had spoken. "I was so mad when I saw what he had done, I told him he had no right to modify my invention and that I am withdrawing my license option offer. I said that I had already consulted on the matter with a patent attorney, a friend of mine, and with Les Suggs from The Company Legal department. They both agreed that there is no doubt the invention is mine alone and that I was free to offer it to whomever I wished!"

Albert Tanaka grimaced, then suddenly broke into a chuckle. "I bet he had never heard that from anyone before!"

"When I was about to leave his office, V.P. said, 'We shall see. I don't view it like that.'" Tessa bit her lip. "Maybe if I keep a low profile, he'll forget and steal from someone else for consolation."

" V.P. suffers from amnesia of convenience. He forgets inventors' names, but he has a long memory when he chooses to remember. Maybe you're right, a peace offering of some sort to appease him might work. He has had his eye on our sub-attomolar protein analysis method—perhaps this might placate him?"

Albert Tanaka smiled encouragingly, but Tessa Euler was suddenly assailed with a sinister sense of foreboding.

▲

Six months passed by and Tessa Euler agreed to add V.P. Barron's name to the patent application for the novel, ultra-sensitive protein analysis method she had developed in collaboration with Albert Tanaka. In fact, V.P. had also insisted they include Dr. Todd Dean and his technical assistant, Mary, as co-inventors even though their collaborative efforts involved only two irrelevant sideline experiments.

"But Mary just took instructions as a tech and all she did was prepare three solutions for Todd!" Tessa protested to Dr. Tanaka. "And Todd did not contribute to our invention! He just followed our protocol and substituted our peptide analyte with an enzyme substrate. How can V.P. justify adding their names as equivalent co-inventors on our patent?"

" V.P. never justifies any of his actions, Tessa. Mary and Todd have other uses for V.P. and including their names on our patent is how he rewards them. He is—" Albert Tanaka paused as he saw Mary emerge from the walk-in refrigerator, a test tube rack in her hand and a sly look in her eyes. He waited for her to leave the lab. "Let's have a talk over lunch and away from The Company eavesdroppers. Be careful what you say when those two 'big ears' are around," he advised. "You did say you will keep a low profile?" he reminded with a friendly smile.

Tessa agreed.

Over lunch at a quiet restaurant not frequented by The Company employees, Dr. Tanaka raised the issue of the impending review.

"I am worried, Albert," Tessa confided. "After the run-in I just had with V.P., do you think there is any chance I will get the promotion V.P. has been promising me this last year?" she inquired. "I do have ten years research experience and I hear that Todd Dean, who obtained his Ph.D. two years after I did, is already two levels above me."

"As I promised, Tessa, I have proposed you for promotion. You more than fulfill the necessary job criteria for the position of Staff Research Chemist!"

Tessa spent the next couple of weeks immersed in her research activities. She found her work in Albert Tanaka's group stimulating and exciting, and she was in excellent spirits for even V.P. Barron had recently taken to greeting her frequently on the corridors with a light-hearted witticism. He even laughed at her quick banter. On several occasions he stopped by her lab to take what seemed like a genuine interest in her research results. He also attended their project meetings with Todd Dean, who now headed the Enzyme Research Project, to see how the adaptation of their ultra-sensitive method to low-level enzyme detection was progressing.

A week before the ART department's review day, Dr. Tanaka invited Tessa into his office and smiled encouragingly. "I think, Tessa, you've been a very good employee!" he praised with a hint of good-natured sarcasm. "I have to leave town for the week. Surprisingly, V.P. asked me to review on his behalf the outside research project with Amgo, Inc. But I will be back in time to give you your review. In the meanwhile, it'll give V.P. enough time to sign all the necessary paperwork for your promotion. He's been dragging his feet, but don't worry, Tessa. Everything is going fine!"

Tessa eagerly looked forward to obtaining the promised, long overdue change in her job status. Then, three days before her review, she found a note on her desk from Loyola Fraise, stating that she was expected to attend a meeting the following morning at eight-thirty sharp in V.P. Barron's office.

Her feelings of elated anticipation for a possible promotion and salary raise, soon turned into a sense of uneasiness as she tried to discover the reason for the meeting.

"I can't say! I mean, V.P. is at an off-site meeting today," Loyola Fraise replied with unusual curtness. "You'll just have to wait and see."

"But surely you must know, Loyola!" Tessa tried some friendly persuasion. "After all, you arrange all of V.P.'s meetings. I'd just like to know if I have to prepare anything or bring along any data. Is it about our protein analysis project?"

Loyola Fraise switched off her computer, pulled on her jacket and picked up her handbag. "It's past four-thirty already and I have an appointment to get to!" she said and brushing past Tessa she hurried toward the elevator.

Tessa followed her with rapidly mounting apprehension. "Loyola! Please, what is this meeting all about?"

"I can't say, Tessa," Loyola stubbornly persisted with averted eyes. "Ask Albert. He's your boss!"

"But I can't! Albert won't be here for two more days!"

"Oh, yes. That's right. V.P. sent him off–"

The elevator doors opened and Loyola rushed inside. As she turned to press the button Tessa clearly saw an embarrassed expression on her face.

"I can't say…I really can't! V.P. didn't tell me!" she stammered and as the elevator door was slowly closing, she added on a sudden impulse, "Jay Rush will be there!"

Tessa Euler frowned in puzzlement. Jay Rush was from the Employee Relations department! Why would he be present? Maybe V.P. wanted him to approve the regulation of her job status? But that was very unusual. It was common practice for the direct supervisor to handle these matters. Tessa was really upset that Dr. Tanaka was away at this crucial time and she had no one to turn to for advice.

Her musings were interrupted by Mary, who walked by and with a smug smile, remarkable for its sugary sweetness, asked if she intended to go home in her lab coat.

"I guess it's time you put in more overtime hours," she said with a sarcastic curl to her lips.

"What do you mean?" Tessa snapped. "I often work long hours."

Mary gave a short laugh. "That's what you think, isn't it?" she said as she stepped into the elevator.

The malice was clear in Mary's voice and insolent manner.

In a flash, Tessa knew what she had to do! She hurried to the shopping mall.

The following day, a couple of minutes before eight-thirty, Tessa leaned against the cool tiles in the ladies restroom to steady her pounding heart. She closed her eyes and took several deep breaths, then looked at her watch. It was eight twenty-four.

Tessa glanced at her reflection in the mirrors and gave herself an encouraging smile. She wished Dr. Tanaka was there to support her, but there was nothing she could do at this moment, except compose herself and see what this highly irregular meeting would reveal.

At least nothing in the self-confident appearance she projected, attired in a neat, conservative, dark blue suit and a crisp, white blouse, hinted at her inexplicable nervousness.

Decisively, Tessa reached into her leather briefcase and switched on the small tape recorder she had bought the previous afternoon at the mall. She took a deep breath and walked briskly toward V.P. Barron's imposing office.

Loyola Fraise returned her greeting with a nod and stiffly indicated for her to proceed into V.P.'s office.

Dr. V.P. Barron, a sanctimonious smile on his face as she entered, sat back in his high-backed, black leather chair, elbows resting on the armrests, his fingers touching as if poised for prayer. The wall behind him was covered with gold-plated patent plaques and The Company's certificates honoring his many achievements.

Tessa was surprised to see Todd Dean, as well as Jay Rush, seated in front of V.P.'s polished, mahogany desk, laughing at some comment V.P. must have just made.

"Tessa! Come in! Please, take a seat!" V.P. invited with false geniality. He indicated the low settee opposite his desk, flanked on each side by potted plants.

Tessa carefully placed her briefcase onto the low coffee table in front of the settee. She sat up straight, immediately realizing that her placement was a premeditated act to give her a height disadvantage, though at her five feet four inches, this would not have been difficult even if she had been offered a chair of equal height with the three men. Obviously, V.P. wanted to provoke in her a feeling of inferiority. Tessa's direct look and cool poise, however, swept aside such attempts at dominance and Todd fidgeted uncomfortably as she glanced at him.

Jay Rush turned to V.P. for approval to start the proceedings.

V.P. Barron silently motioned to Loyola, who was hovering curiously just outside the office, to close the door and then turned with a pharisaical expression to Tessa.

"I think you must know, Mr. Jay Rush, our Senior Personnel Officer in charge of employee regulations and compensation. Since Albert is not here, I decided that Todd's position more than qualifies him to represent your supervisor in his absence," he said, his head swaying from left to right. He tapped the tips of his fingers together and after a pause, continued, "Tessa, we need to talk about a serious issue. Perhaps it was partly my fault for not addressing this sooner, but with reviews coming up in a couple of days, we felt this was the appropriate time." He motioned to Jay Rush to continue.

What serious matter? And who was 'we'? Tessa wondered, fighting to keep her outrage under control. And how could that fresh, inexperienced, insinuating rat, Todd Dean, represent her boss? She had more years of research experience than he did, except that V.P. had given him a higher position in The Company!

"Tessa–Dr. Euler," Jay Rush began with exaggerated formality, "I think you should read this first before Dr. Barron explains his reasons further for this important meeting."

He handed Tessa two typed pages with The Company logo on the header. Tessa realized it was a document intended for filing in the personnel department's employee records. She was glad the hand she extended to accept the memo did not shake and betray her emotions.

Tessa forced herself to ignore the silent pressure of three pairs of eyes focused on her and concentrated on the contents of the memo.

She read the header several times and could hardly believe her eyes as she saw that the memo, addressed to her, was from both V.P. Barron and Albert Tanaka!

Her brain screamed at the betrayal by the very colleague and supervisor she had trusted without reserve. How could he? Did he remove himself on purpose to let V.P. do the dirty work? Then, she recalled how unwavering his support had always been and Loyola's remark that V.P. had "sent him off."

She glanced up and seeing the hard glint in V.P.'s eyes, her analytical logic took over. She reread the header. Yes, her boss's name was typed next to the statement, 'Direct Supervisor'. But it was obviously only a necessary formality. She noted that 'Albert Tanaka, Ph.D.' was printed in brackets below ' V.P. Barron, Ph.D.', and Albert had not signed his initials. So V.P. Barron alone wrote this letter!

"Take your time, Tessa," V.P.'s glib voice broke the silence. "Don't feel pressured. Isn't that so, Jay?"

"Yes, yes, of course," the personnel representative nodded, glancing surreptitiously at his watch, while Todd Dean, chewing on his right hand forefinger nail, sighed audibly.

Tessa returned her eyes to the memo. Suddenly she remembered the comforting presence of her hidden witness, whirring quietly in her briefcase, chronicling every syllable uttered.

"I would prefer to read this aloud, if I may?"

"Go ahead, Tessa, refresh our memory banks," V.P. agreed at once. He laughed out briefly. "I heard that only feeble authors can recall their compositions verbatim. My memory always fails me!"

Jay Rush and Todd Dean responded with an ingratiating chuckle.

Dr. Tessa Euler lowered her eyes to the page and in a clear, steady voice, which even surprised herself, read to the unbiased recorder:

"*From Dr. Euler's frequent requests to both her direct supervisor, Dr. Albert Tanaka, and the Senior Vice President, Director of ART, Dr. V.P. Barron,, it is evident she believes she merits a regulation of her present Research Chemist status to Staff Research Chemist. After careful consideration of her demands, however, we find that we cannot justify her promotion.*

"*There are several important areas of professional maturity in which Dr. Euler must first show substantial improvement before her promotion can be considered. Her ten years of research experience, seven of which were spent in academia not in an industrial research setting, cannot automatically qualify her for the requested position in ART. Furthermore, her scientific publications were on basic research topics not industrial applications and, therefore, are insufficient criteria for promotion within ART. Although Dr. Euler has shown promise in adapting to her current research project on sub-attomolar protein analysis methods, she must demonstrate a greater degree of independent problem-solving ability, competence in designing, planning, and meticulously conducting and recording data.*

"She has yet to demonstrate a satisfactory level of diligence expected of the ART staff with respect to innovation and active time spent performing assigned tasks. This brings into question her limited accomplishments. Her data will require greater scrutiny and independent validation in the future.

"Most importantly, she must learn the meaning of teamwork spirit within our research department and should concern herself less with her own selfish, outside interests. A greater understanding of our corporate culture, based on the principles of loyalty and generosity toward The Company, is required.

"Last, though by no means least, her perceived arrogant attitude has a negative effect on her coworkers and Dr. Euler should seriously consider improving this before any regulation of her status can be granted.

"We have confidence in Dr. Euler's ability, if willing, to fulfill these requirements in due time. Her progress will be monitored closely. Witnessed by Dr. Todd Dean; signed by Dr. V.P. Barron."

Tessa was so shocked by the libelous accusations against herself that for a couple of moments she just stared in silent disbelief at the pages in her hands.

How could anyone compose such falsehoods? She raised her eyes and looked questioningly at V.P. Barron. From the cold, sadistic gleam in his eyes, she realized he was enjoying every minute of her discomfort. Why? What had she done to deserve such malignance? Confused thoughts raced through her mind.

The Company intercom chimed, paging an employee and breaking the silence in the office. In a sudden flash of understanding, the answer came to her as clearly as if someone had announced the words on the intercom system itself. It was incredible, but there could not be any other explanation.

V.P. Barron was punishing her, taking revenge for her refusal to relinquish her invention! What a vindictive, vicious personality lurked behind that benevolent, smiling mask he presented to the world. Without compunction, he would destroy her scientific reputation and any future career prospects either in industry or academia. She knew she now had no alternative, but to fight for her survival!

With a composed face, she put the accusatory document on the table. "I am afraid I do not fully understand all the points raised in this letter. Please, would you explain?" Her voice sounded distant to her ears, almost unreal. There was not a hint of the strong emotions she was feeling.

She glanced at Todd Dean. He flushed, crossed his legs, defensively folded his arms across his chest and concentrated on the crystal pen and inkwell set decorating V.P.'s desk.

"Naturally, Tessa," V.P. Barron replied smoothly with a half-smile at Jay Rush. "It is perfectly simple. Before you can advance in The Company, you must show greater professional maturity and match your opinions of your own abilities to your actual accomplishments!"

"That is precisely what I have done, Dr. Barron, in my written request, which I forwarded to you over a year ago," Tessa replied in as even a tone as possible. "Dr. Tanaka agreed with my requests and so did you at that time, if you would care to remember?" She looked toward Jay Rush, whom she hoped was an unbiased witness. "Dr. Albert Tanaka will, I am sure, confirm this and also that I have successfully fulfilled all my research goals!"

Jay Rush raised his thin eyebrows. "Are you saying Dr. Barron's assessments are not correct?" He glanced with an obsequious smile at V.P. "As you must know, Dr. Barron is a man of great experience, Dr. Euler! You would do well to listen to his advice!"

With a mixture of anger and dismay, Tessa turned away, realizing she could not count on any support from this prejudiced personnel representative. Her resolve strengthened as she became acutely aware she stood alone against these three adversaries.

"I disagree most strongly. The statements in this letter do not offer any useful advice whatsoever!"

With distinct pleasure, she saw the self-satisfied smile vanish from V.P.'s face and she quickly continued. "I have more than twenty accredited publications in peer-reviewed, international journals, which have been very well received in the scientific community. They form the basis of the work in which I am currently involved. It was because of my experience in this field that I was hired by you to work and apply my expertise in the very project I am now working on." She glanced at the letter. "I cannot see how anyone would believe that experience in academia is irrelevant to research in industry! After all, many of the inventions reduced to practice in industry began life in an academic setting. And I know you can't deny, Dr. Barron, that we have many consultants from academia at this very moment advising us at The Company. If all their academic experience was worthless, I'm sure we would not be paying for their contributions!"

"That may well be true, but when you join my ART department, you must live up to higher standards!" V.P. Barron replied and with a derogatory grimace and a flick of his hand dismissed academia from his office. "You must prove your scientific abilities here, to my satisfaction!"

"In my three years with The Company, Dr. Barron, I have contributed more than fifteen novel invention disclosures, which is more than any other young researcher in your department!" Tessa countered, glancing at Todd Dean. "Your name, Dr. Barron, is practically on all of them and Todd's and Mary's names have been added as co-authors on my most recent patent application!"

V.P. half-nodded. "Yes, we are, which only proves that you must yet show you can think and solve problems independently!"

Tessa was incensed and stunned. Independent?! She raged silently as she recalled how V.P. Barron had insisted to Albert Tanaka that all their names should be added to her patent disclosure! With iron will, she reigned in her anger before replying, "The novel algorithm for the detection of sub-attomole amounts of proteins was conceived and developed independently by me. Dr. Tanaka will vouch for that!"

"Albert may be a good scientist, but he is too easily influenced and his scientific judgment suffers from this weakness. That is why I have decided that in future Todd will validate the results of your sub-attomole analyses."

"But Todd is neither an analytical chemist nor a physical chemist with the necessary experience. I understood that Dr. Tanaka, who is a physical chemist, is the specialist and project leader who validates my results!"

"I don't view it like that!" V.P. Barron used his favorite phrase. "You should shake off your arrogant, academic attitude. In ART, *I* decide who is qualified to pass judgment on various projects. That is why I decided on Todd and Mary to evaluate your data!" He paused and added, "I have heard of your opinion of Mary, but even though she is only a technical assistant, she is, in my opinion, more than equivalent to a staff research chemist. I expect you to treat her as an equal from now on!"

Tessa was outraged by such deliberately insulting remarks, but her logic told her that V.P. was trying to provoke her into making some statement she would later regret. She, therefore, replied in a calm voice.

"Anyone is welcome to review my results, if they feel themselves qualified. My research data are all documented in detail and I have shared my results openly with all my colleagues. Todd, I don't believe we had too many difficulties communicating!"

"No…I mean, yes…Mary had some problems with your expressions…your accent, and she doesn't understand your way of doing higher math, your formulas and things like that…." Todd's voice petered out. He bit his full, lower lip in obvious embarrassment as it dawned on him that he had just contradicted V.P.'s glowing assessment of Mary's abilities.

V.P. Barron shot an annoyed look at his protégé, who shifted uneasily in his chair. A waft of Todd's aftershave mixed with sweat impinged unpleasantly on Tessa's senses.

"What Todd was trying to say is that your protocols lack clarity, Tessa!" V.P. elaborated.

"In which case, how could Todd have reported to Dr. Tanaka that Mary has successfully carried out all the analyses by following the experimental protocols, which I wrote for them?" Tessa looked directly into Todd's bloodshot eyes, which quickly darted away. "And as you know, Todd, I also solved the problems, which you had in your own enzymes research project."

"Well, we did have some success…once, when you gave us the reagents, but last week Mary couldn't repeat the results again," Todd said defiantly.

"Then why didn't you come and see me?"

"Because we couldn't find you anywhere!" Todd lied outright.

"Yes, I can see this seems to be a real problem with your job performance!" Jay Rush interjected, holding up his copy of the accusatory letter.

"I'm afraid it is," V.P. wiped the traces of saliva from the corners of his loose mouth with a white monogrammed handkerchief and his head swayed in regretful agreement. "You see, Tessa, does not put in sufficient active lab time–"

"How can you say that?" Tessa exclaimed sharply. Her frustration and wrath were turning caustic and beginning to fume like concentrated nitric acid exposed to the air. "I am either in my office or in the lab almost every morning at least one hour before our official start time at seven-thirty and I often leave after five in the evening, long after everyone else has gone home! I even come into the lab over the weekend, if the experiment requires it!"

V.P. Barron's slim hands formed a loose triangle, flexible fingertips caressing each other. With raised eyebrows and a cynical twist of his lips he said, "But *I* never see you!"

"I do have witnesses!" Tessa retorted. "I can't help it if Todd and Mary do not keep to the same long work hours!"

"Perhaps. But that is just your opinion! Mary and other members of my ART department tell me a different story. You know, we can always check with The Company security log-in books."

"You know very well, Dr. Barron, how lax The Company security is. No one ever signs in and we only need to flash our badge at the guards to be allowed to enter!"

"Signing in after hours is your own responsibility!" Jay Rush said with a frown and Tessa recalled that he was a member of the ineffectual security committee.

"As an honest employee, that is!" V.P. added with a malicious half-smile.

Tessa was appalled. "Are you implying that I am dishonest?"

"Not exactly, but this is just another example of your overall, slapdash, arrogant attitude," V.P. accused. Curling his slack lips, he added, "You believe yourself to be above The Company rules and regulations. You have too many self-interests that do not coincide with those of The Company!"

Now he was coming to the truth behind this entire charade, Tessa thought. She was determined to draw him out so he would voice his reasons for the record on the impartial tape.

"What kind of self-interests, Dr. Barron?" she feigned ignorance and cast a deliberately questioning look at the unsympathetic Jay Rush.

"When you joined ART, Tessa, all your patentable ideas, if in any way related to your present work or other work within ART, should become the property of The Company!"

"Yes, I agree, but only those inventions I made *after* joining The Company or, if the research at the university in New Zealand would have been financed by The Company!" Tessa protested. "And it was definitely not!"

"But we do not view it like that!" V.P. raised his voice for the first time. He pointed a long, accusing finger at her. His diamond and onyx ring glittered in the sunlight. "To give but one glaring example, you have selfishly decided not to give the patent application on the lipolytic enzyme analysis method to The Company!" He leaned back in his chair and after taking a deep breath, continued, "You have much to learn, Tessa, about loyalty to The Company. I am willing to help you, but it cannot be done in one day!" His hypocritical, benevolent smile returned. "In the meanwhile, we will keep track of your willingness to change your attitude over the next year. Jay will ensure, in all fairness, that your compensation will be commensurate with your professional progress!"

Jay Rush nodded his agreement and checked the time on his watch again. "You will have to excuse me, Dr. Barron. I have another meeting now, but I will make sure the proceedings of this meeting are filed."

"Where will this letter be filed, Mr. Rush?" Tessa asked, more for the sake of the recording device than her own curiosity.

The personnel representative looked at her in surprise. "In your permanent personnel reference files, of course. Where else?'

"But every supervisor I go to work for will be able to read this!" Tessa exclaimed indignantly.

"Naturally! We are not in the habit of hiding personnel records in this Company!" Jay Rush replied with an affronted snort.

"Look at it this way, Tessa," Todd interjected in an attempt at wittiness. "Your successful transformation and professional progress will also be registered!"

V.P. nodded and laughed with approval as he stood up and everyone followed suit.

"You see, Tessa, you are not alone. We are all willing to help you achieve our ART standards. Todd, Mary...," V.P. Barron opened the office doors and indicated his secretary, who was standing before the filing cabinet beside the office door, "even Loyola is willing to keep an eye on your progress and help you adjust!"

The threatening warning underlying his apparently genial words did not escape Tessa.

Loyola chuckled and a knowing look on her face told Tessa she had been eavesdropping.

"We are all one happy family in ART," she tittered. "We stick together and we don't tolerate disruptive behavior!"

"That's right!" V.P. Barron looked pointedly at Tessa Euler. "We give everyone one chance and then we move on to the more serious business of formal reprimands!"

Tessa Euler returned to work the following day, exhausted and tired from a sleepless night during which she had tried to decide what she should do next. She had listened to the recording over and over again and was pleased with her reactions under pressure. One thing was certain, if the accusatory letter was filed in her personnel records her career prospects were bleak if not completely ruined. However, did she dare fight such a powerful Company man as V.P. Barron? And which options were open to her anyway?

She called the Personnel department several times during the day, but was told by the friendly, talkative secretary that Mr. Ken Hunt, the department head who usually dealt with such matters as giving advice to personnel, was unfortunately off-site, attending an 'Advanced Personnel Management' seminar. He would not return for a month. Since Mr. Hunt's deputy was away on sick leave, Mr. Hunt had left Mr. Jay Rush in charge, but he was unavailable at the moment and could not answer her questions. The secretary promised to forward her requests.

Tessa persisted and called one last time before the end of the workday. The secretary told her that Mr. Rush said he was too busy to talk with her. Maybe he will see her sometime after the weekend, since on Friday, tomorrow, he would not be in.

Tessa had no choice but to spend another night tossing and turning, pondering her abysmal situation, and await the return of her supervisor, hoping her trust in him at least had not been misplaced.

▲

*D*r. Albert Tanaka returned on the official departmental review day, and was stunned by the events that had taken place in his absence.

V.P. Barron had taken the day off from work, but Loyola Fraise informed him that Tessa had already been given her "well-deserved" review and Dr. Barron had decided to set aside Albert's review of Tessa's work performance until he feels she merits it.

"I hope she will stick to the ART department rules in the future!" Loyola unprofessionally reinforced V.P. Barron's words. "V.P. says it is up to you, Albert, to make sure she follows through. He expects you to sign this document too!"

Dr. Tanaka silently took the "letter of accusation" and returning to his office read it with a pensive and deeply troubled mind. He then phoned Tessa to come to his office and as she rushed in he motioned to her to close the door.

"You were told what happened, Albert?" Tessa asked as she saw the frowning expression on her project leader's face.

"Yes, I read the letter, but I would like to hear your version."

Tessa, who had impatiently awaited Albert Tanaka's return, had had the foresight to bring along her tape recorder.

"I think it is best that you hear this for yourself," she said taking the small recorder from her skirt pocket. She switched it on and began to play back the tape. V.P.'s voice sounded loud and clear.

Albert quickly reached forward and switched it off. "Good Lord, Tessa!" he exclaimed in a shocked whisper. "Do you realize they would most probably have you fired for this if they found out? I take it you didn't tell them they were being taped?"

"No, why should I? After the callous way they treated me, I had to have some independent proof!"

Albert's solemn face broke into a broad grin. "You know, Tessa, that was a brilliant idea, I must say!"

Tessa withdrew a pair of new headphones. "I bought these," she offered with a smile. "I thought you might want to listen to the tape privately."

Albert Tanaka accepted the headphones. He chuckled and shook his head in admiration.

An hour later, he called Tessa back to his office. She could not recall ever having seen him look so grim.

"What did you decide to do, Tessa? Will you quit?"

"I can't, Albert. If I do, this compromising letter will haunt me for the rest of my working life. My career is in jeopardy!"

"That is the conclusion I came to as well," Albert said solemnly. "As far as I can see you have only one alternative left."

Tessa slowly nodded. "Yes, I know. I heard that one could file a grievance. I decided to file it against V.P."

"Are you sure?" Albert Tanaka seemed to be probing the depth of her resolve.

Tessa gave him a direct, unwavering look. "Yes, I am determined, Albert. There is nothing anyone can say or do to stop me!"

"Aha, I see," Albert paused thoughtfully for a brief moment. He then broke into an encouraging smile. "Did you talk to Ken Hunt in Personnel yet? He is a good man and will advise you on how best to proceed."

"I called the Personnel department, but he's away for the month and Jay Rush, I think, is avoiding me on purpose."

"Be careful, Tessa. If I recall correctly, someone wanted to file a grievance several years ago, but waited too long. There is a three-day deadline, if I'm not mistaken. So, if you really want to go ahead with it, you have…," he glanced at his watch, "exactly one hour left to fill out the necessary form and have it signed."

As Tessa resolutely stood up to leave, Albert said, "I wish you luck, Tessa! I will stand by you, but you will have to fight this battle alone, if I am to be of any use to you as an unbiased witness. Do not expect too much justice! I know of no R & D employee, who would dare to take a stand against V.P., or for that matter, against any manager around here. The chances of succeeding are slim. Only a few I have known have tried but then decided to leave instead. But I do understand, Tessa, that you have to go through with this to save your career and professional reputation!"

Albert Tanaka suddenly reached back onto his bookshelf and handed Tessa a framed verse, hand-written in black ink. Tessa admired the perfect beauty of the calligraphic strokes.

"My old Ph.D. advisor gave me this bit of philosophical advice when I left to take up my first job in industry. Keep it on your desk. It might help to keep your spirit up in the rough days ahead:

> Challenge troubles face to face,
> Don't quit, until you've won the race.
> Retreat, if it seems wise,
> Don't take defeat as compromise.
> In circumstances dire,
> Don't be guided by your ire.
> Then with resolve and daring-do
> To sunny shores, you'll sail right through
> Life's raging, churning waters!"

The simple verse was often a source of inspiration to Dr. Tessa Euler in the coming month as her normally tranquil work environment was transformed into a whirlpool of speculations, innuendoes, and spiteful rumors.

The notorious Company gossips were consulted with never-ending curiosity in the corridors, in cubicle offices and behind almost every manager's closed office door. Employees who, under most circumstances pointedly ignored such "low-life", now strained their ears to catch a whisper of the "latest news on the grievance". None rivaled Mrs. Dona Trivi-Nuthing, however, for she did have access to both the opinions of management through her husband, Dr. Dan Nuthing, and the secretarial network through her extensive personal gossip-mongering acquaintances.

The Personnel department secretary, Cathy, soon became the most visited and sought after source of information. Since she was of an extremely obliging and open nature, a confidential secretary who confidently confided all she knew, soon found herself in the enviable position of having offers for more free lunches than she could possibly accept. And what juicy morsels of information did she have to impart for the price of her favorite enchiladas and strawberry daiquiris?

Tessa had to admit with a cynical smile when she overheard Dona Trivi-Nuthing relating to Mary in the adjacent lab, all the events of the Friday on which she officially registered her grievance, that Cathy was at least truthful.

"Cathy told me that since Jay Rush was away on that Friday," Dona related with relish, "Tessa's case had been handed over to that newly hired guy called Leo. And Leo had no idea it's the unofficial Company policy to try to dissuade—or to permanently squelch, as Dan says—any employee who's out for management blood."

"And what did that fool do?" Mary asked eagerly and barely containing her spiteful emotions, added, "I'd kick her out on her know-it-all ass! I can't stand it when she gives me those typed protocols, like she's something better than anyone else just because she's got a Ph.D.! I just can't stand to work for this woman!"

"I know! But Leo was apparently impressed, who knows why, and quickly pulled out some old Company regulations about grievance proceedings. Can you believe it, he even advised her on how to fill out the form!"

"What?" Mary was horrified. "That's stupid! I can't believe that bitch dared to file against V.P. himself. Can you imagine? Against such a fair and brilliant Company man!"

"And Cathy said that Leo even wished her luck! Of all the nerve!"

"Well, all I say, is get rid of both Leo and Tessa! The Company will be all the better off for it!" Mary voiced her venomous opinion. "But what does poor Loyola have to say now that her boss has been so unjustly attacked?"

Dona Trivi-Nuthing sniggered. "She has her own ways of getting back at that New Zealand, stuck-up know-it-all!"

So it happened that word of Tessa Euler's filing an official Company grievance against the most senior vice president, director of ART, spread like wildfire throughout The Company.

Within days Tessa began to feel the mixed reactions and consequences of her unprecedented action.

Encouraged by V.P. Barron himself, Loyola Fraise faithfully ensured that as many managerial levels as possible were fully appraised of Tessa's selfish motivations, her willful arrogant character, and her dangerous tendencies toward insubordination.

Though not every manager believed such malignance, it soon became crystal clear to Tessa that the vast majority thought it was not exactly in their best career interests to acknowledge any friendship with her in the corridors or in meetings. Even the project manager of the Protein Analysis Project, on which she was currently working, seemed to look right through her and pointedly ignored her contributions at their progress meetings.

As far as management was concerned, Dr. Tessa Euler, had become an "invisible Company employee".

The reactions from her senior scientist colleagues in ART, however, were more sympathetic. Dr. Albert Tanaka was true to his word. He was always available for her to voice her fears and misgivings, and he tried to dispel them with words of encouragement.

He allowed her to take the necessary time from her lab work to write a detailed rebuttal of the accusations to V.P. Barron's letter. This she submitted to the Personnel department for filing as part of the official proceedings, which, she understood, would eventually be reviewed by someone in upper-management, though Leo was not as yet certain who that would be.

In the meanwhile, veterans like Dr. Nigel Jansen and Dr. Wayne Greschwin, gave her reassuring winks, pats on the back, and openly spoke words of encouragement in their offices and the labs.

"It's a shame how technical people are treated around here," Dr. Nigel Jansen commented with an angry frown one day while chatting to Tessa and Wayne in the lab. "And maybe we are in part ourselves to blame for it. Few of us would dare to take an open stand like you, Tessa, against that thieving bastard…excuse my language, but maybe it is time that someone did!"

"Our nincompoop managers are allowed to get away with too much, if you ask me," Dr. Wayne Greschwin added. "The less they know, the higher they go! And in all my time with The Company, I have yet to meet one who is not an over-inflated and overpaid administrator without the proper qualifications! You did the right thing, Tessa. We will support you all the way. You are a darn good scientist, and they don't make many like you these days. Keep it up! V.P. is crazy to want to destroy your career prospects!"

"This is your strengthening fire," Dr. Nigel Jansen encouraged. "You'll be tougher than steel when all this is over!"

As the weeks passed by, Tessa often wished it were all over. On a daily basis she experienced how easily her own peers in the department had been intimidated by the almost hysterical atmosphere created by Loyola Fraise and perpetuated by Dona Trivi-Nuthing.

As if infected by some strange, contagious disease, one after another, they began to avoid her with sheepish, embarrassed glances.

"I can't be seen talking to you," several of her younger colleagues whispered when they happened to meet in the recesses of the lab or behind the closed walk-in refrigerator door. "Loyola says V.P. wouldn't like it and I'm afraid to cross him!"

The very colleagues who had criticized V.P. on many occasions for his autocratic managerial style, now trickled into her office after hours and confided nervously, "I hope you win, but it could mean my job, if I openly said so, you understand?"

"Don't quote me; I'll deny everything!" said her cubicle office neighbor, a tall male scientist, who had been very outspoken in the past. "Everything I ever said against V.P., I didn't say!"

Her male peers, who had confidentially shared information about their salaries with her, also feared the consequences of their frankness. "I know we joked when we congratulated you for being the lowest-paid Ph.D. we've ever met," three of them told her over lunch in a small secluded restaurant, "but you won't tell that we shared this information, will you? We could all be in trouble for revealing our wages. You know the managers don't like it if we start comparing. The discrepancies are too large, but we never said that either, okay?"

Loyola did indeed do her duty well. Four times a day she or Mary policed the department, looking to record Tessa's presence or preferably absence in her cubicle office or in the lab. Loyola kept a diary and alerted to this subtle form of harassment, Tessa reluctantly asked the senior scientists to sign and witness a report card she had made for herself, four times a day, proving that she was indeed at work all day, including overtime hours.

Two weeks after filing the grievance, Leo informed Tessa that Dr. Barron had sent a follow-up letter to the Personnel department.

"Is it in answer to my rebuttal?" Tessa asked.

"No," Leo said, " V.P. was not supposed to see your rebuttal. He had merely decided to add his opinions to your filing the grievance."

However, after reading V.P. Barron's second letter, which was addressed to her, it was obvious to Tessa and Dr. Tanaka, that V.P. must have an informer in the Personnel department. The letter was a point-by-point reply to her rebuttal. The senior scientists in ART unanimously suspected Jay Rush.

Tessa decided to write another rebuttal to V.P. Barron's second slanderous composition, which in fact only reiterated the same points made in his first letter of accusation.

Her persistent actions triggered a new wave of attack, inspired by Loyola and Mary. Many mornings, Tessa would find typed notes on her desk suggesting, from persons unidentified, that she should leave The Company. Several of her peers even called her with words of "well-meaning" advice that she really should quit, because as far as they had heard, she didn't have a chance of winning. Tessa filed the notes and after the fourth such call told her well wishers as politely as she could to mind their own business!

▲

*I*t was at this time the Head of the Personnel department, Mr. Ken Hunt, returned to The Company with a certificate of achievement from the Excellence in Employee Relations and Management Psychology course. He was full of enthusiastic ideas and concepts on how to apply all his newly acquired knowledge for the good of The Company.

On his first day back, before his secretary got in, he decided to "get a feel" for The Company again. He started his early morning stroll through the R&D departments, happily deliberating how he would begin his new program of closer personnel, management, and employee communications. With this in mind, he was pleased to see how well V.P. Barron was already interacting with his department members as he noticed the polite and apparently cordial manner with which Dr. Tessa Euler and Dr. V.P. Barron greeted each other as they entered through the department doors.

Therefore, it came as a complete shock when Cathy finally arrived and excitedly related the grievance scandal that had been the talk of The Company for the past month.

Deeply disturbed, Ken Hunt immediately sent for Leo, who handed him Tessa Euler's file with V.P. Barron's letters of accusation and her rebuttals. To Cathy's surprise, she heard him actually praise Leo for his appropriate actions in the matter.

Later that afternoon, after reading Tessa's file, he held a long session with Jay Rush.

"How dare you allow Dr. Barron to draw our Personnel department into such a mess!" Ken Hunt scolded.

"But... V.P. Barron is such a senior employee, a great scientist and an outstanding manager. I assumed he had the right to ask me to be present," Jay Rush stammered uncomfortably before his irate boss.

Ken Hunt, generally a good-humored man, ground his teeth angrily. "You assumed, did you? Well, you may have just made an ass of you and me and this entire department! We are not here to support atrocious management practices that run The Company reputation into the mud! Dr. Euler described your role in this mess in her rebuttal and any fool can see your bias!"

Ken Hunt stood up to his full six-foot height and towering over Jay Rush gave him a stern lecture from his course notes.

"We, in the Personnel department, must ensure that employee-management relations are improved. We are here to put out the fires not fuel them!" He paused and sat down while Jay squirmed in the deliberate silence. In an ominous tone, Ken Hunt inquired, "What do you think will happen, if Dr. Tessa Euler goes outside The Company and sues us for discrimination against her as a woman, not to mention harassment?"

"Well, she can't possibly win," Jay Rush protested. "Not against V.P.!"

"Oh, and is that your personal opinion, or advice from our Legal department?" Ken interrogated with undisguised sarcasm. "You did consult with them, didn't you?"

Jay Rush flushed and shrugged. "It hasn't ever been necessary to do so before," he desperately sought plausible excuses. "I mean, you know as well as I do that no employee in The Company has ever won their grievance against a manager, never mind such an influential one as Dr. V.P. Barron. They all have to leave sooner or later! How was anyone to know Dr. Euler would write such an extensive document?"

Ken Hunt sighed. "Never underestimate our researchers. Hell, we hire them into R&D for their inventiveness!" He smiled wryly. "And let me remind you, Jay, that The Company managers are not The Company owners! They are employees, like everyone else around here. Their exorbitant compensations and perks do not exempt them from our Company employee rules and regulations!"

Ken Hunt was a changed man after his course and was determined to reform his Personnel department policies.

"From what I read in Dr. Euler's file—and by the way, I consulted with our VP Legal, Hugo Lawson himself—she has an excellent chance of winning her case outside." He raised a questioning eyebrow at the now distressed subordinate and pointing to V.P. Barron's second letter asked, "Did you forward her rebuttals to Dr. Barron?"

"Well, Personnel always has worked closely with management and a man in V.P.'s position has access to any employee's files...."

Ken Hunt ran a hand over his forehead in frustration. "From now on, Jay, I will handle this prickly case. You will tell V.P. that you no longer have access to her files. They are sealed as a result of the grievance proceedings!"

Jay nodded, eager to please his boss. "And I'll look into her wages. I can't think how it could have escaped our notice?"

"Yes, give me all the records of her wage status and a comparison with other Company R&D employees with equal years of experience and education."

Ken Hunt took a folder from the shelf beside him. "I recommend that you copy the contents in here and read these lecture notes. We will be introducing some excellence in employee-management relations courses of our own in the near future!"

<hr>

Several days later, Tessa Euler was invited to a meeting with Ken Hunt, where she was given an unbiased hearing and a date was set for a formal discussion with Mr. Phil Fox, vice president of R&D. Ken Hunt patted Tessa Euler on the back in a friendly gesture as they stepped out of his office, saying, "Don't worry, Tessa, I am sure everything will be resolved fairly!"

Cathy, straining her ears, caught his words and soon the telephones of all the secretaries were buzzing. Loyola Fraise was appalled when she heard from Dona Trivi-Nuthing, with her usual measure of exaggeration, that Tessa had been promised Phil Fox would meet all her demands.

V.P. Barron was furious and made an urgent appointment to see The Company President, Mr. Wally Steen.

Wally Steen's immediate reaction to hearing that an employee had dared to file a grievance against one of his vice presidents had at first been one of surprised anger. Without inquiring further, he wholly sympathized with his staff manager. The thought even crossed his mind that there was no place for such a "troublemaker" in The Company.

However, as he observed the self-important face of the ART vice president as he approached his Captain's desk, something in his manner reminded him of a slippery eel. Wally Steen had never quite forgotten how, many years ago, when he was just a junior accountant, V.P. Barron had berated him in front of his boss about a minor accounting inconsistency that was later proven to be a mistake in V.P.'s own budgeting. Yes, Wally thought, Dr. V.P. Barron was too big-headed by far. Furthermore, Wally secretly doubted V.P. really was the sole originator of all the bright ideas and patents in his department, which V.P. Barron expounded in his accomplishment reports every year and which obliged him to grant this vain vice president a substantial bonus.

When he saw the deeply affronted expression on V.P.'s face, Wally became curious about this "troublemaker", who had been able to so seriously rattle this implacable man.

"How can I help you, Victor?" Wally asked, offering the chair opposite his desk. He refused to call him V.P. It sounded as if he were the only vice president in The Company.

"I suppose you know, Wally, about the scandalous grievance Tessa Euler has filed against me?" V.P. Barron asked in a whining tone. His eyes searched the president's suntanned face for a sign of sympathy.

"Yes, I heard," Wally replied in a noncommittal manner.

"She is an insubordinate, arrogant woman. At The Company we believe in free flow of information, but Tessa Euler holds everything to herself! I tried to reason with her, but she selfishly persists in pursuing her own interests!"

Wally Steen raised his bushy brows. "And what did you do to provoke the young woman into filing a grievance?"

"I merely explained, for her own good, that she should learn to shape up to the standards of behavior expected in The Company. She overreacted. In fact, she was quite hysterical at the review meeting," V.P. Barron prevaricated.

"I see, you mean like a typical female?" Wally commented dryly, testing the depth of the vice president's prejudice. There was something in the tone and the manner with which V.P. Barron related the events that did not quite ring true to Wally's ears.

"Exactly! And now she has approached Ken Hunt and influenced him into believing her side of the story. I heard he has already promised her success in her false grievance claims!"

"And what are her claims?" Wally asked, increasingly intrigued.

"Her claims are preposterous!"

"But what are they?"

"She believes she has the right to patent an idea, which she insists she had conceived before starting her employment in The Company. But it isn't at all clear she didn't get the idea while in ART. Over a month ago, I handed in a similar invention disclosure! And she also wants a promotion, which in my judgment she does not deserve at all!"

"So you precipitated a grievance?" Wally needled him on purpose.

"That was entirely her own idea!" V.P. Barron protested, while Wally wondered whether he had ever made such an admission about anyone's ideas before.

"And why don't you agree with the regulation of her status that she claims is overdue?"

"Impossible! Just the thought of such a thing has already sent a tsunami of emotions through ART! Everyone is upset and she has already had enough of a negative influence on work relations among the staff in my department!"

Wally Steen frowned. V.P. Barron's tirade sounded more emotional than he liked. His instinct told him there was something fishy about the situation, and he did not want it to get out of hand.

"Why exactly did you come to see me, Victor?"

"To ask you to remove Ken Hunt from the upcoming grievance hearing with Phil Fox. He is much too biased against The Company interests. Jay Rush, who is familiar with the situation from the beginning, would serve the purpose much better! After all, Ken's attitude may even prompt Tessa Euler, who is already emotionally unbalanced, to seek outside legal assistance. She has no concern for The Company reputation whatsoever!"

Wally Steen stood up, terminating their meeting. "I will look into this, Victor, but I will not tolerate any interference from you. You are the accused party and you must await the independent decision of The Company like your accuser."

V.P. Barron left the president's office frustrated, while Wally Steen permitted a mischievous smile to creep into his eyes. Did he finally have a chance to get back at V.P. Barron through this Company "troublemaker"? He asked his secretary to place a call to Phil Fox.

▲

*O*n the day of the grievance hearing, Tessa Euler was accompanied by Ken Hunt, who remained the official grievance proceedings officer, to the luxurious tenth floor conference room adjacent to Wally Steen's office.

Tessa had never before seen these corporate headquarters. From the moment she stepped out of the elevator into the carpeted corridors, the atmosphere of wealth and extravagance was unmistakable. She wondered how much understanding The Company president, who spent all his time in the surrealistic atmosphere of such plush surroundings, could have for the realities of work life in R&D? He was never seen to even walk along an R&D corridor!

The president's secretary, with her long wavy hair and hour-glass figure in a sea-green suit looked like the figurehead of the ancient galley in the oil painting on the wall behind her. She smiled kindly at Tessa and ushered them into the conference room through the heavy oak doors.

The Company president looked up and broke off his conversation with Hugo Lawson by the buffet table, set with fine china tea and coffee cups, silverware and serving plates laden with delectable finger sandwiches and a sumptuous fruit platter. He surveyed Tessa with curious blue eyes and extended a large welcoming hand in cordial greeting.

"Pleased to meet you, Dr. Euler!" he smiled. "Have you met our Vice President for Legal Affairs, Mr. Hugo Lawson?"

"How do you do?" Tessa said and shook hands with the tall, gray-haired man.

"I must say I've heard a great deal about you," Hugo Lawson said on a brief chuckle. "And I have read your grievance and rebuttals. They are very well written. Did you have outside legal help and advice?"

Tessa realized this question had a deeper meaning than mere polite conversation.

"Not for the sections dealing with the scientific aspects of my rebuttals," she replied, diplomatically avoiding a direct answer. If she admitted she had studied Thomas Paine's *Rights of Man* for inspiration and had gone to the library to read through legal books dealing with employee rights, she knew she would appear at a disadvantage.

Hugo Lawson and Wally Steen nodded to each other in mistaken understanding, while Ken Hunt, to whom Tessa had given the truthful version during their confidential conversation, busied himself with a slice of carrot cake.

"Coffee?" Wally played the genial host. "Or maybe you'd prefer a cup of tea?"

"Yes, please, tea will be fine. Thank you."

While Wally went out of his way to gallantly fill her cup with hot water and Tessa made her selection from the array of tea bags, he chatted, "I understand you're from New Zealand. I've sailed in many regattas down under. Do you sail?"

"In the City of Sails, Auckland, we almost all love sailing," Tessa smiled. "Dr. Newman, my old professor at the university, is devoted to yachting."

"John Newman?" exclaimed Wally Steen.

Tessa replied in the affirmative.

"I know him well! We were on the same team last year. I met him in the Visitors' Match Race in Auckland harbor, when my wife and I first visited New Zealand several years ago!" Wally was genuinely pleased. His whole perspective on this young lady standing before him changed in that very instant. She just had to be a bright scientist. He firmly believed that sailors must have their wits about them. No wonder she had spunk. Dr. Tessa Euler was, after all, a yachtswoman!

"Do have a seat. May I call you Tessa? All that doctor business is too formal between yachtspersons! Call me Wally, all my crew members do, isn't that so, Hugo, Ken?"

They all agreed and sat down in a pleasant, relaxed mood, as the doors opened and Phil Fox hurried in, a copy of the grievance proceedings in his hands.

"I'm sorry, I'm late, but I had an urgent telephone call," Phil Fox began and faltered as Wally Steen, his eyes dancing mirthfully, motioned to him in an attempt to convey some sort of a message.

Tessa turned round curiously, just in time to see the red hue of embarrassment suffuse Phil Fox's face as he turned his back to shut the zipper he had forgotten to close on his pants.

Wally and the other two men exchanged humorous glances, while Tessa tried to maintain a straight face. This was meant to be a serious meeting! But when Phil turned back she nearly burst into laughter. He must have leaned over too far and caught his tie in the zipper and the knitted tie began to fray. He had to excuse himself and turn his back once more to remedy the disaster.

Wally could no longer contain himself. He winked at Tessa and said, "Phil, if you continue in this way, Tessa, will have you for indecent exposure!"

Ken Hunt and Hugo Lawson anxiously looked for Tessa's reaction as Phil Fox joined them at the table, his face flushed and grinning like a silly schoolboy. Fortunately for them, Tessa did have a lively sense of humor and she responded with a smile, but quickly added, "I only object to deliberate and premeditated acts of harassment and… discrimination."

Her comment instantly brought the proceedings back on course. Wally opened the file with a serious expression and they questioned her for the next hour about her objections and treatment in ART, her wishes and her reasons for her discontent. She defended her position with a composed self-assurance Wally Steen admired. There was no sign of any tendencies toward hysterics in this woman. By Jove, he could hang V.P. Barron from the yardarm if he wanted!

"We can't really pass judgment on your technical abilities," Phil Fox said eventually. "I can barely recall the last time I saw a lab notebook–back in my lab class days–long before I moved on to the serious business of managing R&D. So, we will hand over a selection of your invention disclosures and one or two of your lab patent notebooks and protocols for evaluation to a couple of senior scientists in The Company."

"Dr. Barron has already proposed Todd Dean and Mary O'Malley, if the need for such an evaluation arises," Ken Hunt said. "He suggested Mary for her judgment as technical assistant."

"But they are not unbiased!" Tessa protested.

"Yes, I think so too," agreed Hugo Lawson. "After all, Todd Dean has witnessed the first letter of accusation."

"And Mary reports to Dr. Dean," added Ken Hunt. He glanced kindly at Tessa. "I also have to say that it is highly irregular that Dr. Albert Tanaka was not consulted, as Dr. Euler pointed out in her rebuttal. He is Dr. Euler's supervisor and he told me he has written a performance review that does not support Dr. Barron's accusations."

"And where is Dr. Tanaka's review?" asked Hugo Lawson, thumbing through the folder. "Why isn't it included here?"

Ken Hunt cast a meaningful glance at Wally Steen. "According to Loyola Fraise, Dr. Barron's personal secretary, the review is awaiting Dr. Barron's signature of approval."

"I told Victor to stay out of it!" Wally Steen scowled. "Phil, you decide which of the scientists are suitable to evaluate Tessa's work and add an outside consultant to the list. You don't have any objections, Tessa, do you?"

Tessa said she did not but nevertheless resented that her technical abilities were being questioned and assessed in this way. She had no choice but to acquiesce and set aside her professional pride.

▲

A month passed by during which Tessa forced herself to concentrate on her experiments and to ignore the chilly atmosphere in ART.

She could not altogether ignore her feelings of resentment and slighted professional self-esteem when she learned Phil Fox had conceded to V.P. Barron's demand. Her notebooks would be compared to Mary's, in order to check that her protocols satisfied and matched the expected ART standards.

The support from the senior scientists, however, was unwavering. Dr. Albert Tanaka was called to testify on her behalf once, which he did wholeheartedly and without hesitation. She was given a confidential hint that the selected scientists, who included Dr. Alan Hawk, Dr. Wayne Greschwin and a colleague of theirs from the Future Development Technologies department, were all appalled by the sloppy experimental data entry and record-keeping in Mary's notebooks. It was obvious the only precise experimental protocols stapled in her notebooks were those given to her by Dr. Tessa Euler.

Although this enabled Tessa to breathe a small sigh of relief, nothing could assuage her anxiety over the impending decision.

Tessa would never forget the day, Loyola Fraise made a point of typing a "pink slip" with her name on it as Tessa came by to pick up her monthly paycheck. As V.P. Barron came out of his office, a false smile played on Loyola's lips as she said, "I'm only practicing on this new form, V.P. Don't you think Tessa's name looks good on a pink background?"

As Tessa forced herself to smile at this malicious comment and V.P. Barron chuckled as if it was the joke of the month, Loyola's telephone rang.

With a glance at the switchboard, she said, "That's for you, Tessa. I'll get it! Yes, this is the ART department. Loyola Fraise speaking. Yes, yes, I'll let her know." She replaced the receiver. "Ken Hunt would like to see you in Wally Steen's office."

Loyola glanced meaningfully at her boss and patted the pink form. "I'll keep this…just in case!"

Tessa Euler, head held high, rode the elevator to the exclusive domain of The Company's elite. She chuckled as she suddenly thought of Aristophanes's classic Greek play, *The Birds*, where the privileged few dwelt with the gods in their *Nephelococcygia*. This corporate realm was just as much a *Cloud-Cuckoo-Land* that separated the managerial deities from the mere mortal employees!

The secretary beamed a welcoming smile and escorted her into the presidential office. Wally Steen came toward her and welcomed her with his usual firm handshake, then indicated to her to take a seat in one of the three armchairs grouped around the glass-topped coffee table.

Ken Hunt, already seated, gave her a reassuring nod.

"Well, Tessa, I'm glad to tell you the storm is over!" Wally Steen said, settling down with relaxed ease in the armchair opposite her.

"Mr. Steen and Mr. Fox have made their decision, Tessa," interjected Ken Hunt, clearly eager to minimize Tessa's suspense.

Tessa's heart began to thump. Her mouth suddenly became dry. She nodded her understanding and looked into Wally Steen's intense blue eyes.

"Okay, I'll get to the point," Wally said. "It has been decided that your research work does indeed meet the standards expected of a scientist at the higher level of Staff Research Chemist. Your status will be regulated."

Tessa shuttered her eyes and restrained herself from a show of buoyant emotions. The negotiations were only just beginning. She accepted The Company president's judgment with a polite smile. Wally Steen was impressed.

"But we did not find any evidence whatsoever," Ken Hunt hurriedly interpolated and stressed the words, "of any discrimination against you in The Company."

"And so my wages will also be regulated, commensurate with those of the other…employees on the same level with the same years of experience and education?"

Ken Hunt and Wally Steen exchanged a quick glance and Tessa began to feel the full force of the corporate justice system facing her.

Ken Hunt cleared his throat before replying. "Not regulated, Tessa, just implemented according to the usual fair practices of The Company."

"It is not the years of experience or education, which automatically entitle an employee to a position in The Company," Wally

Steen continued. "Tessa, you have to understand that management reserves the right to decide."

Tessa frowned. "But how can an employee ever be certain he or she has been fairly treated in comparison with all the other employees?"

"The employee has to place his or her trust in the good judgment of managers and the Personnel department," Wally Steen explained. He noticed the doubtful look in Tessa's eyes. "It's always been like that. A manager can hire, according to The Company need, one employee for one wage and the next minute another for a higher wage, even if the second employee's education and experience are lower than those of the first."

Tessa hesitated before responding and Wally prompted. "Go ahead, Tessa. Yachtspersons don't hold back. Air your views. I'm interested!"

"But if an employee is more qualified, he or she will contribute more and deserves a higher compensation!"

Wally Steen glanced again at Ken Hunt, who interjected, "We, in Personnel, try to ensure that this does take place."

"No, no, Ken," Wally shook his head. "Personnel cannot interfere in the decisions a manager makes about the people working for him! That would be disastrous! A bureaucratic shambles!"

Tessa noticed that Ken Hunt did not agree for he fixed his gaze on the sunlight reflecting from the beveled glass of the coffee table, but she could not keep silent.

"Your argument presupposes that the manager's judgment is without bias," she countered and received a nod from Ken Hunt.

"We're not *all* perfect, and I admit Victor has his management faults."

"Then, may I request a written apology from Dr. Barron for his slanderous behavior toward me?" Tessa said with an earnest look.

Wally Steen was visibly taken aback by this request. After a brief pause, his eyes lit up and he gave way to heartfelt laughter. "I like your sense of humor, young lady! There's a bite of the salty sea breeze in it! But I'll have to deny your wishes on this point. I'll deal with Victor's management style myself. If it'll make you feel better,

I must say, it leaves a lot to be desired!" He leaned back in the armchair and added dryly, "Tessa, there are more important issues to be considered in your case. Bear in mind that qualifications, degrees, certificates all mean nothing. What counts is how you get along with people at your workplace and not what a good student or scientist you were before you became an employee! As far as I'm concerned, you could be a Nobel Prize winner and you'd have first to prove your worth to The Company management!"

"But scientists are usually hired on the basis of their resume and bibliography, listing publications, previous experience and education. This provides hard evidence that one is able to perform assigned tasks! If all that doesn't matter, what does?"

Wally Steen leaned forward and gave her a direct look. With a crocked smile he said, "When I joined The Company many years go, I heard the then vice president of Research and Development give some damn good advice to a young scientist, who proudly displayed his Ph.D. thesis. I still remember that sound verse:

> Forget your glorious Ph.D.,
> Talents and ability,
> With these your prospects will be marred,
> For rising up the ranks is hard!
> Practice, instead, some sly deception,
> What matters really is Perception!"

He chuckled, while Ken Hunt laughed aloud and Tessa smiled in polite response. A sense of overwhelming cynicism swept over her.

"You see, Tessa, that's the only darn thing that matters. Perception! Opinion!" Wally continued with his advice. "Believe me, it is much easier to get ahead if people have the right perception about you. The value of your abilities and accomplishments can be easily disputed, as you just found out!"

"Mr. Steen, wouldn't you rather have an employee who really accomplishes something than one who just pretends to be working all the time?" Tessa persisted.

"Of course, but equally important is a show of team spirit, a willingness to conform to The Company culture. Changing your boss's mind is always harder than presenting the right image from the very beginning!"

Tessa silently wondered what he defined as the 'right' image? How could she have conformed to V.P. Barron's nefarious wishes? Should she have simply allowed him to misappropriate her intellectual property and ruin her career prospects for the sake of The Company team spirit?

"Remember also, Tessa," Wally blithely continued, unaware of the demoralizing effect his advice was having on the young Company researcher facing him, "that libel and slander are premeditated acts. Victor has his quirks, as we all do, but such intentions are hard to prove." With a cynical twist of his lips he added, "Though, he is known for his strong opinions on almost every subject, except sailing, thank God!" He rolled his eyes heavenward. "In The Company an open and honest evaluation of an employee by a superior is merely an expression of his opinions and cannot be considered as public malignance!"

"But if his accusations become a part of my permanent personnel files, they can potentially damage my career since they become accessible to any of my future supervisors!" Tessa protested, ignoring Ken's look that advised her to give in.

"You have our assurance that none of this will be included in your personnel file," Wally Steen said. "Isn't that so, Ken?"

"Yes, absolutely," Ken confirmed, quickly rising to his feet and preparing to leave. "You can come and check anytime."

Tessa accepted his promise. "Thank you, I will!" she said, a determined gleam in her eyes.

Suddenly Wally barked a laugh. "I like that! I really like your spirit, young lady! Please, stay and let's talk about Auckland, my favorite City of Sails!"

$\mathcal{T}$he decision in favor of Tessa Euler brought her back into The Company ranks of acceptable employees.

Managers, whom she had never met, greeted and even congratulated her. Her proposals were once again given keen attention at the project meetings and as the ice around her gradually thawed in the department, she became a curiosity to be visited, questioned, and viewed with wonder.

Tessa had sampled The Company justice, but both Tessa and Albert Tanaka knew that her sweet victory had a bitter aftertaste.

Feeling far from victorious, she sensed that Wally Steen's judgment in her favor was strongly influenced by his mischievous one-upmanship against V.P. Barron and her knowledge of sailing and Auckland regattas, rather than any desire to see Company justice served.

A week after her meeting with Wally Steen, she received a letter from Phil Fox confirming the regulation of her status and wishing her success in her new position. The vice president of R&D, however, also informed her that: "...*despite the lack of any management need for your promotion, you have been granted a regulation of status by The Company contingent upon your performance in this higher level position over the time of the next review period. We are certain your qualifications will permit you to achieve such objectives.*"

Albert Tanaka confirmed that he had also been told she was now on a probation period for the next year. It appeared that V.P. Barron was still able to exert his will with Phil Fox.

Furthermore, though her first paycheck indicated that her status had been regulated, it would reflect only in the title on her business cards, not in her bank account. Her wages fulfilled the barest minimum requirements for her recent promotion. Tessa knew from previous consultation with her colleagues, and from confidential words whispered in her ear by the senior scientists, that two younger, less experienced male researchers, recently hired into ART, were still making significantly higher incomes.

Her change in status, she was informed in Phil Fox's letter, was generously considered as effective from three months ago, the time of the initiation of the grievance proceedings, but none of her requested retroactive adjustments in salary ever appeared.

It seemed clear that even Ken Hunt's good intentions, for he had at first agreed with the reasonable nature of her requests, were falling rapidly by the wayside.

In the meanwhile, it became obvious to Tessa and her supervisor that it would be wise to cut short their time in the ART department. Albert Tanaka arranged for himself and Tessa to transfer with their project, which was conveniently nearing completion of the research phase, into the Future Development Technologies department.

This, in fact, became a definite necessity for V.P. Barron purposely ignored Albert Tanaka and spoke only distantly polite words when absolutely necessary. He resented what he viewed as Albert's lack of support for his position, while at the sight of Tessa Euler, his eyes snapped unforgivingly and the frozen smile on his face never reached the hard look in his narrowed pupils.

After V.P. Barron was seriously berated by The Company president for his "atrocious management practices," V.P. Barron found solace for his defeat by instantly promoting Mary to Tessa's previous position, usually reserved only for entry-level Ph.D.s, and Todd Dean another two levels above Tessa. Both received a substantial merit increase in strict accordance with The Company fair practices. This generated many hard feelings among the other R&D employees, who began to consider Tessa Euler's struggles in an increasingly sympathetic and favorable light.

The department productivity slumped, but V.P. Barron marched on regardless.

He rewarded Loyola Fraise's loyalty with a new title of "ART Research Organizer", with a bonus check for her outstanding performance. No one could quite figure out what her novel job description required of her. Loyola, however, interpreted it by bestowing a condescending smile on those in favor and reserving the right to remove the Ph.D. titles from library circulation lists and newly ordered name plates for the unfortunate few who had been perceived as insubordinate to V.P. Barron's wishes during the grievance proceedings.

Since the senior scientists Dr. Nigel Jansen and Dr. Wayne Greschwin fell into that exiled category, they silently removed their name plates bearing the offensive Ph.D., from their doors and placed them in a less conspicuous position in their offices.

Ken Hunt's mild protests at such unreasonable actions went unheeded by Phil Fox, who felt that he could not permit a complete humiliation for a manager in V.P. Barron's position.

"It would not look good for The Company if management appeared too vulnerable to its subordinates," he told Ken Hunt between golf swings at the usual monthly management off-site meeting. "Tessa Euler received more than a fair deal from The Company for all the trouble she caused! She is what I would call a genuine troublemaker!"

At that very moment, Tessa was discussing the possibility of leaving The Company with Albert Tanaka and Wayne Greschwin.

"Well, management is considering some changes, such as a new employee assessment system called MBO—Management by Objectives—so that the accomplishment of pre-set goals in R&D can be more fairly assessed," said Wayne.

Tessa gave a cynical smile. "Management by *objections* is more likely!"

"What we have here," Albert Tanaka quipped, "is management by *vice!*" He paused, while they all laughed in agreement and with a knowing look predicted, "But sit tight, Tessa. I hear that a new wind of change is blowing our way!"

THE REORGANIZATION PILL

Hurry, quick! We've got to stall,
Profits have begun to fall!
Mergers in our future loom,
What measures will forestall our doom?

Investing funds in R&D?
A wasteful, useless, spending spree!
Projections for ten years ahead?
Just fill the mind with untold dread!

We need more Management Control,
To dig us out of this deep hole!
A short-term cure for every ill:
The Reorganization Pill!

Rumors were running rampant throughout The Company. The Wall Street stock market reports and the *Financial Times* all recorded unfavorable slides in The Company shares. Clippings from newspapers circulated among the employees and decorated the corridor and cubicle office walls, where whirlpools of agitated debates could be heard throughout the day.

The official bulletin boards, however, were devoid of any news. Management flippantly ignored the floundering Company morale. The latest addition to the news board, a new monthly slogan designed by The Company President, Mr. Wally Steen, insouciantly announced to the R&D department: *"Shape Your Ship: Make Your Teamwork Shipshape!"* To the anxious employees, this slogan soon became a painful stab in the eye.

While the cauldron of speculation bubbled, the desperate troops in R&D gave vent to their frustrations in sarcastic, black humor. Someone had suspended a grotesque plastic chicken by its neck from the ceiling, while the sight of papier-mâché effigies that clutched pink slips and peered menacingly from behind several potted plants elicited raucous, stress-relieving laughter.

In all of Dr. Nigel Jansen's twenty-five years with The Company he had never witnessed such general depression. He frowned at the blatantly evasive responses everyone received from the managers' secretaries. At all levels, The Company managers were unavailable for comment.

What was management planning? What were they up to? Come to think of it, where the hell were they, if The Company was truly facing financial ruin? Nigel and his colleagues asked one other.

Nigel had neither seen nor heard from his own laser chip focusing, or LCF, project manager nor had any of the other members of The Company systems management group appeared in R&D for the past ten days. Annoyed at himself for succumbing to such unsettling thoughts, Nigel turned his otherwise rational mind to planning experiments for the next month, whether The Company lasted that long or not!

The sudden ring of the telephone brought an uncharacteristic four-letter word to his lips.

He raised the receiver. "Yes!" he barked and was surprised by his own curt tone. "Good morning! Dr. Nigel Jansen speaking!" he added in a more mellow tone.

"Hi, Nigel! This is Brad!" the LCF Project Manager greeted jovially. "Had a bad week? You sound crabby this morning!"

After so many years with The Company, Nigel did not hesitate to interrogate his project manager. "I'm fine, but tell me what's going on in The Company, Brad. Everyone's very concerned! Or hasn't our sensitive management tuned in yet?"

"Of course, we have!" the affronted manager replied.

"Well, you've got a fine way of showing it!"

"No need to get sarcastic, Nigel! There's nothing to worry about! If you'll take a look at the notice board on Monday, there'll be an announcement that we're planning a most revitalizing reorganization of The Company that will benefit all the employees. First, Genie Prat has been promoted to the position of Strategic Planning Manager for Technical Projects." There was a pause as Brad added on a somewhat sour note, "She's on the program management team now."

"You must be kidding!" Nigel interjected, aghast. "She's only got a two-month short course in management and no background in science whatsoever! It was bad enough when she was in charge of laboratory safety affairs, but how can she make strategic plans for technical projects?"

He well remembered the short, brash, peroxide blonde with the piercing black eyes. Her precipitously high heels reminded Nigel of her high-flown aspirations and seemed as sharply pointed as her long nose; the strict lines of her black business suits were as harsh as the voice, which grated with irritating regularity at every mandatory laboratory safety meeting Nigel had been obliged to attend.

He recalled that in all the meetings he had ever had with the aggressive woman over the last several years, the sum total of her comprehension of technical issues could be compressed onto one of their minuscule laser chips, not that it would provide any illumination thereafter. He painfully recalled how he had tried to explain to her on more than one occasion that just because osmometer and osmotic pressure reader, ultra-centrifuge and ultra-sonic devices had some similarity in their respective nomenclatures, they were vastly different pieces of lab equipment with very different safety requirements. He had failed. She became angry, defensive and turned her back on him, then stomped out of the laboratory.

"So, who's responsible for this latest gaffe?" Dr. Jansen asked.

Brad cleared his throat. "Our Company President, Mr. Wally Steen, of course. He thinks Genie's a genius, sharp and...."

"What, Brad?" Nigel prompted. "What else endeared her to Wally?"

Brad could not help venting a little of his own resentment. He'd had his eye on that position for a while. "I trust you to keep quiet about this, Nigel, but the rumor mill says she's Wally's wife's sister-in-law." Ah, yes, so that was the explanation for this anomaly, Nigel thought. A woman in an upper-management position was unheard of in The Company. "Though that's really neither here nor there," Brad added, hastily trying to downplay his rash outburst. "The fact is, she has a lot to say on all technical and strategic issues—and I guess there must be a need for someone like that in this organization."

Nigel kept his opinions on the merits of Genie Prat's technical and strategic drivel to himself. "What is the other surprise you were talking about?"

"It's why I really called you. As one of our ten most senior R&D scientists, we want you and your pals to get together and prepare your proposals for a new R&D compensation system!"

Nigel leaned back in his chair and scratching his ear in disbelief said, "Are you saying that corporate management is now seriously considering the parallel R&D Technology Compensation Scheme we proposed five years ago?"

"You bet! Complete equality in both promotion and salary ladders for scientists and managers. Wally is gung-ho about it! We really mean to iron out the inequities, which you guys pointed out last time. We'd also like you to present your viewpoints at Wally's staff meeting, outlining your future plans and needs for long-term research."

"No problem! My list and plans have long been ready if someone will truly be willing to listen for a change."

"We're all ears!" Brad laughed genially. "This Company is in for a total makeover. A brand new culture. A forward-looking reorganization that'll boost the shares sky-high and polish our image!"

Brad's stereotypical management/leadership course phrases irritated Nigel. "I'm more concerned with the reality of R&D funding than creation of virtual images!"

"Of course, and that's why we want you to attend our meeting with Wally on Friday next week, where you'll get your chance to present the R&D perspective!"

———————————▲———————————

The notice, promised for Monday, finally appeared on the news bulletin board on Wednesday afternoon. By that time, The Company employees all knew a reorganization was being planned.

It was not the ten senior scientists—working enthusiastic, long hours every day to prepare the detailed R&D equitable compensation and promotion proposals—who leaked the management plans. Indeed, no one needed to. The daily trail of food carts, laden with gourmet snacks, that had faithfully followed The Company program management team every morning, lunch, and afternoon since Monday, indicated to one and all that important management discussions were in progress behind the president's closed, tenth floor executive conference room.

Inside these hallowed quarters, Mr. Wally Steen bit into a chocolate-dipped strawberry and sympathized with the message on the personalized number plates of his new Company Mercedes: *'Any Ruse for a Pleasure Cruise.'*

He wished he could think of one now as the Senior Vice President, Director of the Applied Research Technologies department, Dr. Victor Paul Barron, again raised his pet issue.

"Before we get to the matter of the R&D budget," he said in his habitually complaining, whining tone, "I think we should consider the future in the application of research technologies and the title of my department should reflect this correctly."

Dr. Victor Barron, or V.P. as he preferred to be called since his first days with The Company thirty years ago, looked challengingly across the table at the ten-year veteran Director of Future Development Technologies department, Dr. Mike Vander. Since their very first encounter, the two managers were as antagonistic as a snake and mongoose.

The near-paranoid rivalry between the two men was well known to The Company president. He half-opened his mouth to speak, but Mike Vander swiftly interjected.

"But future implies research with a vision!" His mouth split into a challenging grin.

"Are you implying–" V.P. Barron raised his voice in outrage but was cut short by Mike Vander.

"All I'm saying is that we are still waiting for you to deliver some sort of viable invention that could be developed into a product with a future! When you do, I'm sure your proposed new title will be appropriate!"

V.P. Barron's slack mouth quivered and his prominent Adam's apple bobbed up and down as he swallowed. His head, which moved about as if on a long and flexible stalk, turned a deeply offended look at the president.

"You all know that I myself have authored over seventy patents, many of them turned into products your people are working on; and I know there is not one major product currently under development that hasn't come from my forward-looking ART department!"

Mike Vander grimaced. "And there isn't one we're not having development problems with!"

Wally Steen attempted once again to intercede, but V.P. Barron beat him to the verbal battlefield.

"If you insist on viewing your department's deficiencies as problems," he countered in a smooth, oily voice, "I can't see how you can even think of a future!"

"Hold it, gentlemen!" Wally Steen finally succeeded in cutting in across the bow. The other ten members of his staff management team murmured their consent, weary of this weeklong tug of war. "You two can discuss this later on. Now, let's recapitulate our decisions on R&D's reorganization and plan of action, before Nigel Jansen joins us in a couple of minutes for an update on the technologists' viewpoint."

Wally Steen ran through the condensed summary of the minutes of the meeting that his secretary, sitting beside him, had been typing on the portable computer.

"Requirements for increased R&D productivity: improved communication, tighter budget controls, more accountability from the R&D research staff–"

"Don't forget, Wally, better documentation in compliance with safety regulations and more technical record-keeping to facilitate our Strategic Planning Objectives," Ms. Genie Prat's shrill voice interjected as she gave Wally a thin-lipped smile.

The Company president nodded with an avuncular smile in her direction. "Quite right, Genie. SPOs. We'll get to those later." He glanced back at the list before him. "Also more patentable, Company-oriented inventions and ideas–"

"And to safeguard our future, more investment into research on the feasibility of novel technologies," V.P. Barron interpolated with an arctic glance at his rival. "I have to emphasize that more Company funds must be allocated to the applied research division of R&D...I mean, to the future Applied Research Technologies department!"

Wally Steen winced. Not again! He cast a grateful look in the direction of one of the program managers, who remarked dryly they had heard enough of that and suggested they move on to the next item on the agenda: the Technologists' Compensation Scheme.

"What's your opinion on this major issue, Wally?" he asked. "Is The Company ready for such a radical change?"

Genie Prat frowned with aggressive concern. Not wishing to be left out as murmurs of agreement circulated around the president's table after the previous question, she hurriedly interpolated, "Do we have a strategy?" She wanted to ensure that her recent promotion should not be forgotten. "Technically, speaking," she added to underscore her close acquaintance with technical matters.

"That's what we're here to decide," Wally replied. He was a great believer in deferred payments and delayed decision-making. "Let's hear your thoughts!"

"The Company may wish for a forward-looking image, but what amounts to charitable and wasteful handouts to all R&D scientists is quite a different matter," the VP of Finance said, helping himself to an apple puff pastry desert from the tray beside him. "We must address the issue of The Company budget," he continued. "We have to ask ourselves, can The Company profits cover such an overload?"

He always asked questions whenever he was expected to give answers. In this way he never needed to commit himself. This time, his strategy was infectious. After all, the entire program management team had just recently attended the same course on strategic leadership.

"And what is this I heard about a bonus-sharing scheme with technologists?" the Production Chief Manager asked, disbelief evident in his deep voice.

"That's right! Are we proposing to fritter away all the profits and share them with absolutely every bench-bod in R&D?" Genie Prat threw in, disdainfully.

"What's the budget slack?"

"And how much shall we have to sacrifice from our bonus fund?"

The concerns expressed were mirrored in the eyes of all members around the conference table.

It occurred to Wally Steen that with a curtailed bonus he might not be able to afford another new yacht he had planned to buy. Mike Vander recalled he had promised a new Mercedes to his wife. Genie Prat bit her thin lower lip and thought of the taxes on the huge mansion she and her husband had just bought. V.P. Barron had his eye on a diamond signet ring he had commissioned for himself. In general, Wally's managerial staff had little difficulty in picturing all manner of ways in which they had planned to support the consumer-driven economy of the nation with their upcoming bonuses.

The VP of Production and Manufacturing leaned forward and laughed nervously. "Sharing profits with technocrats sounds to me like a crazy proposal leftover from one of those outdated utopias that have just crumbled around the world!"

Exclamations proclaiming complete agreement and hearty laughter filled the conference room. Nobody heard the knock on the door.

"Excuse me," one of Wally's two secretaries called out, popping her head inside. "You asked me to let you know when Dr. Nigel Jansen arrives. He's here now."

Wally invited Nigel in with an open, welcoming hand wave.

"Come in, come aboard, Nigel!" He glanced toward Genie Prat and added, "We've now got a technical person on our team,

Nigel. So, you won't feel so left out!" Genie grinned defiantly at Nigel, who gave a tepid smile in return. "Hope all's well with our great inventors down in R&D?"

Nigel drew breath to reply, but the president preferred to answer his own questions.

"Fine and full of new ideas requiring masses of funds, I'm sure!" Wally focused on the stack of overheads and the thick pile of paper containing the scientific proposals in Nigel's hands. "I can see you've been working hard. Let's hear it! Are we ready?" He glanced around at his management team and all members resignedly concurred, and as if to fortify themselves for the upcoming ordeal, they quickly began to refill their plates with the remaining gourmet morsels.

Nigel readied the projector and distributed copies of the agenda and the technologists' proposals. On Wally's nod, he began his R&D presentation.

Part one was short and to the point. He concluded with a list of the most essential laboratory equipment requirements to boost the future research projects. Despite the semidarkness of the room, Nigel could clearly see the pained, barely concealed yawns and disinterested expressions that greeted the suggestions he and his colleagues had worked on with such enthusiasm. He hurriedly moved on.

Part two was even more straightforward with plenty of cartoon illustrations. Surely, this would hold their short attention span? He outlined the R&D contributions and proposed a reasonable compensation scheme for the technical staff, which included a salary ladder with bonus sharing parallel to that of the managerial staff. Judging by the furtive glances exchanged and raised eyebrows of the program management team members, Nigel knew he had finally struck close to home.

"In R&D we feel strongly," Nigel concluded, "that The Company scientists, as the inventors of novel technologies, should be in charge of the long-range technical strategic planning objectives." He paused. Genie Prat was choking on her coffee. Good. His point had struck home. "As well as have a voice in the research and development decision-making processes, especially when our research plans are presented to the investors and board members!"

The light in the room was switched on, the projector and its whining fan switched off. In the silence Nigel cautiously awaited the managerial response.

"Very well presented!" Phil Fox, vice president of R&D, praised. He chuckled and added, "But believe me, Nigel, the last thing those investors of ours understand is science!"

"And by the way, you do have a voice in the technical SPOs now, Nigel!" Wally Steen said, indicating an aggrieved Genie Prat.

"As your new strategic planning manager for technical projects, I will decide for you on these matters," Genie added, her sharp nose piercing her inviolable managerial airspace.

Mike Vander laughed. "Who knows, Phil," he said, ignoring Genie Prat's comments. It still rankled that he had not been given this position. "The investors might invest several million in some fancy technical proposal. Boy, they're so naïve, if you told them we had a cure for Martian flu, they'd be knocking down Wally's front door, begging to invest!"

In the general laughter, Wally Steen interjected, "Be careful, we don't want to be accused of stock price manipulation or we'll all be thrown in the brig!"

On a somewhat more serious note he turned to Nigel Jansen, who was finding such derogatory remarks about the very people who were taking a personal monetary risk to support R&D efforts in The Company in exceedingly poor taste. Especially when voiced by managers, whose technical understanding was dubious.

The Company president continued. "Nigel, you guys in R&D did an outstanding job with your presentation!" He smiled on his team and repeated his pet phrase, "Well, let's have your thoughts."

Dr. Nigel Jansen sat down and leaned back, looking expectantly at the faces of The Company top level management.

"I fully agree with the proposal for more input and involvement by the technologists," Mike Vander said, shooting a meaningful glance at Ms. Prat.

Genie bristled. "As I said, I know all there is to know about strategic technical issues!" Her beady dark eyes suddenly noticed the deepening frown on Dr. Nigel Jansen's brow. She might need his help to maintain her authority in this new position, so she conceded, "And I know where to go for what I don't know. Nigel here does have some expertise."

"Some expertise, sure," Nigel said with a wry twist to his lips. After twenty-five years as a senior scientist and internationally recognized expert with more than 150 peer-reviewed publications, was that how much The Company valued him? No one rose to his defense.

Mike Vander had time to think. Wally looked so damn pleased with Genie's words that perhaps he should ingratiate himself a little. As if on an afterthought he added, "As I was saying, research guys should have an input but only whenever it is really required."

"We were hoping for a more permanent representation in The Company's SPOs with respect to R&D planning," Nigel interjected. "Informed decisions can't be made without detailed technical knowledge."

As Genie opened her slash mouth to protest, V.P. Barron cleared his throat. Her new title irked him as well. The only person truly qualified to make strategic technical decisions was the man whose face he saw every day in the shaving mirror. "Naturally, Nigel, and that's why we ask you to write reports on the results of your research…so that I can…I mean, this program management team can make the best decisions and strategic plans for the future of R&D in The Company."

"Wally has already suggested more documentation is required from R&D," Genie hurriedly interpolated. "Your research should be presented to us in a form understandable to strategic management, without all the unnecessary scientific expressions and long-winded formulas!"

"We must function as one team, guys!" reminded the vice president of International Marketing from the far end of the table. He was getting worried about the current slackening in sales figures. There would be no future products in the pipeline, if program management did not encourage and support R&D efforts.

Nigel shook his head in frustration. "No, no, no! I'm afraid that's not our idea of teamwork! We meant *direct* participation. Not just through more report writing, which will simply increase the unproductive work load and delay the accomplishment of scientific objectives!"

His words triggered agitated debate. The VP of International Sales aimed an encouraging grin toward Nigel as the other team members concertedly disagreed with Nigel's proposals until Wally ended the discourse by raising his voice.

"Gentlemen and lady! We can't decide on this important issue today. Any feelings or counter-proposals on the subject of the new technologists compensation scheme?"

A distinctly uncomfortable silence was the only reply to his query. Nigel compressed his lips. He had faced this managerial concrete wall five years ago, but he decided he would speak out his thoughts bluntly this time.

"Look, you can't deny that the technologists in R&D are the inventors of products on which The Company depends, yet already an entry-level technologist with a Ph.D. is paid less than an entry-level manager with a B.S. degree or sometimes even only an MBA short-course. And you know very well that in The Company, researchers never catch up. They don't have a cat's chance in hell of doing so! A scientist cannot progress up the managerial ladder and there is no equivalent scale of responsibilities to enable a scientist, even after thirty years of experience, to progress to a salary, never mind the benefits, equivalent to a VP!"

Somewhat shamefaced glances were cast at Nigel and he added, "If The Company wants to attract the best young talents and specialists into our R&D departments, we must consider more funding for R&D and introduce some form of incentives for our technologists!"

"Don't you guys spend enough already?" asked the manager who could not resist the puff pastries. "All those chemicals and equipment–"

"The depreciation costs are phenomenal!" interjected the VP of Accounts and Budgeting. "I can't believe you really need all those fancy, expensive instruments you listed here."

Nigel's irritation mounted. "We listed only the most essential items. It is of great importance to The Company's future that we do quality research and we need up-to-date equipment!"

"In the days when I was doing research," interjected Mike Vander, "we got by with a mouth pipette and Bunsen burner...and we were still inventive and did quality research."

Nigel wanted to tell him what he could do with his flippant statement but just smiled cynically as the manager continued, "Come to think of it, I just remembered that I saw a large, wholesale freezer unit for a bargain price advertised at an upcoming auction. Freznet, Inc. is going under…we'll get that for you!"

"I'll get it!" interjected Genie Prat, aggressively.

Nigel sighed deeply. Oh, no! If Genie Prat goes to the auction they'd probably end up with a liquid nitrogen tank large enough to freeze a mammoth, he thought to himself. He was about to protest but Genie continued with determination. "I'll make up a strategic plan for all the requested research instruments!"

"That's it! You can rub your magic lamp, Genie, and give 'em all they want!" joked Wally Steen.

"Great idea! We can both go to the auction," said Phil Fox, seeing his opportunity for a closer acquaintanceship with Wally's favorite Genie. "I saw the ad and liked that bargain on the computers to help with the safety documentation…besides, there's a great vineyard nearby makes Byron's Dell, a superb Chablis. You'd love it, Wally!"

"May I join you?" the VP finance eagerly volunteered. "I'll have to keep an eye on the R&D budget."

Nigel's head was beginning to throb. "We do not need a secondhand or new freezer! It's a waste of money!" he raised his voice crossly.

Stares full of annoyance at his interruption were directed at him as he added, "But we have to invest in the future. To think about the future of R&D in The Company, five, ten years from now our Company must have some products waiting in line!"

"Who knows what lies that far ahead?" Wally shrugged. He knew that in ten years, if not sooner, he intended to be happily retired and cruising the high seas in his yacht. "Our investors won't stand for it! They want products yesterday. So you'd better sit down with Genie. Make some R&D SPOs and tell everyone down there to get cracking, Nigel!"

"Researchers' demands are as impractical as their research theories," Mike Vander laughed. He glanced at Genie. "What we need is more quality control in the development and production processes."

"Exactly!" rasped Genie. She bestowed a thin smile on Mike Vander. "Quality assurance, safety and strategic planning…technical planning!"

"Without investments in future research, Mike, you won't have anything to develop!" Nigel retorted, ignoring Genie's prattle.

His words were a cue for Dr. V.P. Barron, whose head was moving constantly, shaking to show his disagreement with Mike Vander, an indecisive circle in response to Genie Prat and then nodding vigorously in agreement with Nigel. "I…I have to say that Nigel hit the nail on the head!" He finally succeeded in cutting in. "The future is what counts and where better to invest than in my future Applied Research Technologies department?"

Wally Steen supported his head on his left hand and doodled on the meeting agenda. Several staff members stood up and strolled casually to the buffet table to refill their coffee cups and sample the remaining Chilean grapes, Hawaiian pineapple slices and other exotic fruits.

Nigel Jansen found solace for his frustrations in thoughts of the experiment currently underway in his laboratory.

V.P. Barron stubbornly persisted. "As I always say, the title of my department correctly reflects that science is an art…ART and art is by nature unpredictable."

"You can say that again," murmured Mike Vander from the buffet table with a grimace at his grinning friends.

V.P. Barron ignored him and continued. "After all, the charter of The Company is to look forward! To go with our reorganization, we must…."

Wally suddenly looked up from the agenda notes, his eyes gleaming with mischievous amusement as he interjected, "Yes, yes, Victor, we all know your department's title should reflect this! I promise you, I'll make sure it does!"

V.P. Barron was highly gratified and he smiled triumphantly as Wally closed the meeting. As an afterthought The Company president suddenly remembered the lone researcher's presence.

"Thanks for your presentation, Nigel. It was great, just great! We'll give it very serious consideration!"

*T*wo weeks later, the decisions of the program management team made all The Company skeptics happy and transformed the idealists into cynics and disgruntled employees. The first expression of the new reorganization plan to raise productivity was an announcement from management that there would be a company-wide move of departments.

Ms. Genie Prat was instrumental in the purchase of an unwanted desiccator instead of the unrequested freezer. Someone mentioned it dried and preserved samples, so she thought it might serve just as well. She also brought back an outdated electron microscope, which nobody in the department needed and was not a part of any of the projects underway. Since this latter piece of huge laboratory equipment required its own room, she then participated in the plans to move R&D to a more suitable location within The Company to accommodate this expensive, unwelcome, "bargain" item. With Wally's approval she had decided all this fell within her technical strategic planning objectives mission.

Sarcastic jokes whispered throughout R&D told that management had mistaken activity for productivity, but when a dinosaur company shifts sleeping positions, the global financial markets have their own perspective. The Company image in the world of technology instantly began to improve.

In-house, the less kind comments became the most popular. The statement of the month was made by an employee, who preferred to remain anonymous: "I'm not surprised management decided to reorganize...after all, they only play with a single deck of cards, and all they can do is reshuffle it!"

During the months that followed, all R&D research work ground to a standstill. Dr. Nigel Jansen and his colleagues bitterly endured the constant interruptions to their research activities. The R&D employees were certainly not idle, but their job description would have been better suited to "movers and packers" than "inventors and experimenters."

New R&D laboratories were eventually established on the ground floor facilities that had previously housed the accounting offices. Protests that these facilities had not yet been prepared for such basic R&D requirements as exhausts for the chemistry labs, gas lines, electric wiring, and special floor and bench mounting for sensitive equipment were all dismissed by Genie Prat, Phil Fox, and flippantly brushed aside by Wally Steen. In their eyes, the scientists were merely "unreasonable, whining technocrats" full of excuses, which would delay and undermine the good efforts of The Company management.

"The shareholders' trust in The Company must be upheld," Wally Steen stated in his monthly proclamation.

Besides, everything could be installed later, Dr. Nigel Jansen was told by his project manager, Brad. However, Nigel persisted and objected that work could not continue or start under these conditions. He and his senior colleagues wrote several memos to that effect but to no avail. The reconstruction of the new R&D facilities had already cost too much, Wally Steen replied firmly.

"What the hell do these guys want?" was the question at the top of the agenda at the next program management meeting.

"Who knows?!" Genie Prat threw her hands up in frustration. Her eyes snapped as she recalled how Nigel Jansen had berated her for not showing him her proposals before they were approved. How dare he talk to her as if she did not know what she was doing! "They're constantly complaining. That Nigel Jansen is the worst troublemaker. None of the technical SPOs approved by you and Phil were welcomed."

"They'll be the ruin of The Company!" Phil Fox concluded. "It only proves they don't deserve the compensation they demanded!"

"How can we let them participate in our strategic planning when they make such absurd requests?! And Nigel Jansen had the nerve to talk about investors!" grumbled the outraged VP of public relations.

"Okay, so you think, guys, what R&D needs is more firm management control?" Wally Steen asked, impatient to close the meeting, and received quick, unanimous concurrence from all his management staff.

Meanwhile, the legal and marketing offices prepared to move into the previous R&D laboratories and accounting swapped offices with personnel, which in turn moved into the purchasing division offices. Five months slipped by and finally The Company returned to a semblance of outward stability.

In accordance with Wally Steen's command for stricter budget controls, a new layer of middle project management, reporting directly to the upper program management team was introduced to facilitate the interpretation and handling of the larger volume of documentation now required from the R&D technocrats.

Dr. Nigel Jansen frowned and swore at the memo, which he shared with Dr. Mike Atkins, his colleague from the Bio-engineering department. He fully sympathized with his friend's caustic remark, "There's always money available for more managers, but when I asked for a small sum to set-up an inexpensive additional unit to house a few more rabbits that I need for immunization to support the successful immunology development project, they flatly refused!"

"Afraid of competition from more of their own kind, I guess, " Nigel replied dryly.

"What d'you mean?"

"I've long ago come to the conclusion, Mike, that our Company managers are like Jackrabbits, stuck in the act of procreation. The more they reorganize, the more they end up breeding their own kind!"

───────── ▲ ─────────

When Phil Fox eventually called an R&D information meeting, the old rumors of a new equitable compensation scheme surfaced. With renewed trust in the altruism and company guardianship of their management, all the R&D employees enthusiastically crowded into the R&D conference room.

Sitting at the front were Drs. Mike Vander and V.P. Barron, exchanging general comments on the weather for the sake of appearances and acid remarks about Ms.Genie Prat, whom they both by now disliked. Mike Vander's attempts at a closer relationship with Genie Prat had not resulted in any favors from Wally Steen. The two VPs of R&D both, therefore, agreed that Prat's contribution to the reorganization had been far too highly praised by her boss. Besides, it rankled that she was busy right now sailing at an off-site meeting with Wally Steen and a few Company clients.

Phil Fox welcomed the R&D employees and raising his already high-pitched voice by an octave, he began to speak. Expectant silence fell on the room.

"First, I'd like to reassure you that The Company is here to stay. So don't panic; there'll be no takeovers or layoffs! I also have a number of important announcements to make concerning the R&D reorganization. After lengthy deliberation over the budget situation, we have decided to introduce an equitable compensation scheme for technologists!"

Hearty cheers and clapping greeted this statement. VP Fox held up his hand to cut short the applause. "I have to warn you not to be impatient. It will take some time to organize and your input and suggestions are welcome. In keeping with our reorganization, our President, Mr. Wally Steen, would like you all to memorize our new company motto...." He switched on the overhead projector, and on the screen a three-dimensional picture of a yacht on a choppy sea appeared. On its flag was the motto: *"Hoist the Sails! Be Prepared for the Gales!"*

"With these words of wisdom in mind, we will soon overcome any minor storms and reach the calm waters of success!" Phil Fix concluded.

Thus, the meeting was brought to a close, leaving the R&D employees to return to their work with no definite promise and an atmosphere of dissatisfaction and resignation. In fact, nobody believed anymore that the equitable compensation scheme would ever materialize.

However, less than a month after this meeting, a list of new promotions was published throughout The Company. With great interest everyone swarmed around the announcement, but the R&D employees' hopes were shattered once again for the only change was that all the program managers had now been granted the new title of Technology Research Manager. They were thus officially classified together with the most senior research staff, which brought a cynical smile to the lips of more than one active R&D scientist, whose benefits were dwarfed by those of the newly added counterfeit researchers.

"And they're so out of touch with real research, there isn't a sane scientist who'd hire them even as a novice lab assistant, if they paid for the privilege!" Dr. Nigel Jansen commented as the R&D staff learned the meaning of the term "status quo."

What about the promised, long-range investments in R&D? Of course, there would be investments, they were reassured. However, it soon became apparent to the senior scientists that the investments would first take a sort of minor diversion into the new technology research managers' travel and meeting funds. There would also have to be funding set aside for managerial short-courses from which The Company middle-management eagerly memorized the appropriate technical "buzzwords" with which to impress on everyone how very well suited they were to managing any assigned research project.

Dr. Nigel Jansen, protesting this reorganization and lack of additional R&D support and professional staffing, was warned it was his responsibility to ensure that the R&D scientists do not discuss their income levels. Why? Nigel wondered. Confidentially, he was told by the VP of Finance that it would not shed a good light on The Company management if the shareholders and investors would not agree with the new compensation scheme and send around snooping analysts, who could start interfering with the allocation of Company funds.

Persistent rumors that The Company might be taken over by a competitor firm resulted in an emergency upper-management staff meeting. The President/CEO, Wally Steen, along with the recently promoted Corporate VP of R&D, Phil Fox, and the two corporate executive officers, VP/Finance/CFO and VP/Legal Affairs, quickly drew up some amendments to the new Company reorganization/ contingency plan.

They added that in case of a takeover, the CEO and his VP/ executive officers would receive a compensation in the form of five full-years' salaries plus a minimum parachute sum of about fifteen million dollars. The other executive officers and VP/managers, according to rank, would receive one to three years' salaries and a negotiable bonus. This proposal was hurriedly submitted to the Board of Directors and instantly approved by the impartial Executive Compensation Committee. After all, everyone agreed the proposed change-in-control and severance arrangements were in compliance with the industry norm. The fact that several of the non-employee, independent members just happened to be Wally's long-time sailing cronies, naturally had no influence whatsoever on the favorable nature of the committee vote!

The executive officers' futures having been secured, a final contingency plan was put into action. Just in case the corporate takeover partners would, by any chance, decide to retain their managerial services, the executive officers grudgingly decided to make a few concessions to the technological compensation scheme. For the sake of a good corporate image, they agreed to include some incentive benefits for a handful of the most outspoken R&D scientists.

Drs. Nigel Jansen, Alan Hawk, Wayne Greschwin and Albert Tanaka, among the most senior R&D project leaders, were selected. They were assigned a new title of R&D Technocrat and were told that they would be entitled to receive a yearly profit bonus. However, for the R&D Technocrats the incentive bonus would depend solely on a favorable review of their perceived performance by management and, unlike the Technology Research Managers, would never exceed fifteen percent of their yearly incomes.

Since the yearly incomes of the selected scientists were so embarrassingly lower than those of the vast majority of the most junior members of the managerial staff, Wally Steen decided it was time to show some generosity. At the very next board meeting he suggested it would be good for the new Company image if they could report to the shareholders that scientists were now also included in the new profit-sharing bonus scheme.

Nigel Jansen and his colleagues understood perfectly well that they were the recipients of a few crumbs from the managerial gourmet table. They shrugged and busied themselves with experiments, their only refuge from the frustrations of Company politics.

------------▲------------

*D*r. V.P. Barron's wish was granted.

Wally Steen renamed his department from Applied Research Technologies, or ART, to Future Applied Research Technologies, abbreviated FART.

On the morning after this latest change appeared on the bulletin board, Dr. Nigel Jansen entered the department and saw a group of his colleagues chatting and laughing in front of the bulletin board. He soon realized what had triggered their mirth. On a chuckle Dr. Alan Hawk whispered to Nigel that V.P. Barron was enraged over what he said was a deliberate mischief Wally Steen had played on him, since he had given explicit instructions for the abbreviated title to be published in bold, red letters.

"So what do you think of Wally's latest prank, Nigel?" Alan Hawk asked with amusement.

With a cynical smile Nigel studied the wicked abbreviation of V.P. Barron's department title. "What else can we expect from our CEO and his management staff," he replied on a dry laugh, "but this inevitable consequence of The Company's 'Reorganization Pill'!"

THE WINDS THAT BLOW

The Company waits; the winds of change blow,
A genuine change, or just a false show?
In which direction will the future flow?
Will vices stay or will they go?

The predictions of the senior staff in the Future Applied Research Technologies department had an uncanny way of materializing. It was perhaps because the research and development staff was expected to look into the future. Of course, it could also have been because they were, over the many years, the first to know how very effective The Company management practices had been in plundering and wasting without investing. How callously had The Company management drained all incentives out of the research idea tanks!

Many of the senior researchers, who had been very productive and enthusiastic during The Company's halcyon years when they themselves still managed their own projects, now merely pitied the younger scientists. Disillusioned, they responded cynically whenever a new idea was proposed, saying they would be better off taking a cue from the self-centered corporate culture.

A flyer entitled *Management Advice to R&D* was circulated among the research staff at a meeting organized to discuss long-range research objectives. A much-admired and respected thirty-year veteran researcher composed it just before his retirement:

> *From every project, new or old,*
> *Make sure you get your worth in gold.*
> *Who cares if projects fly or slip,*
> *What counts is in your money clip!*
> *To get all this from R&D,*
> *There's one sure means, I guarantee,*
> *Delay—it's job security!*

The President's "ship", as Wally Steen like to call The Company, had no more reserves to fuel future products. It was running, or rather cruising, on empty and the R&D staff was just too malnourished and disgusted to pick up the oars, while management continued to party on the upper decks.

As managerial off-site meetings once again increased in frequency, no one took much notice.

The R&D departments were the first to feel the consequences of a frantic three-week management planning session. To their initial delight, they were all granted a week of vacation, but several days later they learned it was not a freebie but a compulsory unpaid leave! When they returned, funds for costly equipment on order, overseas scientific conference attendance, and hiring of new assistant level employees for ongoing projects in development were all temporarily put on hold.

The staff in R&D was accustomed to such budgetary constraints in the past and brushed the announcements aside as yet another myopic management decision. However, questioning eyebrows were soon raised as business-related newspapers began to report Company layoffs. A few hundred people in the South American and Taiwanese manufacturing divisions were shrugged off lightly, but when the closure of a major East Coast operation that sold what had been believed to be a staple Company product was announced, employees became personally concerned.

They all agreed it was somewhat unusual that the Corporate VP of R&D, Phil Fox himself, called an employee information meeting where he almost bent over backwards to reassure one anxious group after another that it was "…all a natural consequence of the current market pressures. Nothing to get worried about. All companies are suffering from the same problems of stifling government regulations and, of course, foreign competition that is eroding our fair market-share both at home and abroad. The Company is doing just fine!"

Shadows of doubt lingered in the minds of The Company R&D staff and Wally Steen's latest slogan, proclaiming, "*Whatever the Weather, We'll All Win Together!*" did nothing to assuage their mounting concerns. Why sure up the ship unless there was a storm ahead?

The employees, as always, heard more about The Company plans from a plethora of local business newspapers, reporting on a takeover battle that was underway.

A couple of weeks later, the storm blew in with the announcement from Wally Steen that negotiations for what The Company management downplayed as a "beneficial merger" with a major international company, Global Systems, Inc. had been completed. His memo read: "*The Company shall now become the Pacific Division of Global Systems, Inc. Let me assure all employees there is absolutely no immediate change contemplated in our management or business strategy. I would like to take this opportunity to thank all employees for their outstanding contributions over the Company's 50 golden years.*

"*As the Global Systems Pacific Division, we will be a formidable competitor on the high seas of world trade and we can look forward to a bright and prosperous future as we sail into global success. Congratulations! Walter Steen, President/CEO.*"

Global Systems, Inc. was already well known to many of the senior R&D staff members and they felt an invigorating tingle of anticipation. This multinational company had a reputation for investing heavily into long-range research and owned major research facilities in Europe, Canada, and the East Coast of the United States. They only hoped they would be recognized as valuable contributors and they began preparing their resumes listing their publications, inventions, and technical expertise.

At least the technical staff had some solid expertise to offer, and many of them wondered with a cynical smile whether for once their top-lofty R&D managers would not have preferred to be called "eccentric behind-the-benchers" with some definite knowledge and research skills with which to bargain.

Thus, the R&D staff members observed, with no small measure of amusement and interest, the dramatic effect on The Company managers at the unexpected arrival of two teams of outside business analysts. Global Systems, Inc. had sent one team to analyze the financial statements and the other to assess the R&D projects and resources. Voices were raised in indignant protest, but The Company managers soon consoled themselves that rumors of white-collar layoffs really meant the research staff in white lab coats. After all, they were to blame for the lack of present and future products and ideas!

However, when the analysts began to take a detailed look at the background expertise of the managers, the bulletin board every week announced that a handful had decided to follow the corporate vice president of R&D, Phil Fox's example. They jumped ship! Under pressure, the managers simply could not justify their numerous shaky qualifications, which did not match the basic requirements for managing scientific research projects.

As the analysts told a group of senior scientists, in their usual forthright manner, "You wouldn't believe what we uncovered. Some MBA diplomas were outright forgeries and not worth the paper they were printed on. There were even a couple of your so-called technical managers who had resorted to creative publishing. They used computers to insert their names on multi-author papers listed in their resumes. They obviously thought we wouldn't take the trouble to cross-check with the scientific journals." The senior analyst winked a hint. "It's a very crafty, or perhaps better said, a 'foxy' move?"

Only mildly surprised and very much amused, the researchers understood these words were aimed at the departed Corporate VP R&D, Mr. Phil Fox.

The senior analyst continued with a dry laugh, "But Global Systems didn't hire us to practice timeworn management book advice. We didn't come here to catch The Company managers doing something right and shower them with 'praisings'!"

Two weeks into this attrition, an eye-catching notice was found one morning pinned to the bulletin board on the R&D corridor. On a disposable, toilet seat protector were written the words: "Manager's Diploma: Excellence in The Company Leadership Award."

Although The Company management made a point to say how much they disapproved, the mischievous act brought the outside analysts and the R&D staff even closer together.

To the delight of the researchers, the senior analyst one day commented, "I can't believe you guys are still breathing with all those asphyxiating layers of middle-management." He shook his head and with a chuckle added, "Does this sound familiar, guys?

Phrase after phrase,
Bluster in a blaze,
No spinning in this maze,
No weaving in this craze,
Eyes in distant gaze,
Everyone parts ways:
It's The Company that pays,
For Management Malaise!"

The agreement was unanimous. It described their management to perfection and the senior analyst smiled. "If it's any consolation, our consulting firm has seen this before in other companies like yours. You're lucky Global Systems decided the ground The Company's built on and the technical expertise in R&D are worth enough of an investment to bail you all out!"

In the meantime, the managers who decided to weather the storm together with "Captain Wally"–after all, where else would they get, for so little work, so much 'say and pay'–awaited with baited breath the arrival of the new Global Systems, Inc. management. But how should they present themselves, they wondered. What image did the new corporate culture appreciate in a manager? And from which corner of the globe would it come? Germany, France, Ireland, Canada, or the good old USA?

Yet, they did not have long to wait before the face of the new management, meticulously assessing the acquired Company prospects, from R & D to Manufacturing, was to reveal itself.

▲

Look! What just surfaced out of the can!
Is it a worm, or The Company man?
A survivor, well-versed in each
Management move,
Whose precise contribution you
Never could prove.
Yet by all he's perceived as a
Great Employee,
But he asked once too often,
"What's in it for me?"

*I*t was about this time that a new Company scandal broke out.

And it was the worst possible moment in The Company history for such a shameful event. What made it so painful was that it involved someone who, despite his management faults, had long been considered as a faithful Company man. It was none other than the Senior Vice President, Director of FART, Dr. V.P. Barron.

In V.P. Barron's opinion he had suffered a humiliating defeat after the President, Wally Steen, settled the grievance in Dr. Tessa Euler's favor. He had thought that a two-week vacation immediately following, what was in his opinion, a grossly unjust CEO decision, would help him to forget such a blatant miscarriage of corporate justice. It did not. Objective self-analysis had never been a part of V.P. Barron's nature.

So, when he returned to work and opened his desk drawer to find his copy of Tessa Euler's patent disclosure proposal, which she had offered to The Company and then withdrawn, the temptation was just too great to resist.

Though his Company-wide reputation was paved with the work and ideas of his colleagues and subordinates, he had never as yet actually given away any such proposals to interested firms outside The Company. The prestige, high managerial salary, bonuses and shares he had received in the past from The Company had been quite sufficient to satisfy both his significant ego and his lifestyle.

But this time, V.P. Barron felt that he had been greatly slighted. Everywhere he looked he thought he saw sly smiles on the faces of researchers and even his fellow managers. His almost paranoid imagination told him they were openly mocking him, all because The Company president had dared to pass judgment on a senior manager in favor of a young, expendable scientist!

He craved revenge against Tessa Euler and felt he deserved some compensation for his undeserved maltreatment. Anyway, he thought he wasn't really taking anything that belonged to The Company. Tessa Euler had withdrawn her offer!

He knew, as a member of Wally Steen's executive management staff, The Company would soon be taken over by a large competitor and he saw this as just the right time to get something more for himself.

What else is in it for me? he reasoned.

Thus, V.P. Barron contacted a long-time business acquaintance in a small company, Enzimo, Inc. in San Francisco. The Company had dealt with them several years ago on an outside development project and V.P. Barron knew they had a thriving research interest in enzyme assay kits. Tessa Euler's lipolytic enzyme, substrate and analytical method would fit perfectly.

V.P. Barron retyped Tessa Euler's disclosure data and flew out to meet his counterpart, Dr. Mark Mandel, Enzimo's vice president of research. He offered it as something he had worked on many years ago but in which The Company was no longer interested. He should know—after all, he was the research director!

Mark Mandel was very impressed with the technical information and they closed the deal that very same day. Several weeks later, V.P. Barron received a substantial payment in cash, as they had agreed.

When the takeover agreement was signed, V.P. Barron, his ego pacified by his successful deal, happily planned on capitalizing on Global Systems' Inc. substantial R&D investments and confidently saw himself holding a leading research position. Perhaps even as president, if Wally Steen retired?

The presence of the analysts may be striking fear into the hearts of the other Company managers, but not so much as a shiver touched V.P. Barron. He was supremely confident and with his usual, polished manner, welcomed the analysts and handed them his impressive resume.

V.P. Barron, unfortunately, did not know that Global Systems, Inc. was also in the closing phases of a merger with Enzimo. He also did not imagine for a moment that Tessa Euler would send her invention disclosure to the Global Systems research director, Dr. August Gust, from the U.S. East Coast division, who the analysts had told her would be visiting The Company to review the R&D departments. It, therefore, transpired that Dr. Gust and his staff reviewing Enzimo Inc. projects became aware of two identical, very ingenious inventions. Puzzled and intrigued, Dr. Gust visited The Company a week earlier than he had planned.

Tessa Euler was excited and delighted as she was summoned to see Dr. Gust. Had they decided to take her offer? However, she was shocked to discover that Dr. Gust came close to accusing her of duplicitous dealings. Had she tried to sell her invention to two companies simultaneously?

"I don't know who did it, but it wasn't me!" she protested in outrage. "Why don't you ask the person who bought my stolen work at Enzimo? I'd really like to know, who sold it to them!"

Dr. Gust delegated this investigation to his senior analyst and within a couple of days the unpleasant truth surfaced. Dr. Mark Mandel was only too eager to please his new bosses.

It, therefore, transpired that the winds that sweep clean, also swept V.P. Barron out of The Company. He arrived at work one day and after a brief half-hour meeting, spent the rest of the day packing up his office, while Loyola Fraise, his devoted personal secretary, distraught and tearful, told anyone willing to listen of her former boss's many failings that had led to this shameful incident. Everyone soon knew that V.P. Barron's parachute was not even gold-plated!

The consequences of this scandal added pressure on Wally Steen. Faced with growing accusations from the bristling Board of Directors of "guilt by omission; failing to control his management in recent years; losing personal contact with The Company innovators and not recognizing the importance of novel technologies that would give a sustainable competitive advantage," he decided to announce his retirement.

At a buffet lunch in his honor, arranged in the presidential company conference room, he was presented with an oil painting of his yacht, commissioned by his secretary. In his pocket were his 'golden sails', awarded to him by the Board of Directors the day before, which would undoubtedly carry him in the ultimate luxury through his retirement years.

Wally was in fine spirits. With a mischievous glance at the smiling Dr. Gust and his replacement, the new President of the Global Systems Pacific Division, Dr. Larry Gale, he made his parting comments. "I have enjoyed many glorious years with The Company and I could not ask for better memories as I sail around the world. With such an auspicious combination as Drs. Gust and Gale, I am confident that my old ship will surely not lack a good strong wind to fill her sails!" He paused for the laughter and applause to subside before adding, "We all have many choices to make in life, and I made mine. It's one thing a good sailor always heeds: 'Never piddle against the wind!'"

EPILOGUE

A truly fresh and invigorating wind of change swept through R&D; Dr. Tessa Euler and her colleagues were very pleased they had weathered the storm.

Many changes in management policies were made, and these were especially visible in R&D. There were no project managers, who were not also the most technically qualified in the project topics. Middle-management layers were decimated. The new Senior Vice President of R&D, Dr. Gust, who also took on the task of research director, was always accessible and contributed to the projects from his own extensive research experience. He sternly brushed aside any suggestions that his name be automatically added to patents and publications from his researchers, preferring to write his own.

Plans for future research and development of new products were made for many years ahead and involved all the research staff. To the delight of the jaded researchers, their proposals were indeed appreciated and incorporated into the R&D research goals. There were even special funds set aside for participation at international scientific meetings, at the discretion of the research staff.

The Pacific Division's profits soared, which pleased both the employees and the Global Systems shareholders.

At the first annual shareholders' meeting, Dr. August Gust, as one of the key speakers, reported on the successful reorganization of the R&D departments.

He concluded, saying, "After an in-depth discussion with our research and development staff regarding the many possible reasons for the downfall of The Company, the research staff presented me with this most interesting R&D caveat. I would like to share it with you all!" The verse was projected onto the screen.

The composition from R&D received a standing ovation from the shareholders. The President, Dr. Larry Gale, quickly declared that with such honest communication and cooperation between the new management and R&D, the new company must surely be on its way up!

He had the warning framed and distributed from the board-room and throughout Global Systems, Inc. as a reminder of the consequences of *Management by Vice.*

Give the Gift of

MANAGEMENT BY VICE

to Your Friends and Colleagues

CHECK YOUR LEADING BOOKSTORE OR ORDER HERE

❑ **YES**, I want _____ copies of *Management by Vice* at $19.95 each, plus $3.50 shipping per book. Canadian orders must be accompanied by a postal money order in U.S. funds. Allow 15 days for delivery.

My check or money order for $_____ is enclosed.

Please charge my ❑ Visa ❑ MasterCard

Name _____

Organization _____

Address _____

City/State/Zip _____

Phone _____

Card #_____ Exp. Date _____

Signature _____

Please make your check payable and return to:

Book Clearing House
46 Purdy Street
Harrison, NY 10528

Call your credit card order to: 800-431-1579
Fax: 914-835-0398
Email: bookch@aol.com • URL: www.book-clearing-house.com